Look out for

Blart II: The Boy Who Was Wanted
Dead Or Alive – Or Both

BLART

The Boy Who Didn't Want to Save the World

Dominic Barker

BLOOMSBURY

Acknowledgements

I would like to thank Michael Barker and Nancy Miles for all their help and encouragement during the writing of this book.

First published in Great Britain in 2006 by Bloomsbury Publishing Plc
36 Soho Square, London W1D 3QY

A CIP catalogue record of this book is available from the British Library

ISBN 978 0 7475 8074 4

All papers used by Bloomsbury Publishing are natural, recyclable products made
from wood grown in well-managed forests. The manufacturing processes conform to
the environmental regulations of the country of origin.

Typeset by Dorchester Typesetting Group Ltd
Printed in Great Britain by Clays Ltd, St Ives Plc

5 7 9 10 8 6 4

www.bloomsbury.com/blart

To Alison

Chapter 1

It should be made clear from the start that Blart never wanted to be a hero. He had not been brought up on tales of bravery and courage in the face of overwhelming odds; he had been brought up on a pig farm. He had not read the myths and legends of the dim and distant past where noble men and women gloriously chanced all for others; he had looked at the pictures in his grandfather's books which were mainly about diseases that pigs got. He had not learnt to ride a horse or to sword fight or to risk his life for the honour of a beautiful woman. He had learnt that if you want to catch a pig you sneak up on it from behind and take it by surprise.

Which is why it is not unusual that, as our story opens, we find Blart leaning over the rail of a large sty with a bowl of potato scraps in his hand preparing to feed two of his grandfather's champion pigs.

'Here, Wattle,' encouraged Blart. 'Come on, Daub. Have some dinner.'

Wattle and Daub did not wait to be asked twice. When

most of your life is spent wandering round and round a manure-filled pen then dinner is bound to be a highlight. Blart watched appreciatively as the two pigs chomped and munched their way through their meal. He felt that there was no more attractive sight on earth.

Eventually, pulling himself away from the pigs' sty, Blart headed back towards the farmhouse. Nature had laid on a beautiful picture for his trudge home. The burning sun setting behind the opposite hill, igniting the lazy clouds which hung idly in the air and reflecting off the river which eased itself through the heart of the valley. The long shadows reaching across the lush fields. The slivers of smoke rising from the chimneys of the village. The horse and cart idling down the road towards home. But Blart looked mainly at his boots. They were muddy boots and hence did not so much as hint at displaying Blart's reflection, which was probably a good thing because Blart was not a prepossessing figure – his head was too big, his eyes were too small and close together, his nose looked as if it had been squashed into his face and his mouth constantly hung half open. Below his dirty neck things didn't get any better. His body managed to be too short while his legs were too long, and this was accentuated by his ill-fitting grey woollen jumper which hung down far too low, combined with his maroon trousers made from the cheapest cloth which were too short and featured holes in most inappropriate places. All in all, Blart's physical appearance was really in need of a winning personality or a variety of impressive skills to counterbalance it. Unfortunately, he had neither.

However, when Blart stomped into the farmhouse kitchen without wiping his muddy boots at the door, there was something that made even him look twice. They had a visitor. Blart's grandfather disapproved of visitors, on account of the fact that they talked to you and tried to be friendly. He had put it about in the nearby village that Blart had some kind of mysterious and extremely unpleasant disease that was highly contagious to everybody who wasn't a member of his family. This had prevented most visitors coming but it had also meant that Blart couldn't go to school. The only day he tried all the other children ran out of the room screaming, for which they could hardly be blamed as they were only following their teacher's example.

But back to the visitor, who wore a large grey cloak with a hood.

'Blart. This gentleman wants to see you,' said his grandfather.

Blart had never ever had a visitor of his own before. Well, at least not a human one. Sometimes the pigs had managed to get out of their sty and come to find him.

'What do you want?' demanded Blart rudely.

'Boy,' said a terse voice from under the cowl, 'know ye that I have come many miles through many dangers across strange lands and seas to see you today and what I have to say is of great import.'

'Is it about pigs?' asked Blart.

'No,' conceded the cowled figure after a short pause. 'No. It isn't about pigs.'

And with those words the stranger shook off his hood to reveal a bald head and a thin craggy face adorned with a straggly white beard. But what was most noticeable about his face were his eyes. For such an old man he had the deepest, clearest blue eyes. Eyes that briefly silenced even Blart.

'My name is Capablanca and I am the greatest sorcerer alive today,' announced the wizard with more than a touch of pride.

'Do a spell, then,' demanded Blart, who was not the kind of boy to go around believing old men were wizards just because they said so. 'Turn this table into a pig.'

'What?' exclaimed Capablanca.

'Are you deaf?' said Blart.

'No, I am not,' answered Capablanca. 'But I'll turn you into a pig if you won't listen.'

'Wow, great,' said Blart. 'Would you?'

The wizard was taken aback by this response. Sighing, he stood back and went very still. Time seemed to stop ever so briefly in the little room and there was a flash of blue from the wizard's eyes and a swift blast of gushing wind, so swift that it might not even have been there at all. And the table did indeed become a pig. A surprised pig who immediately began to charge round the kitchen.

'Do it again! Do it again!' screeched Blart in delight.

'No,' said Capablanca. 'I shall turn all your pigs into tables,' he added menacingly.

Finally Capablanca had hit upon a way of frightening Blart, who decided to shut up and listen to what the wizard had to say. The pig kept running and both the wizard and Blart were forced against the walls to avoid being knocked over. Gradually, though, before Blart's very eyes, the pig began to look less and less like a pig and more and more like a table, until it was completely a table again.

There followed a long pause and then, dramatically, Capablanca began.

'I have come to take you with me, boy. For it is our destiny to travel to far-flung lands, to undertake deeds of great glory and to endeavour to save the world from a terrible peril.'

Chapter 2

We all know what should happen when a healthy strong boy of fourteen is offered the chance to save the world from peril. He should grasp the chance firmly with both hands. He should not hesitate. He should pause only to arm himself with **his** trusty dagger and then he should put his bold feet forward to meet the challenges that lie ahead.

'I'm not going,' said Blart stubbornly.

'You'll be a hero, boy,' said Capablanca.

'I don't want to be a hero.'

'Bards will write epic poems in your honour and balladeers will sing of your great deeds.'

'I want to stay here with my pigs.'

'You could have more pigs.'

'More pigs?'

'You could have the biggest pig farm in the world.'

Blart was tempted. However, far stronger in Blart even than the desire to own the biggest pig farm in the world was the desire to say no to somebody who had asked him to do him a favour.

'No,' said Blart.

The wizard sighed. He decided upon a new approach.

'Sit down, boy,' he said. 'And let me tell you some history.'

Though it was against his nature to do as he was told, Blart found himself obeying. His grandfather sat down too, though he made sure he pulled his chair well away from the table.

'Now,' began Capablanca, 'we must go back far into the past.'

Blart sighed. This didn't sound much fun.

'A long time ago, at the dawn of time, the earth was made by the Creator, and soon after he created seven lords in human form to oversee the development of the world. These lords were Andromeda, Baikal, Centaur, Dub, Efcheresto, Fluther and Zoltab. The Creator made these lords immortal, trained them himself and, when their training was complete, divided the world into seven great sectors and gave each of the lords one to administer. But he made them all swear a solemn oath that they would work only for the good of mankind but without ever interfering directly in their affairs, that they would never try to use their power for their own glory and that they would never under any circumstances attempt to take on human form and stalk the earth as men. To this they all agreed. The Creator departed and left the world in their hands. All seemed well. But one lord did not abide by his word. Zoltab was tempted by power and by evil.

Nobody is sure why, but it is suggested that he first became frustrated because his name was last on the register at the Creator's training school and he developed an inferiority complex. We will never know for sure. Zoltab broke his oath and tried to use his power for his own glory and to raise himself to the status of the Creator and have men worship him. There was a terrible battle with the other lords. Zoltab was defeated, but the other lords could not kill him because he was immortal so they imprisoned him deep in the bowels of the earth. Once more, all seemed well.'

'I do like a happy ending,' said Blart's grandfather. 'It rounds off a story nicely and sends you off to bed with a warm feeling.'

'Stay, old man,' said Capablanca. 'For this story has no end.'

'Modern, is it?' said Blart's grandfather disapprovingly.

'It is both ancient and modern,' replied Capablanca gnomically. 'Know ye that some foolish men did band together and work for the return of Zoltab. For many centuries the Cult of Zoltab has worked in secret, sending out Ministers to convert others to their evil cause through lies and cunning and deceit. Their influence has steadily increased until today they lie poised to take power throughout the world. They await only one thing – the return of Zoltab. And his return is near because for all these centuries the Minions of Zoltab have been digging to free him. They have died in their thousands but they have continued to dig.

And so they have created the Great Tunnel of Despair which soon – how soon I do not know, but very soon, mark you – will reach Zoltab in his underground prison. They will free him and he will rise filled with vengeance after enduring aeons of confinement, attempt to take control of the world, and there will be famine and disease and pestilence and death. This must be prevented and in order to prevent it Blart must come with me to do battle against the Ministers and Minions of Zoltab and to place a Cap of Eternal Doom on the Great Tunnel of Despair. So concludes my sobering narrative.'

There was silence at the table, broken only briefly by a belch from Blart that he did not attempt to cover with his hand. Finally, Blart's grandfather spoke.

'It's a good tale that you tell, I'll not deny that, but it seems to me that there are a few holes in it.'

'Holes!' The wizard was outraged. 'Old man, let me tell you that I have spent hours and hours in the Cavernous Library of Ping, which contains so many books that if you stuck them end to end they would reach into the heavens and touch the most distant stars. For ten long years I have worked in that library from dawn until dusk. I have concocted my narrative from thousands of different sources, checking and cross-referencing each event dozens of times.'

'Well, I say there's holes,' insisted Blart's grandfather. 'And stop calling me "Old Man". I'm in late middle age. You talk about the return of Zoltab as though it were a big problem and that there'll be death and disease and famine and the other thing.'

'Pestilence.'

'Yes, peskyness or whatever. But what about these six other lords? They got rid of Zoltab before. They'll just do it again, won't they?'

'Ah,' said Capablanca with the smug air of a man who knew that he had an answer. 'The first time Zoltab broke his word and attempted to use his power for his own glory he did so by himself. It was his idea. Therefore the lords could act against him. This time man is acting to bring Zoltab back. The lords cannot act for to do so would be to intervene in the affairs of men. What man has done only man himself can undo.'

'Oh,' said Blart's grandfather, who didn't think Capablanca needed to look quite so pleased with himself.

'Your next hole?' said Capablanca.

'Oh, right,' said Blart's grandfather, who was a little less confident this time. 'Well, look at Blart.' The wizard looked, though not for long. Blart's mouth hung open and his tongue hung loosely out of it. He resembled a rather stupid dog. 'Now, you've been talking about Dark Lords and magic and Cults and Ministers and stuff. It all sounds a bit above the boy's head to me. Don't get me wrong, he's good with the pigs. But that's about all.'

'Ah,' said Capablanca with a look of self-satisfaction on his face. 'In my researches at the Cavernous Library of Ping

I discovered reference to an ancient text rumoured to have been written by the ancient soothsayer Reti in the ice-covered land of Hypermodernia. From it I found out many things, but most important of all I discovered that a lord in human form can only be vanquished by a human whose ancestors are the first-born son (or daughter) of a first-born son (or daughter) of a first-born son (or daughter) and so on going back and back to the dawn of time. For another twenty years I searched, roaming far and wide, examining graveyards and church records in many lands. I could not find such a man until finally I stumbled upon the records of an obscure and unremarkable family, some might even say insignificant –'

'Steady,' said Blart's grandfather, but the wizard was too engrossed in his story to listen.

'I traced it back and back and back to the dawn of time and then forward and forward and forward to make sure I hadn't made any mistakes and then I came here. For Blart is the first-born son of the first-born son of the –'

'I see,' said Blart's grandfather testily.

'And this is what brings me to your isolated pig farm. To take Blart with me to the Great Tunnel of Despair to face and defeat Zoltab and his Ministers.'

There was a silence after that whilst both Capablanca and Blart's grandfather looked questioningly at Blart.

'Blart,' said Capablanca. 'Having heard what I have said and having discovered that you are a chosen one amongst legion of others, will you reconsider your decision and accompany me?'

'No,' said Blart. 'I'm not going. Especially now I know that you're boring as well as everything else. I'm going to bed.'

And with that the last hope of humanity got down from his chair and stomped upstairs, burping loudly and repeatedly.

'Well,' said Blart's grandfather, standing up and indicating that it was time for his guest to go. 'You can't say you didn't try. Goodnight.'

The wizard was ushered into the cold night air, the farmhouse door was shut behind him and mankind was doomed.

Chapter 3

Except, of course that it wasn't. For Capablanca had not spent decades in the Cavernous Library of Ping seeking ancient texts and tracing back innumerable family trees merely to go away because Blart said no. He spent a night out in the open with only his cloak to protect him and got very cold, which did nothing to improve his temper. When the first cock crowed, he got straight up, marched to the farmhouse door and rapped firmly upon it. After a time it was answered by Blart's grandfather. Capablanca gave Blart's grandfather a small bag. Whatever was in it made Blart's grandfather fling the door wide open and usher the wizard in.

Blart had heard the knock on the farmhouse door but he had thought that he'd leave his grandfather to answer it, even though he knew his grandfather's knees were not what they were and it didn't do him any good to be rushing downstairs at his age. Blart had snuggled down deeper into his bed and closed his eyes and dropped immediately into a deep sleep.

Which is of course why he had no warning when his bedroom door was thrown open, his blanket pulled back and he was lifted into the air and placed firmly over the shoulder of the wizard who marched out of the room, down the stairs and out through the kitchen door, not caring one jot how many times Blart banged himself against the walls along the way.

At first, Blart was too surprised and too bleary-eyed to do anything. However, by the time they had reached the kitchen he had caught on to the fact that he was firstly, upside down and secondly, in trouble.

'Put me down!' he shouted.

Capablanca did not respond. Instead he began whistling.

'Help me!' said Blart, catching sight of his grandfather who was standing by the gate looking lovingly at the contents of a small bag that seemed to glisten in the morning sun.

But Blart's grandfather didn't help him. Instead he opened the gate for the wizard and saluted him as he strode past.

'Grandfather,' said Blart in dismay as he was dragged past him.

'Goodbye, Blart,' said his grandfather, waving to him. 'Don't forget to write. Oh, you can't, can you?'

And with that Blart's grandfather shut the gate and walked back towards the farmhouse, counting his gold again and again and again.

Onward strode Capablanca. Looking at him you'd be surprised to think that he could carry a burly fourteen-year-old boy over his shoulder quite so easily, especially when the fourteen-year-old boy in question was screaming and kicking. However, Capablanca had spent many a day in the frozen wastes of Hypermodernia and the experience had toughened him up.

As they approached the nearby village even Blart began to realise that he was not going to be able to free himself from the wizard's grip. He therefore put all his efforts into shouting for assistance.

'Help!' cried Blart. 'Help, I'm being ...'

'Kidnapped' would have been a good word to use at the end of this sentence. 'Abducted' would have fitted just as well. Unfortunately, Blart knew neither of these words and so was unable to alert the villagers to his plight.

'Help! I'm being something I don't know the word for!'

Blart's shouts grew fainter as Capablanca carried him off into the distance.

Eventually the wizard put Blart down. They were by now a good way from anywhere Blart knew. However, there was only one road and he assumed that if he walked back the way they'd come then at some point he would return to his village. This was the first time that Blart had ever thought so deeply about anything and actually reached the level of forming a plan. Unfortunately for Blart, his method of distracting the wizard was not so foolproof.

'Look, a flying pig,' said Blart, pointing behind Capablanca who had sat down on a nearby bank of grass. The wizard turned round to look. Blart immediately sprinted down the muddy road in the direction from which they had just come. He had been carried all morning so he wasn't at all tired.

He had run a good distance before the wizard turned round again. If anyone else had been there at the time they might have noticed a smile flick across the lips of Capablanca as he watched Blart disappear down the road. And then suddenly he was very still, and blue fire flashed briefly from his eyes. In the distance, Blart tripped up and fell on his face in the mud. He stood up, started to run and immediately fell on his face in the mud again. Again he got up. Again he tried to run away. Again his legs got muddled up and he fell on his face in the mud. He got up and did the whole thing again. And again. And again.

After falling over twenty times, Blart paused to think. He turned round to look at Capablanca. Capablanca waved to him. Blart took a few steps towards him. Nothing happened. He didn't fall in any mud. He turned round and walked away from the wizard. Within three steps one leg had tripped the other leg up and he was back in his familiar position – face down in the mud. He did the same thing again. Towards the wizard – no problem; away from the wizard – face down in the mud. With a sigh he picked himself up and stomped back towards Capablanca.

'What have you done to my legs?' demanded Blart.

'Your legs?'

'My legs won't work properly.'

'They look fine to me.'

'That's when I walk this way. When I walk away from you I fall over.'

'Perhaps you shouldn't walk away from me then,' observed Capablanca mildly.

'You shouldn't mess with legs,' Blart said bitterly. 'Legs aren't fair. You make me come away from my pigs and then you make my legs not work properly. This is a rotten day.'

Blart, who was never very good at feeling sorry for others, was extremely good at feeling sorry for himself. He began to cry. Then he began to howl. Then he lay down on the ground and kicked his legs in the air. This really is quite shocking behaviour for a potential hero, as I'm sure you'll agree.

Whilst Blart is sobbing, perhaps this would be an ideal time to clear up something that may have been bothering the more alert amongst you. Blart, you remember, was pulled from his bed by the wizard and carted off to save the world without any opportunity of dressing himself. Some people may be worried that Blart is now weeping in the mud wearing only his pyjamas. Allow me to put your minds at rest. Blart was a lazy boy and he chose, rather than expend unnecessary energy in removing his clothes, to sleep in them, despite them being encrusted in mud and pig droppings, so he was perfectly prepared to embark on his adventure when gathered up by the wizard. Perfectly prepared, but smelly.

Eventually Blart recognised that tears weren't going to do the trick. He stopped crying, rolled over and looked sulkily at the wizard, who smiled cheerily back at him.

'Finished, have we? That's good. Come on.'

'I'm staying here,' said Blart.

'All right. Suit yourself,' said Capablanca, and he strode off.

Blart couldn't believe it. After all that trouble the wizard was leaving him behind. He'd given up. Blart was free. He watched Capablanca continue to stride into the distance. He walked even faster now he didn't have a large fourteen-year-old boy on his back. Soon he would vanish.

Blart's happiness began to ebb away. There was something wrong. He knew it. If only he could work out what it was. Blart kept thinking. The wizard kept walking. Step by step Blart worked out what was wrong. If he walked away from the wizard he fell over almost immediately, so he couldn't do that. If he stayed where he was he would eventually die of hunger, and he didn't like the sound of that. There was only one option left – to follow the wizard, who was disappearing into the distance at that very moment.

Blart got up and, without even pausing to wipe the mud off himself, charged after the wizard.

Chapter 4

All day Blart and Capablanca walked. Through valleys, across streams, up hill and down dale. They passed clusters of little houses with children playing outside and isolated farms where men scythed the grass or ploughed the fields or simply leant against the fence, a stick of straw in their mouths, watching them walk by.

This would have been an ideal opportunity for Blart to study the beauty of the natural world in places he had never visited before. To observe the differences and the similarities and to wonder at the size of a world he had never previously considered. But instead Blart moaned and stared at the ground, unless they happened to be passing some small children in which case he immediately bent down and scooped up some stones to throw at them. Or when they passed a farmer, Blart would pull a horrible face. When he made an effort to look repulsive the effect was truly startling.

As the day drew towards its close and the sun's power began to war.e and their shadows became longer, Blart's mind turned once more to his own needs.

'I'm hungry,' he said.

'Hmmm,' said Capablanca, who was thinking deep thoughts.

'I want some food,' demanded Blart.

'All right,' said Capablanca, and he pointed towards a building in the next valley with smoke puffing steadily from its chimney. 'There's food waiting for us down there.'

'Why is it waiting for us?' Blart persisted. 'Did it know we were coming?'

'It's an inn,' explained Capablanca. 'Like a tavern. They sell food.'

Blart looked uncomprehending. His grandfather had never told him about inns and taverns, working on the principle that if Blart didn't know they existed he could never ask to be taken to one on his eighteenth birthday. Blart's grandfather was a mean man who planned ahead.

'Oh, just follow me,' said Capablanca in exasperation.

And with that he marched down the hill towards the tavern. And Blart who, as we know, didn't have any choice in the matter, followed him.

The Jolly Murderers was an inn with a fine reputation. It served tasty food in large portions in a room dominated by a roaring turf fire. It had a wide range of ales and it had comfy beds that were available at cheap prices. It had stood alone in this small valley for as long as anybody could remember and was frequented by all manner of travellers, some on honest business and some on business that they were less willing to talk about in detail. It was the sort of place Blart had never seen before in his life.

It was not surprising, therefore, that his immediate reaction was one of criticism.

'Yuck,' he said as the wizard led him into the bar. 'It's dirty and smelly and horrible.'

'Hush,' said Capablanca sternly. Inns and taverns are notoriously easy places to get into fights if you start saying rude things about them.

Capablanca strode up to the bar.

'Landlord,' he shouted.

From the back of the tavern a man emerged. He was thin and pale and his greasy hair hung lankly from his head. Capablanca looked puzzled.

'Where is Mr Cheery?' he asked.

'Dunno. He retired,' replied the landlord.

'Retired?' repeated Capablanca. 'But he was but young. He wouldn't have retired.'

'You calling me a liar?' asked the landlord, with an aggressive leer that revealed a mouth half full of yellow teeth.

'No,' said Capablanca hurriedly. 'But all –'

'Do you want a drink or not?' said the landlord.

'Yes. I'll have a pint of your best ale and a glass of water for the boy and two of your superb hot pies for which this hostelry is justly renowned. And we will want a room for the night.'

The landlord disappeared. Capablanca looked around the bar with a mystified expression on his face.

'Retired?' he mused to himself. 'Strange.'

'Oi,' said Blart, giving him a prod in the arm. 'I don't want water. I want –'

'Not now,' said Capablanca. 'Can you not see that I have to think?'

In fact the wizard didn't have to think, but he didn't want to listen to Blart.

They found themselves a table and soon the shifty-looking landlord returned carrying a tray with two pies, a glass of water and a tankard of ale. Unfortunately, the disappearance of Mr Cheery was not the only change to come over The Jolly Murderers. In his absence the inn had swiftly gone downhill. The pies were small and lukewarm rather than big and hot, and filled with gristle rather than succulent cubes of meat. The ale was vinegary. Blart's water, however, was as good as it had been in Cheery's day, but that wasn't much consolation.

The poor quality of the food did not stop them eating it though. Having missed breakfast, this was Blart's first meal of the day and Capablanca was just as ravenous. Neither of them spoke as they ferociously attacked their pies. They overloaded their forks. They chewed with their mouths open. They refilled their mouths before they had emptied them and, to top it off, Blart ended the meal with one of his trademark burps so loud that it echoed off the surrounding walls, drawing stares from all the other drinkers. In all it had taken less than five minutes for them to empty their bowls entirely. The wizard had just decided that a complaint against the standard of the food was not going to get a sympathetic hearing in the face of this evidence when there was a bang and the door flew open and smashed against the wall. Its lower hinge snapped off and flew across the room, hitting the pub dog, Noose, who was lying innocently in front of the fire. Noose began to howl, but nobody paid any attention for all eyes were turned to the doorway to see what came through it.

Chapter 5

It was a tight squeeze but through the door came a big, bronzed, burly, bearded warrior. Even Blart could tell he was a warrior because on his back he carried the biggest sword that Blart had ever seen.

'Greetings,' hollered the big, bronzed, burly, bearded warrior.

'You've broken my door,' said the lank-haired landlord, who had emerged from the back of the bar at the sound of the warrior's arrival.

'Tush and pish,' responded the warrior. 'I gave it a mere tap and it splintered into matchwood. 'Tis no fault of mine.'

'It's going on your bill,' said the landlord.

The warrior had so far made no further progress in entering the room and it soon became obvious why. His huge sword had caught on the doorframe and he was having trouble manoeuvering it in.

'Blast this door! What sort of tiny door is this for an alehouse?' he demanded of the landlord. 'Is it mice and midgets you be hoping to attract with a door like this?'

The warrior bent down and wriggled his bottom in a most undignified way. Then he bobbed up and down a couple of times and suddenly shot through the door, falling flat on his face. He jumped to his feet surprisingly quickly for such a big man.

'Who laughed at me?' he said accusingly, bending down and pulling a small dagger from the inside of his boot. 'The man who laughed at me has laughed his last laugh, for sure. He will not giggle again this side of hell, no, he won't. Is that a smirk I see before me?' he demanded of a small nervous-looking man in the corner.

The nervous-looking man looked away.

'I'll give you the benefit of the doubt. Now, is there anybody here who wants a fight?' demanded the warrior.

Blart suddenly saw his chance to escape from the wizard and to rid himself of the onerous task of having to save the world.

'He does,' he announced, pointing at Capablanca. 'He was laughing when you came in.'

'Who dares do such a thing?' bellowed the warrior. 'You in the cowl.' The warrior indicated Capablanca. 'Go down on your knees and make your peace with God before I chop you into pieces myself.'

The warrior advanced towards Capablanca. The wizard showed no signs of moving. Blart held his breath and wondered if it was wrong to get somebody killed needlessly. The

31

warrior raised his dagger high. Blart decided that on the whole he felt he could live with the guilt.

'Good evening, Beowulf.'

The warrior stopped.

'Capablanca?'

The wizard nodded calmly.

'I heard you were dead.'

'People exaggerate,' observed Capablanca. 'But it has been a long time.'

'So long I did not recognise you,' replied the warrior. 'Many years since we fought side by side against the skeleton hordes at the Battle of Longbarrow Hill.'

'Many,' agreed Capablanca.

'Ay, those were the days, my friend,' said the warrior wistfully. 'But what changes have come over us all. Even you, the great Capablanca, now amuse yourself in a tavern laughing at warriors falling over.'

'I'm afraid my little friend strayed from the truth when he told you that,' corrected the wizard.

Blart felt an urgent need to be somewhere else. What were the chances, he asked himself, that they'd know each other? The warrior's grip on his knife tightened.

'Could you put the knife down?' asked Capablanca gently. 'It's putting the other customers off their drinks.'

'What, this puny thing?' said Beowulf, looking at his knife as though it were as dangerous as an uncooked sausage. 'Of course I'll put it away. Once it's done its job.'

A big slab of hand shot out, grabbed Blart and pulled him across the table. Blart found himself lying face upward with a knife across his neck.

'I shall separate this boy's head from the rest of him. Boys who tell lies should be decapitated,' growled Beowulf.

'Eeeek,' screeched Blart.

'Say your prayers, boy,' ordered the warrior gruffly. 'I am feeling kind so I will not damn thee to hell.'

'I don't know any prayers,' squeaked Blart.

'What?' bellowed Beowulf, but Blart felt the warrior's grip on his neck slacken slightly. 'You don't know any prayers? What sort of upbringing have you had, lad? Go away and learn some. And when you've learnt some come back and I will kill thee then,' he boomed, pushing Blart on to the floor.

'Ow,' groaned Blart as his body smashed on to the hard stone slabs, but neither Capablanca nor Beowulf took any notice. Blart resolved never to learn a prayer in his life because it would mean his instant death. And so yet another young soul was lost to the Church.

'Landlord!' yelled Beowulf. 'Some ale and some food. I have a mighty hunger and a powerful thirst about me.'

The landlord moved like greasy lightning behind the bar.

'What brings thee here, oh, Beowulf the Warrior?' said Capablanca.

'Call me Beo,' said Beowulf with a gruff smile. 'There is no need for formality between us.'

Capablanca nodded.

'Ah, Wizard,' Beo shook his head in sadness. 'You see before you a frustrated man. There are no deeds of chivalry left to do. No damsels locked in castles. No dragons. The Holy Grail has been found. Even if some kind of gallant adventure comes up, before a man can get his armour on and mount his trusty steed there are a hundred knights ahead of him. We've a terrible problem with over-manning.'

Capablanca looked sympathetic.

'And so I'm reduced to debt collecting. I've tried other things but when you've got your own weapon and your only qualification is a lust for blood it's all that's open to you.'

Capablanca shook his head.

'Take it from me, Wizard. There's nobody who enjoys grinding the faces of the poor less than I do.' For a moment Beo looked doubtful. 'Except perhaps the poor themselves. But what can I do? If only I had a quest.'

It is not often that a person is in a position to be the answer to another's fervent wish. Capablanca savoured his moment whilst Beo gloomily contemplated the state of his existence.

'I have a quest for you.'

Beowulf's eyes lit up immediately.

'You do?'

Capablanca nodded. An eager smile broke out on Beowulf's face.

'Is there a dragon?' he asked.

Capablanca shook his head. Beo didn't seem to mind.

'A damsel in distress?'

Capablanca shook his head again. Beo seemed a little disappointed.

'A grail?' he said hopefully.

'None of them,' said Capablanca. Beowulf's face fell considerably.

'Don't mess with me, Wizard,' Beo said menacingly. 'Don't be saying this is a quest when all it is is a journey. I'm not one who enjoys being messed about. Be straight with me and I'll be straight with you. But be crooked with me and you'll be dealing with cold steel.'

'It is a great quest,' snapped Capablanca. 'Know ye that we ride against Zoltab.'

'ZOLTAB!' shouted Beo in his excitement.

'Sssshhh,' hissed Capablanca.

'Your pie and ale, sir,' said the landlord, who had managed to make his way to their table without either of them noticing, so engrossed were they in their own conversation.

'Yes, very good weather we're having,' said Capablanca, trying to change the topic of conversation.

'But I thought Zoltab was –' began Beo.

'An old lord best forgotten,' interrupted Capablanca, making frantic eye movements towards the landlord to indicate to Beowulf that he should be quiet.

'Will sir require any sauces?' asked the landlord.

'No,' said Capablanca in his haste to get rid of the

landlord. 'He won't.'

The landlord departed.

'I wanted sauces,' said Beo indignantly.

'I thought you wanted a quest,' Capablanca reminded him.

'Isn't it a terrible thing when a man can't have a quest and sauces?' muttered Beo, but he complained no further. Whilst he ate his pie, the wizard told him in hushed tones where they were bound.

Blart, who was still sitting on the floor, noticed that the landlord had slunk over to a dark corner where a group of men dressed in black sat close together around a table muttering amongst themselves. The landlord spoke to them, and whatever he said caused the men to sneak a number of dark looks at the warrior and the wizard, who were too deep in conversation to notice. Blart pulled himself up from the floor as it was apparent that nobody was going to give him any sympathy. He sat down next to Capablanca. As he did so there was a loud guffaw of laughter from the table in the corner. It was laughter with an edge to it. Cruel laughter that you might hear from a bully who knows that his victim is lying helpless in front of him.

Capablanca had finished explaining the quest to Beowulf. The warrior raised two objections to it. They were both to do with Blart. The first was that he would now be unable to kill Blart, even after he'd learnt a prayer, as the wizard had made it perfectly plain that Blart was essential to the success of the whole campaign. Reluctantly Beowulf accepted Capablanca's decision. The second objection was that he, Beowulf, was an experienced man of action and, whilst he had respect for Capablanca who had powers that he could never hope to possess, when he looked at Blart he just saw a useless lump.

'What use can this ugly poltroon be against Zoltab?' he asked.

This seemed a good question to Blart. It also seemed a good question to Capablanca.

'That's a good question,' he replied. And then he stopped.

'And …?' prompted Beo, who felt sure that there was something missing from this answer.

Capablanca's brow furrowed deeply. His mouth opened and then closed without any words emerging. He took a deep breath. He closed his eyes. He summoned up his energy and then suddenly out popped the three words that Capablanca found most difficult to say in the whole world.

'I don't know.'

'What?' said Blart and Beo together.

'He's the first-born son of a first-born son of a first-born son dating all the way back to the beginning of time and is therefore the only person able to defeat Zoltab. But I'm not completely clear how it will happen,' muttered Capablanca shiftily.

'But …' said Blart, his voice rising in shock. 'If you don't know and I don't know who's going to tell us?'

'There are times on a great quest when we must trust to

fate,' replied Capablanca.

'That's true,' nodded Beo. 'Sure it wouldn't be a proper quest if we knew everything. We must trust to our destiny to provide us with the answers.'

Both Capablanca and Beo looked serious and philosophical.

'What happens if it doesn't?' said Blart, who was much less convinced by this whole trusting to fate approach.

'Then the world is doomed,' said Capablanca matter-of-factly, happier now that he had a question that he could answer.

'A hopeless quest is even more noble,' added Beo cheerily. 'Count me in. Shall we drink on it?'

'No,' answered Capablanca. 'Blart and I must go to bed. We have walked far today and we will travel further tomorrow.'

'Goodnight to you, then,' said Beo. 'I'll have one more myself for luck and then I'll follow you. Landlord. Another flagon of mead, please.'

'Yes, sir,' said the landlord, making them all jump as he appeared from behind a nearby pillar.

'Cancel that order,' instructed Capablanca. 'We must depart early tomorrow and we must all retire immediately.'

'But a warrior needs his ale,' protested Beo. 'It gives him strength and courage.'

'And makes it very difficult to get him up in the morning,' said Capablanca. 'You must choose, Beowulf the Warrior. Is it to be a quest or a flagon of ale?'

The warrior looked into Capablanca's face and realised the wizard was serious. With an ill grace he threw his tankard to the floor.

'Have it your way, Capablanca,' he said grudgingly. 'But this quest had better be good.'

The landlord showed them upstairs. On the way up Capablanca arranged to move into a room with three beds for he feared that given the chance the warrior would run straight back down to the bar.

The room that they were shown into was far from hospitable. The curtains were covered in mildew, the sheets were smelly and damp and the candle didn't have much wick left. Cobwebs hung from the ceiling and invisible creatures made rustling noises.

'Be out by ten,' said the landlord.

'We'll have the plague by ten,' replied Capablanca. 'You should be ashamed of yourself.'

The landlord shrugged.

'Take it or leave it.'

They took it. They had no other choice. And though Capablanca complained and Beo grumbled and Blart muttered they were still all asleep within five minutes.

Chapter 6

'Death to the enemies of Zoltab!'

Blart's eyes shot open. A shadowy figure stood over him. Something glinted in the moonlight. A knife.

'Aaaarrrggghh.' Blart threw himself out of bed. He heard the thud as the knife embedded itself in his pillow.

'Fight to the death, men,' he heard Beowulf cry.

'Then die in the name of Zoltab,' came the bloodcurdling reply.

'Help,' cried Capablanca.

'Die, old man,' growled another voice.

Blart weighed up his options. He sensed that there were a large number of men in the room. He felt sure that their intentions were not friendly. His two comrades were obviously in trouble. Blart resolved to act immediately. He crawled under the bed, hoping that nobody noticed.

It is difficult to work out what is going on in a fight in a dark room when you are hiding under a bed. Blart heard a lot of bumps and bangs, a number of oaths and quite a few howls of pain. As his eyes became accustomed to the dark, he was able to watch what was happening too. However, he had what can only be described as a restricted view. It mainly consisted of feet and lower legs and it was difficult to get an accurate picture of who was winning from just this evidence.

'Aaaarrgggghhh.'

'Ooooohhhhhh.'

'Uuuggghhhhh.'

'Ouch, that hurt.'

'I'm on your side.'

The yells and screams echoed through the inn. No doubt the landlord would have to give a substantial discount to the other guests in the morning.

Thunk.

A dagger had fallen from someone's hand and landed by the bed. Blart recognised that in the present situation a dagger might come in handy. He reached out and grabbed it.

Thwack! Bang! Crash! Thwack (again)!

'Uuuurrgghhh.'

'Ooooowwww.'

'Aaaaarrrrggghh.'

'I've told you, I'm on your side.'

The fight showed no sign of being decided. Blart continued to watch the movement of feet and lower legs in the hope of working out what was going on and who was going to win and therefore whose side he should pretend to be on.

Loyalty, like honour, was a concept to which Blart had not yet been introduced.

But slowly, ever so slowly, Blart's brain was beginning to work. The man who'd tried to kill him had said, 'Death to the enemies of Zoltab!' He, Blart, was the only person who could defeat Zoltab. Therefore, however nice he promised to be to Zoltab, people weren't going to believe him. Once Beowulf and Capablanca were out of the way they were going to search the room, find him and kill him, and unless they were all really terrible at hide and seek then nothing was going to stop them.

'Get off.'

'Ouch.'

'Die.'

Suddenly Blart realised what he had to do – his best chance of survival was to fight on Capablanca and Beowulf's side now before anything happened to them. And so he rolled from under the bed with a blood-curdling scream, cried death or glory and threw himself upon the intruders. Well, no, actually he didn't. What he did was to try to work out a way for him to participate in the fight without risking his own safety. Amazingly, Blart thought of a way. And the way was …

Feet.

If he could stab the feet of the intruders then he could undermine the attack from below whilst keeping himself relatively safe. Blart was so pleased with his plan that he lay admiring it for a few seconds.

'Help, Capablanca.'

'Save me, Beo.'

Shaken out of this brief period of self-congratulation by the cries of his comrades, Blart picked up his knife and prepared to plunge it into the feet of the attackers. He could almost hear the howls of pain.

And then suddenly he stopped.

There was a problem. He didn't know whose feet were whose. To be fair to Blart, it would be wrong to criticise him for not having made a detailed study of his comrades' feet. Let's face it. Few of us would have considered it necessary as a prelude to military action. It was here that Blart had a stroke of luck.

Bareness.

Of the twelve feet that had at various times passed in front of his eyes only four were bare. These bare feet had to belong to Capablanca and Beowulf. Nobody sleeps in anything but bare feet because covered feet will overheat in the night and swell up, making it difficult to get your boots on in the morning. The surprise attack had left them no chance to put any kind of footwear on and so those with covered feet must be the enemy. Blart was making large leaps when it came to logical thought. He studied the enemy footwear. They had on soft slipper-like shoes chosen to make as little noise as possible in order to maintain the element of surprise in their attack. These soft shoes contained their Achilles' heel.

Blart raised his dagger and stabbed.

'Aaaaarrrrgggaaaaawwwwhhhooo,' was the stunning noise that emerged from the man who owned the foot.

Quickly, Blart crawled to the other end of the bed and sank his dagger into the nearest slippered foot. There was slightly more of the 'wwwwwwhhhhhooo' and slightly less of the 'aaaarrggaa' this time but to those who weren't listening carefully the noise was essentially the same.

By the time Blart's third stab had found its way through an enemy instep, doubts were beginning to enter their collective mind.

'Devils,' cried one. 'There's devils coming through the floorboards.'

'We are not fighting ordinary mortals,' bewailed another.

'I'll never play football again,' lamented a third.

The fourth stab from Blart was decisive.

'More devils,' cried another attacker, who had acquired a ventilation passage in the centre of his foot. 'Run, men.'

Run, in all honesty, would not be a good description of what the attackers did at this point. However, they did limp fast. But one figure did not limp fast enough. By the time Blart emerged from under the bed, the slowest attacker lay on the floor with Beowulf the Warrior sitting on his chest, his mighty sword held aloft and poised to dispatch the intruder to another world.

'Stop!' ordered Capablanca. 'Do not kill him. We need some answers.'

'Ah, go on,' cajoled Beo.

'No.'

'Sure, this is no fun,' lamented Beo. 'The least you expect after a battle is to be able to massacre the defenceless prisoners in cold blood.'

'Maybe later,' said Capablanca in an attempt to mollify the grumpy warrior. 'But first we need some answers.'

They both noticed Blart for the first time.

'Can I kill *him* then?' asked Beo, indicating Blart.

'Why?' demanded Blart. 'I just saved your lives.'

'Did you hear something?' asked Beo.

'No,' replied Capablanca. 'Did you?'

'No,' replied Beo.

'Honest,' persisted Blart. 'I behaved really well. I'm a hero.'

It is often the case when two extreme positions are taken up that the truth lies somewhere between them. Blart had exhibited considerable cowardice by hiding under the bed but then he had redeemed himself by attacking from below. Whilst it was pushing his luck to describe himself as a hero, he didn't deserve to be completely ignored.

'So, who've we got here?' said Capablanca, returning his attention to the captured prisoner.

'I don't know,' said Beo. 'Let's be having a proper look at him.'

And with that Beo dragged the prisoner across the room to the window where the moonlight would reveal his face more clearly.

'Mind my foot!' shrieked the prisoner in a voice which sounded familiar.

'I did that,' Blart reminded them, but to no avail. His two companions showed no sign of having heard.

Blart refused to be abashed by the treatment and pushed forward to see what the moonlight revealed. A simultaneous gasp escaped all three of them. It was the landlord.

Chapter 7

'What kind of a host are you,' demanded Beo, 'to be attacking your guests in their beds? Sure, that's no way to get a good reputation. You'll attract no repeat customers that way, let me tell you.'

The landlord responded with a horrible leer to the criticisms of the warrior even though they were perfectly justified from a business point of view. Below the window the sound of galloping hooves suggested that the other attackers were fleeing.

'Who are you and why did you attack us?' demanded Capablanca.

'You'll get nothing out of me,' spat back the landlord. 'I will answer to a higher power.'

'Great,' said Beo gleefully. 'Do I get to torture him now?'

'Not yet,' said Capablanca. 'For I have an idea which may save us the trouble of torturing this rogue.'

'No trouble,' said Beo lightly. 'Really no trouble at all.'

The wizard reached out and turned up the lobe of the

landlord's ear. The moonshine caught the underside of the ear and shone clearly on an 'm' which was tattooed there.

'The mark of Zoltab,' said Capablanca dramatically. 'I did not think to find it so far west. Things are worse than I thought.'

'An "m",' said Blart, who was puzzled. 'Why isn't the mark of Zoltab a "z"?'

This was such a good question that the wizard forgot that he was ignoring Blart and answered it.

'Know ye that Zoltab's followers are branded according to their rank. A small "m" indicates a minion of Zoltab whilst a capital "M" indicates a Minister. This is a minion of Zoltab.'

'Now can I kill him?' begged Beo, who sensed that he might just get the idea past the wizard if he threw it in quickly.

'No,' said Capablanca. 'He will be able to tell us many things that could help us.'

'Oh,' said Beo, looking crestfallen.

'What have you done with Cheery?' demanded Capablanca. 'You took this inn from him by foul means, did you not?'

The landlord turned his head away to indicate that he would not speak.

A smile broke out on Beowulf's face. He stamped heavily on the bleeding foot of the landlord, who roared in pain. Beowulf's smile grew broader. He really isn't showing himself in a particularly good light.

'He's tied up in the cellar,' said the landlord quickly.

Beowulf looked slightly disappointed.

'Ask him another,' he said to Capablanca. 'A really hard one he doesn't know the answer to.'

'In a minute,' said Capablanca. 'First we must free Cheery. Keep a close eye on the minion when we go down to the cellar, Beowulf.'

They lit a candle from the embers of their fire and rushed down to the cellar. There they found Cheery tied, gagged and frowning. Capablanca undid the knots and removed the gag.

'Thank'ee, kind sirs,' said Cheery. 'I've been hoping someone would come and rescue me.'

'And here we are,' said Beo.

'Let us have a drink to celebrate my release,' said Cheery.

They went upstairs to the bar and lit some candles. Cheery filled three tankards with ale. Beo placed the minion of Zoltab on a nearby chair and stared at him ferociously.

'No ale for the boy,' ordered Capablanca.

'He's a coward,' added Beo. 'You'd still be down there if it was up to the likes of him.'

'I was the one who won it for us,' blurted out Blart in indignation. 'I stabbed their –'

'He's a liar too,' said Beo.

'All boys are liars,' agreed Cheery, giving Blart a hard look before taking his beer away.

'Now,' said Capablanca, leaning forward towards their prisoner. 'We want some answers, minion. Who sent you here and why? How long will it be before the Great Tunnel of Despair is long enough to reach Zoltab and how well is the entrance to it guarded?'

'Ugh.' Cheery spat out the ale he had just swigged from Blart's tankard. 'That's disgusting. To think that I would see the day when a vinegary ale was served in The Jolly Murderers.'

'Sure you'll soon have it sorted,' reassured Beo. 'And you know if you drink five or six tankards it stops tasting that bad.'

Cheery's interjection had distracted them. Briefly they had taken their eyes off Zoltab's minion. This proved to be a mistake because in the short time he was free from the gaze of his captors he had managed to furnish himself with a dagger.

'He's got a dagger,' said Blart, pointing out the obvious.

''Tis a puny thing,' mocked Beo. 'We are four against one here. You have no chance of escape.'

'Put down the knife and answer our questions and things will go easier for you,' Capablanca told him.

The minion laughed.

'Easier for me, a minion of Zoltab? If I were to help you foil Zoltab's return, why, I would be subject to tortures that you cannot imagine. Those who serve Zoltab know that a traitor faces a punishment worse than death. Know ye only that you are too late. Very soon Zoltab will rise from his underground dungeon and take his place as the ruler of the world. That is all I will tell you. I will never speak a word that would prevent the return of my Lord Zoltab.'

'We'll see about that,' said Beo grimly.

'Shall we?' said the minion, and he stuck out his tongue at the warrior. This would have seemed a puerile or childish gesture if it were not for the fact that the minion followed it by raising his knife to his mouth and with one swift strike severing his tongue from its root.

'Ugh,' said Blart.

'Damn,' said Beo.

'We'll never know the reason they took over the inn now,' said Capablanca in frustration.

'Do you think it'll stain?' asked Cheery.

Meanwhile the minion writhed on the floor, his face contorted in pain but no words coming from his bleeding mouth.

Chapter 8

'He's not our responsibility,' insisted Capablanca.

'Well, he's certainly not mine,' replied Cheery.

It was the next morning and the questors were standing outside the inn. There was dew on the grass, a fresh sun in the sky and birds sang from the trees. The natural world seemed utterly unaware that all that was good and pure was threatened by Zoltab's return.

'We rescued you,' said Capablanca. 'And now we've got to go and save the world. And all we want you to do to help is lock the minion in your cellar until we return.'

'I want him out of here,' insisted Cheery. 'I don't want to give him another chance to take over my inn. Who knows how much he's affected trade already?'

'Have you got a well?' interjected Beo.

'At the back,' replied Cheery.

Beo nodded and wandered off.

'Now,' continued Cheery, 'I'd like the world to be saved as much as the next man, but I've got my own priorities and they don't include being a gaoler for one of Zoltab's minions.'

'But we have no time,' pleaded Capablanca.

'Look, I'm very sorry, but I'm a businessman. If it's not good for trade then I don't want to know about it.'

'But the end of the world will be terrible for trade,' argued Capablanca. 'You must think long term.'

'I've said I can't help you and I'm sticking by it. And you haven't paid for last night.'

'You mean that's not on the house?' Capablanca was shocked.

'Ten crowns, please.'

'I demand a discount.'

'What for?'

'What for? Nearly being murdered in our beds. That's what for.'

'All right. I'll knock off two crowns.'

'I'll pay you the full price if you keep an eye on Zoltab's minion until I get back.'

'No need,' said Beo, butting into the conversation.

'I beg your pardon?' said Capablanca.

'He just fell down the well. Tragic accident. We were just wandering along, me talking, him listening, and suddenly he's not there any more.'

'But that well's got a cover on it,' said the landlord.

'Someone's taken it off,' Beo said, shaking his head. 'Kids, I suppose.'

'We're an isolated inn,' said Cheery. 'There aren't any kids around here.'

'Maybe birds, then,' said Beo slightly less confidently.

'Birds?' shrieked the landlord. 'That cover must weigh two stone.'

'Look,' said Beo, pointing his finger aggressively at Cheery. 'I don't know nothing more than the fact that he's in the well. All right?'

Cheery's expression changed to one of horror as he realised the true terror of the situation.

'My water. It'll be poisoned. I've got to get him out.'

And without further ado he rushed off towards the well.

'You didn't push him into the well, did you?' asked Capablanca.

'Me?' said Beo innocently.

'Wow!' said Blart. If you could just go round throwing people into wells then this quest might be more fun than he had previously thought.

And without waiting to pay their bill, the three of them set off to save the world once more.

Chapter 9

'We must go faster,' said Capablanca urgently.

'I can't go faster,' said Blart, sitting down abruptly. 'I'm too tired.'

They had been walking for two days and had left all human habitation far behind them. The land they now travelled through was a mixture of grasslands and rocky hills, but it contained no buildings and no people. Blart had never been fond of people but he would still have liked some of them around to dislike.

'Show some pluck, Blart,' urged Capablanca. 'Zoltab's minions will have wasted no time after escaping from the inn to spread the news of our quest. Their presence in The Jolly Murderers shows that their influence has spread even further than I thought possible. Our quest has become even more difficult and we must assume that his minions will be found everywhere and will be ready to kill us.'

''Tis a powerful shame that they stole my horse when they fled,' observed Beowulf. 'Otherwise we'd have made good speed.'

'And you wouldn't smell so much,' added Blart rudely. He was, however, accurate. The warrior was a big man and he had been sweating for two days.

'Quiet,' said Capablanca. 'Look at this.'

He pointed at a large pile of dung that lay on the grass.

'Why?' demanded Blart.

'Because it is a sign of hope.'

'Is it?' asked Beo.

'Yes,' replied Capablanca. 'For where there is horse dung, there are horses. And this grassland is home to the wild horses of Noved.'

'The wild horses of Noved,' said Beo. 'I have heard of these powerful steeds which are twice the size of a normal horse and can carry three men into battle.'

'The very beasts,' said Capablanca.

'But I have also heard it said,' said Beo, 'that they are impossible to capture because they are so fast and fierce and that a man risks death if he attempts to mount one.'

'That sounds like exaggeration to me,' said Capablanca.

'But it was the same man who told me both things,' protested Beo.

'There is no time for discussions,' said Capablanca hastily. 'We must find a suitable place to catch a wild horse of Noved.'

'What do we do then?' demanded Blart.

'We tame him, of course,' answered Capablanca. 'Now

follow me towards those high rocks. That looks like the kind of place where we might be able to catch one.'

Blart's eyes followed Capablanca's finger. The rocks seemed a very long way away to him.

But Capablanca strode off purposefully and Beo marched behind him. Blart had no choice. He sighed and shuffled after them.

Half a day later, they were standing high above a narrow gulch that lay amid the jumble of massive rocks. After an exhaustive study of the horse dung in the area, Capablanca had concluded that a pack/herd/can't remember what of wild horses must regularly pass through it on their way to the water hole.

'This is perfect,' he announced. 'Now let me tell you my plan for catching a horse.'

Capablanca told them. Beo nodded and agreed. Blart did neither. To him the plan sounded very dangerous indeed. Having previously been opposed to walking, he now began to see its appeal. It might be slow but at least it wasn't going to kill him.

'Couldn't we just walk instead?' he asked.

Capablanca looked exasperated.

'You haven't listened to a single word I've said, have you?' he accused Blart.

'I have,' replied Blart indignantly. 'I can listen to single words. It's just when you stick them together in long bits that

I get bored.'

'Look!' shouted Beo.

They looked.

In the distance there was a plume of smoke. As Blart watched it moved and began to come closer. And then came the sound. A pounding which seemed to make the whole earth tremble. And finally he saw them. The horses. Huge beasts – twice the size of any horse he had ever seen before – galloping towards the gulch.

'Ready,' cried Capablanca.

The first ten horses were into the gulch when blue light shone from the wizard's eyes and suddenly both the entrance and the exit were blocked with rocks. The horses nearest the entrance to the gulch reared back, their forelegs rising in the air. Horses behind clattered into them.

Blart, however, was more concerned with the ten horses that were trapped in the gulch immediately below him. They galloped to the exit to discover it was blocked by rocks, wheeled around and cantered back towards the entrance to discover that that too was now blocked by rocks. Blue light continued to shine from the wizard's eyes and his face was contorted with the effort of maintaining the illusion of the rocks. The horses stopped for a moment, obviously confused by what they could see but as yet unable to work out that they were trapped.

Blart knew now was the time to throw the rope Capablanca had given him, before the horses panicked and began to charge up and down the gulch. Beside him Beo threw his. It snaked through the air, missed all the horses and landed on the rocky ground. Beo's rope might have missed but the horses had noticed it. Whinnying, they shuffled away from it as though it were a snake. Blart spun his lasso into the air above his head as he had done many times at home when preparing to catch a pig. The speed of the rope made it crack. Blart swung his arm faster, injecting more and more energy. And then he let go. It flew down and looped round the head of the largest horse in there – a jet-black stallion that felt the rope tighten around his neck and exploded with anger.

If Beo had not moved quickly to grab the rope then Blart would have been pulled over the edge and would have been trampled to death by the stampeding horses, all terrified by the panic of the captured stallion. But even Beowulf's mighty arms would not be able to hold the rope for more than a few seconds.

'Wizard,' cried Beo.

Capablanca, his eyes still burning blue, grabbed hold of the rope.

'Jump,' yelled Beo.

They jumped.

And crashed on to the back of the horse. The instant they landed the blue light vanished from the wizard's eyes, the rocks disappeared and the stallion bolted out on to the plain, bucking and shaking and kicking as it did so.

'Yee-haw,' shouted Beo.

'Woah,' grunted Capablanca.

'Ooooh, my bottom,' yelped Blart, who felt very much like he was in trouble at home and his grandfather was beating him. Except ten times worse.

The horse ignored all these remarks and continued to attempt to throw them from his back. He rose up on two legs but somehow they clung on. He tried to gallop very fast and then stop very suddenly in the hope that they would shoot over his neck and land in a crumpled heap at his feet. If this worked he planned to trample on them afterwards, because he was a horse who thought ahead.

It didn't. Gradually the horse began to tire. His shakes became less violent, he could no longer get his front feet off the ground and his sudden stops began to resemble long rests. Finally, partly because he was a horse with a surprisingly philosophical approach to life but mainly because he was exhausted, he came to a stop, panting and sweating.

Not trusting the horse not to run away, the questors took it in turns to dismount. There was fruit on a nearby bush and they picked it and fed the horse. Further off was a stream. They led the horse to it and encouraged him to drink. The horse began to feel that there were compensations to being ridden. He'd had to get his own food before. Eventually Capablanca and Beo decided to take a risk. They left the horse without a rider and waited to see what happened. He stayed.

'Good horse,' said Capablanca. 'I shall name thee Magic.'

The horse shook his head and neighed.

'Suit yourself,' said Capablanca, rather put-out.

''Tis a noble beast,' said Beo. 'It should be called Valiant.'

Again the horse shook his head and neighed.

'See if I care,' said Beo, quite offended.

'They're both rubbish names,' Blart informed them. 'I shall call him Pig.'

'Sure you can't call a horse Pig,' Beo told him.

'Ignorant boy,' said Capablanca loftily.

But the horse nodded its head and its neigh sounded much more like a yea, and so Pig the Horse it was.

'I know about names,' said Blart smugly. 'I'm better than either of you.'

Capablanca and Beo exchanged glances. They were both hoping Blart wasn't right too often on the quest, because it could quickly become very irritating.

Chapter 10

The horse had galloped many miles in his attempts to unseat them and the land had taken on a different hue. Gone were the arid plains where they had captured Pig the Horse, as he must now be called, and instead there were once more green hills and trees and plants. Most people would have felt more cheerful with this onset of natural beauty, but Blart preferred the arid plains as there wasn't as much to look at and Blart found looking at things rather boring. However, he did notice one thing. There was a different smell in the air. Or was it a taste? Or was it a smell that tasted or indeed a taste that smelt? Blart didn't know.

'What's that?' he demanded of the wizard.

'What?' said Capablanca, looking around him sharply as though he were about to be attacked.

'That smaste,' said Blart.

'What?' said Capablanca, who had never heard of a smaste and thought it might be a new kind of demon. Wizards were always having difficulty keeping up with new varieties of demon. 'That smaste,' said Capablanca, eventually guessing Blart's meaning, 'is the Eastern Ocean.'

Blart looked confused. 'Ocean', like 'kidnapped', was one of those words that was absent from his vocabulary.

'That smaste, as you call it, is the sea,' explained Capablanca.

Blart's face registered understanding. However, you would have to know Blart for a few days before you recognised this. His face of understanding was still pretty gormless. Blart had never seen the sea before and wasn't sure what he thought about it.

'Bet it's rubbish,' he said, deciding to expect the worst.

'You will soon know,' Capablanca told him. 'For now is the time to depart. We must make for the seaside village of Clegarn. There we will buy provisions, and if we are lucky we may be able to discuss our mission with Nimzovitsch the ex-wizard, who has made his home there.'

'Ex-wizard?' repeated Blart.

'He's retired,' said Capablanca.

And so, having each stroked Pig the Horse a few times to let him know that he was appreciated, they climbed back up on to his back, saying 'Good Pig' and 'Nice Pig' and 'Lovely Pig' in soothing tones as they did so. Apart from one swift shake, Pig seemed perfectly happy to have them aboard and, after a few minor direction problems, began to trot towards the hill where Capablanca wanted him to go. Trotting along on the magnificent beast Blart felt like a king, which was just the sort of delusion that was bound to get him into trouble sooner or later.

Pig the Horse carried them up the hill so easily that they might have been nothing more than fleas riding on his back. Indeed, fleas might have caused him more annoyance by biting him. As it was the only annoyance caused was by Beo, who sang a lusty ballad in which he compensated for the lack of a tune by bellowing out the words at the highest possible decibel level.

The song was called 'The Colours of the Dragon' and was not the sort of thing that you wanted booming into your ear for a whole journey. To give you some idea of the suffering that Blart and Capablanca were forced to endure, here are a few of the verses.

'Oh, the green dragon is the colour of grass
But nowhere near as nice
While grass grows in the fields
The dragon burns your eyes.

Oh, the blue dragon is the colour of the sea
But is no good for swimming
The sea is a home for all the fish
The dragon just likes killing.

Oh, the red dragon is the colour of the rose
But the rose is surely sweeter

You can give a rose unto your love
A dragon would just eat her.

Oh, the black dragon is the colour of coal
It lives near the equator
But coal will warm your house at night
A dragon will incinerate yer.

Oh, the multicoloured dragon is the colour of a garden
A garden in full bloom
But a garden is filled with living things
This dragon spells your doom.

By the time Beo had sung the song three times they had reached the top of the hill. It would be a person with very little soul who was not moved by the sight that met the eyes of the three travellers. Directly in front of them lay the vast ocean. It was a calm clear day and the sea stretched out before them in all its deep blue magnificence. Only a few rocky islands rose up to disrupt its infinite smoothness but the sea was marvellously unconcerned by their intrusion. Have a bit of space, it seemed to say. I have more than enough myself.

Perched on the edge of the water was a tiny village. A harbour sheltered the village from the sea and a jolly red fishing boat was sailing towards it. Smoke rose from some of the chimneys and dogs and children could be seen scampering hither and thither in some impenetrable game that only they knew the rules to. The strong yet soft colours of the scene blended together so effortlessly that the works of nature and the works of mankind seemed to be in complete harmony.

'There,' said Capablanca with a hint of wonder in his voice. 'This is what we are fighting to save.'

'Indeed we are,' said Beo supportingly.

'It's boring,' said Blart. 'Boring old green and brown and blue.'

'Boring?' exploded Capablanca, who liked his beauty spots. 'Boring? This, lad, this is beauty.'

'I like pigs better,' said Blart.

'Grrr,' said Capablanca, who was wondering if he hadn't made a mistake in his research at the Cavernous Library of Ping. After all, his eyes weren't what they were. Could Blart really be the boy to save the world?

Chapter 11

Well, if he wasn't, it was too late now, Capablanca told himself glumly as they trotted into the village of Clegarn. Zoltab's minion had said that his master would soon be rising from his underground prison and it would take far too long to read all the books again. Ten years too long.

As they entered the village, the children stopped their games. The sight of two men and a boy riding the biggest horse they had ever seen proved much more attractive than repeatedly running round in circles shouting, 'You're it now.' Somehow word spread, as word often does mysteriously spread in small villages, and the children's mothers appeared in their doorways to see the magnificent beast.

Blart had never seen people look at him like this. They seemed to be impressed. He swelled out his chest and held his head high as he pretended not to be listening to the complimentary remarks that came from the people they passed.

'He's amazing.'

'He's handsome.'

'He's powerful.'

'Shame about the ugly kid on his back.'

Blart chose to ignore that last remark. They stopped at what appeared to be the centre of the village. You could tell it was the centre of the village because there was some sort of small plinth there and a shifty group of men leaning against it. As they climbed down from the horse one of the men detached himself from the group and slunk over to them.

'What did you pay for that horse?' he demanded of the wizard.

Capablanca was taken aback by this forward question.

'Why … er … well … nothing.'

'You was robbed,' the man informed him.

'Oh,' said Capablanca, rather confused.

'I'll take him off your hands,' offered the man.

'What?'

'Big horse like that must eat a lot. But I like horses and I'm a kind man so I'll look after him.'

'We want to keep him,' Capablanca insisted.

'I'll give you one crown, then, to show my goodwill.'

'But we don't –' began Capablanca, but he was overtaken by an outraged roar from Beo.

'One crown?' yelled Beo indignantly. 'This horse is worth a hundred crowns.'

The man smiled broadly and transferred his attention to the warrior.

'Ten,' he said.

'Ten?' said Beo.

'Twenty.'

'He's not for sale,' insisted Capablanca.

The man ignored the wizard and continued to talk to Beowulf.

'Now, how's about you and I go into that tavern and have a little drink and we can discuss this matter further.'

'A drink would be nice,' agreed Beo.

'He's not for sale,' repeated Capablanca.

'I'll just have one,' said Beo, 'whilst you're getting the supplies.'

'Sell that horse and you'll spend the rest of your life croaking,' threatened Capablanca.

'Don't worry,' said Beo, and he headed off to the tavern with the man, who seemed to laugh very loudly at everything the warrior said, which shows that a sense of humour is a very personal thing.

The wizard shook his head.

'Right,' he said to Blart. 'I'm going to buy some food and a saddle. You stay here and look after Pig.'

The wizard headed off to the two shops in the village, one of which sold food and one of which sold saddles, which was very convenient.

Blart stood by the horse. The men leaning against the monument all stared at him. He turned away. The women in their doorways all stared at him. He turned away again. All the children were on the other side of the little square and they were staring at him. Blart looked down at the ground. It may have been his imagination but he had the distinct feeling that the ground was staring at him.

And then, whilst he was looking at the ground and feeling very uncomfortable, he was struck by an idea. This didn't happen often to Blart and so it shocked him rather like a sudden punch in the face would shock most of us. He staggered to one side with the force of it.

'He's going to fall over,' commented one of the children hopefully.

The idea was this. He could get on Pig and ride off. They'd never catch him on Pig. Pig was the fastest horse in the world. And then when he got somewhere he could sell him and get ten or twenty crowns for him like the man had said. That was where the idea stopped.

With a huge effort, for as we know Pig was very big, Blart hoisted himself up on to the horse's back.

Once he was high up he no longer minded people staring at him. In fact, he rather liked it. He met the gaze of the watchers with a haughty glare of disdain, revelling in his superiority over all of them.

'Come on, Pig,' he whispered, and the great horse began to move, gathering speed as it moved to the edge of the little square. Blart felt a rush of happiness. He was free. He wasn't going to have to save the world or face things like perils. He was going to get thirty crowns for his horse and spend it all on himself. He was …

Face down in a puddle and everybody was laughing at him.

You see, what Blart had not had the foresight to see was that if a wizard could put a spell on him, making his legs trip him up as he ran away, he could do the same to a horse.

And he had.

Blart lay in the puddle hearing the sounds of laughter all around him. This was obviously the funniest thing that had happened in the village for a very long time. The laughter that echoed around Blart was not the sort that explodes and then dwindles down to a giggle very quickly. No. This was the sort of laughter that rolled over him in waves, and whenever it seemed to be on the point of disappearing it would suddenly rise again to a howl as one person remembered how funny it had looked to see the horse stumble strangely and Blart fly over his head, his big proud smirk suddenly altered to an expression of abject panic and fear and then disappearing altogether with a dramatic splash into the only puddle in the whole place.

Blart's reaction was totally understandable in the circumstances. He resolved to keep his face in the puddle and then he would never have to look at all the people who were laughing at him. Understandable, but essentially impractical.

So he raised his head and the sight of his muddied face was enough to set the crowd off again. He noticed Capablanca coming out of the saddlery. Dolefully, he stood up and led Pig the Horse back to the wizard.

'I got the only three-person saddle they had left,' the wizard informed an uninterested Blart. 'They're the only people in the whole country who make three-person saddles so we're very lucky.'

Blart did not respond.

'I might as well talk to myself,' said Capablanca, throwing the saddle on to the back of Pig the Horse.

'I'm all wet,' Blart blurted out.

'Listen, lad,' said Capablanca as he secured the saddle. 'The sooner you get used to the idea that you're going to save the world, the drier you'll be. Now come with me. We must go to pay our respects to the ex-wizard Nimzovitsch.'

'What about Beo?' asked Blart.

'We'll come back for him later,' said Capablanca. 'Nimzovitsch lives in a small cottage just outside the village, and Beo isn't at his best in small places. He tends to destroy them.'

Chapter 12

Together they rode out of the village until they saw a little cottage in the distance.

'Can you think of a more pleasant place to retire to?' observed Capablanca.

They rode closer. The cottage became less idyllic the nearer they got. The front gate was off its hinges, the windows were cracked, and the garden was overgrown with weeds and nettles.

'Come on, Pig,' Capablanca urged the horse. 'I fear foul play. Zoltab's minions may have been here.'

'They might still be there,' pointed out Blart. 'Maybe we should leave them alone.'

'Coward,' said Capablanca. 'I have bonds of honour to Nimzovitsch. When I was a young sorceror he tutored me in much wizard lore. It would be an act of shame not to come to his aid now.'

'I can live with shame,' said Blart.

When they reached the gate they dismounted. That is,

Capablanca dismounted and then pulled Blart off after him.

'Let us approach the house carefully,' said Capablanca.

'Let's not approach at all,' suggested Blart.

A faint cry emerged from the cottage just as he finished speaking.

'What was that?' said the wizard.

They both listened.

'Help,' came the quavering cry once again.

'I can't make out what he's saying,' said Capablanca, whose ears were not as keen as Blart's.

'I think he said "Go away",' said Blart.

Capablanca looked puzzled.

'Are you sure?'

The cry came again but this time it was louder, as though the frail owner of the voice was putting every last ounce of effort into attracting attention.

'Help!'

This time Capablanca heard for himself. He looked accusingly at Blart.

'He must have changed his mind,' said Blart innocently.

Capablanca grasped Blart by the ear and pulled him towards the door of the cottage. At the door they stopped.

'We must be careful,' said Capablanca. 'Zoltab's minions could be waiting.'

Capablanca opened the door and peered in. He could see nothing. The room was filled with steam.

'Help!'

'Don't answer,' whispered Capablanca to Blart. 'The steam could be a ruse to hide Zoltab's minions so they can ambush us.'

Blart nodded to show he understood.

Capablanca took a step forward. Blart took a step forward. Capablanca took another step forward. So did Blart, hitting a large piece of furniture as he did so.

'Ow!' said Blart loudly.

'Ssssh,' hissed Capablanca.

'Who's there?' said the voice that had cried for help. 'Identify yourself, or I shall turn you into a rat.'

Capablanca didn't answer straight away. If Zoltab's minions were waiting to ambush them, then identifying himself could be very risky. But then being turned into a rat didn't appeal much either.

Blart, however, piped up immediately.

'My name's Blart. I look after pigs and I'm with Capablanca who doesn't.'

Capablanca bristled at this description. As the greatest sorcerer in the world he wasn't used to being described as someone who didn't look after pigs.

'Capablanca,' said the voice. 'Capablanca. Is it really you?'

The steam was beginning to dissipate through the open door and the details of the room were gradually appearing.

'Yes,' said Capablanca.

The steam continued to disappear and Blart and

Capablanca were now able to see that they were standing in a kitchen. On the stove there was a pot from which the steam was pouring. And on the kitchen floor was a frail old man. And on top of the frail old man was a huge white blob of sticky goo that was pinning him to the floor.

'Nimzovitsch!' cried Capablanca. 'What has happened to you? Who has done this to you?'

'Get it off me,' said Nimzovitsch.

'Blart,' commanded Capablanca, 'take the pot off the stove while I assist Nimzovitsch.'

Blart did as he was told even though it cost him a burn on his hand. Meanwhile, Capablanca knelt by the wizard and began to pull the huge blob of white goo off him handful by sticky handful.

'I will find and punish whoever has done this to you,' Capablanca assured Nimzovitsch. 'No wizard can be treated like this. Blart. Help with this goo.'

'I don't want to,' said Blart. 'It will get on my clothes.'

This was the first time in his life that Blart had shown the slightest concern about getting dirty.

'There is an old wizard who needs your assistance,' said Capablanca. 'You are a young boy. It is your duty to help and respect your elders.'

'Why?'

'Because that is what people who have embarked on noble quests do. They help others.'

Blart looked unsure.

'Or they get turned into rats,' added Nimzovitsch from his prone position.

Reluctantly Blart knelt down and began to scrape the goo off the old wizard. And once more the stick had worked where the carrot had failed.

A few minutes later, they had managed to pull off enough white goo to allow the wizard to stand up. Capablanca helped him to his feet.

'Who did this to you?' Capablanca asked. 'Was it Zoltab's evil minions?'

Nimzovitsch didn't answer straight away.

'Do not be afeared to speak,' said Capablanca. 'I am on my way to defeat Zoltab's minions. If they have humiliated you then defeating them will give me even greater pleasure. Can you tell me their names or what they looked like?'

Nimzovitsch looked a little sheepish.

'You must tell me,' said Capablanca. 'Everything I can learn about my adversaries will assist me in my great quest.'

Nimzovitsch sighed and then he spoke in a thin, reedy voice.

'I was making stew,' he said.

'I beg your pardon?' said Capablanca. This was not the answer he had been expecting.

'I was making beef stew,' repeated Nimzovitsch. 'And I thought to myself, "What goes nicely with beef stew?"'

Capablanca was too astonished by the turn the conversation had taken to answer.

'And then,' continued Nimzovitsch, 'I thought to myself "Dumplings".'

'Dumplings,' repeated Capablanca.

'Dumplings,' confirmed Nimzovitsch. 'So I prepared my dumplings. But when I had prepared them they were too small and I hate small dumplings. I decided to make some new ones. But I had run out of ingredients. I thought to myself, "How else can I make small dumplings into big dumplings?"'

The bizarre speech from the old wizard had left Blart and Capablanca dumbfounded.

'"I know," I said to myself,' continued Nimzovitsch, "I will cast an enlargement spell on the dumplings and they will grow." So I did. But something seems to have gone awry for the dumpling increased vastly in size, shattered the bowl I was holding it in and pinned me to the floor. And then the dumpling kept growing because I couldn't remember how to stop the spell. Meanwhile the stew boiled dry on the stove and filled the room with steam. If you hadn't come, I would have been smothered by my own supper.'

'Why didn't you just mix the small dumplings together until they became one big dumpling?' suggested Blart.

Nimzovitsch considered the suggestion and his face became angry. No wizard likes being made a fool of by a young lad.

'It's all very easy being wise after the event,' he said irritatedly. 'I was faced with a tricky culinary dilemma.'

'I'm sure you were,' said Capablanca soothingly.

'I think you're stupid,' observed Blart less soothingly.

'Be quiet,' Capablanca snapped. 'One day you too may be old and a little confused.'

And it is true that wizards are not free of the absent-mindedness and general befuddlement that can come with age. However, in their case a little confusion can have far more drastic consequences. A little slip-up when saying a spell, and suddenly they can turn themselves into toads and ruin what could have been a very happy retirement. It is for this reason that retired wizards are encouraged to avoid using magic.

'Let us sit down and talk,' Capablanca said to the old wizard. 'Blart. In payment for your rudeness you may clean the kitchen floor.'

'Why should I?' demanded Blart. 'He made the mess. He should clear it up.'

'If you don't then I'll let him cast his next spell on you,' threatened Capablanca.

Blart considered. If Nimzovitsch could make this much mess with a dumpling, imagine what he could do to him. Blart decided to do some cleaning.

Meanwhile Capablanca and Nimzovitsch retired to Nimzovitsch's study for a talk.

Capablanca emerged just as Blart was wiping up the last of the goo.

'We must go without delay,' he informed Blart.

'Why?' said Blart, who wouldn't have minded a brief rest after his exertions.

'Nimzovitsch tells me that from rumours he has heard in the village it is likely that Zoltab's minions are closer to their goal of releasing Zoltab than I had previously thought.'

'What are you listening to him for?' demanded Blart. 'He's just nearly killed himself with his own dinner. He probably doesn't know anything.'

'He is of sound mind,' insisted Capablanca. 'He simply makes occasional mistakes. But he has given me an idea that might help us speed up our progress and give us more chance of preventing Zoltab's return.'

'What is it?'

'It's ...' began Capablanca. And then he stopped and looked doubtful. 'I don't have time to tell you now,' he continued brusquely. 'We must return to the village and collect Beowulf. Nimzovitsch fears that there may be minions of Zoltab there already who will take note of every stranger that passes through.'

Nimzovitsch came into the kitchen from his study. He looked blankly at Blart.

'Who are you?' he asked.

'Let us go,' said Capablanca to Blart.

'Would you like to see me make some custard?' asked Nimzovitsch.

Blart fled to the door. He had no wish to be drowned in custard.

'Farewell, Nimzovitsch,' said Capablanca. 'You are a great and noble wizard who has helped me on my epic quest.'

'I can make scones too,' replied Nimzovitsch.

Chapter 13

They left the cottage and, swiftly mounting Pig the Horse, rode back to the village square to look for Beowulf. They did not need to look far. As they entered the village square Beo emerged from the tavern supported by two men. Other men from the village spilled out of the inn after them. In a short time the warrior had managed to get to know a lot of people.

'Greetings, Capablanca and thingy!' shouted Beo when he spotted his comrades. 'I want you to meet two new friends of mine. Fine friends they are too. I'd like you to meet Mr Motte and Mr Bailey.'

The wizard nodded curtly in the direction of the two men but his eyes remained locked on the warrior.

'If you've sold that –' Capablanca began coldly.

'Sssssshhhh,' replied Beo, putting his finger on to the wizard's lips. 'Know what you're going to say. Saying I'd sell the horse. As if I,' here he turned indignantly to Motte and Bailey for moral support, who nodded understandingly, 'as if

I,' he repeated, 'would sell a horse. A horse that is needed for a quest to defeat Zoltab.'

'Quiet,' urged Capablanca.

'Well, it's true, isn't it?' said Beo with an air of injured pride. 'These good people say "sell your horse" and I say, "Sorry fellas. Can't oblige. Got to use the horse to go and fight Zoltab."'

'Beo,' hissed the wizard, 'shut up and get on the horse. Blart, help him on to Pig.'

Unfortunately Beo had in his drunken state managed to forget that Pig was in fact a horse.

'I'm not riding a pig,' said Beo stroppily, pushing Blart away. By now he was no longer simply addressing the immediate group but was speaking to all the inhabitants of the village. 'I ask you,' Beo appealed to the general populace, 'is it right? Is it right that I, Beowulf, am going to have to ride on a pig? I, who would have been a fully fledged knight by now if they hadn't expelled me from knight school for plunging a weapon into a fellow pupil's bottom. He said, "lance my boil". How was I to know it wasn't that sort of lance? It was a mistake anybody could have made. And now people want me to go on a quest on a pig. Sure it's not on. In knight school they said it is not only important what you do, it is also important how you do it.'

'Beowulf, pull yourself together.'

But Beowulf did not reply to Capablanca. Instead he replied to the crowd which had by now gathered in the village square.

'You see him? It's all right for him. He wanted to be a wizard and that's what he is. Capablanca the Wizard. Off to defeat Zoltab. But me, I wanted to be a knight and I've tried being chivalrous and I'm always on the lookout for dragons but I've got to settle for being a warrior. It's not –'

Nobody ever knew what the warrior was going to say next. For suddenly he was lifted from the ground.

'Whoa!' shouted Beo as he rose into the sky. 'Help!'

Blart could see blue light flashing from the wizard's eyes.

'Capablanca!' pleaded the warrior. 'Put me down!'

Beo flew through the air until he floated above an over-flowing horse trough. The blue light disappeared from the wizard's eyes. Beo dropped into the cold water.

'Aaaargh,' he cried.

'Hurrah,' shouted the crowd.

Pig trotted over to the trough.

'Get on,' Capablanca ordered the spluttering warrior.

Beo's belligerence seemed to have been temporarily washed away by the ducking. Meekly he climbed on to the back of Pig the Horse. Capablanca wheeled Pig the Horse round and faced the crowd.

'Who will rent me a boat and a crew?' he asked. 'My comrades and I must sail forth urgently.'

Nobody in the crowd spoke up.

'I will pay well,' Capablanca told the crowd.

Still nobody took up his offer.

'I beseech you,' urged Capablanca, pointing to the

harbour where ten sailing ships were anchored. 'Our journey is of great importance. Surely somebody will help.'

But the mention of Zoltab by Beowulf had ensured that no sailor in the village wished to skipper a boat for them. The crowd slowly began to disperse, muttering amongst themselves as they departed. The questors were stuck.

'What possessed you to mention Zoltab and our quest?' demanded Capablanca.

Beo did not answer.

'I was forced to use magic before you revealed anything else,' continued the wizard. 'But that too will attract attention. We can only hope that none of Zoltab's minions were hidden in the crowd.'

And so Capablanca nudged Pig forward and the great horse trotted out of the village square and back through Clegarn towards the great cliffs that lay high above the village. But though Pig trotted as impressively as ever nothing could hide the fact that the questors were going backwards.

Had Capablanca seen the village square a few moments after their departure he would have known his hopes about Zoltab's minions were forlorn. As soon as the questors left a number of shifty-looking men slunk out of their cottages. After an urgent whispered conversation they scurried down to the harbour, and some time later two boats with dark sails set forth into the open sea – on what business nobody knew.

Chapter 14

'I only had two flagons of ale,' insisted Beo.

'Two?' repeated Capablanca.

'Well, maybe three,' admitted the warrior.

'Three?' repeated Capablanca.

It turned out that Beo had drunk ten flagons of ale.

'I thought if I got them drunk then I could get more information out of them,' Beo explained.

'But instead you got drunk and blabbed all the details of our quest,' Capablanca reminded him. 'And now nobody will supply us with a boat and so we're stuck on the wrong side of the Eastern Ocean.'

'I never said the plan was foolproof,' insisted Beo. 'But it was a noble and brave undertaking, worthy of a knight.'

And with that Beo sat back on Pig the Horse and looked at the sea with the air of a man who was much misunderstood but, because of his fine character, was prepared to accept it without complaint.

'What are we doing up here?' Blart demanded of

Capablanca. 'It's making me feel dizzy.'

They had ridden up to the cliffs high above Clegarn. Before them lay the vastness of the ocean, calm and easy and deeply blue. But immediately below them it took on a different character as it hurled itself repeatedly against the rocks and then slipped back to gather strength for its next assault. Here the deep blue was replaced by an angry white foam. Blart had looked over the edge briefly and then pulled his head back. The water below had seemed to call to him and he had felt unsteady and nervous that he might fall.

'So, why?' repeated Blart.

'Yes, why?' echoed Beo, who had decided that he had spent long enough being noble and misunderstood.

'Now there's no need to get worried,' said Capablanca.

Blart immediately got worried. Beo got worried too, but he was a warrior and so he didn't show it.

'It is something that Nimzovitsch the wizard told me about the wild horses of Noved. Horses like Pig,' said Capablanca.

'Who's Nimzovitsch?' demanded Beo.

Capablanca briefly explained about Nimzovitsch. Blart noticed that Capablanca emphasised Nimzovitsch's wisdom and knowledge while glossing over his weakness for becoming trapped under dumplings.

'I spoke with Nimzovitsch,' Capablanca continued, 'and he told me a great secret about the horses of Noved. Horses like Pig.'

'What is it?'

Capablanca paused dramatically.

'Pig the Horse can fly.'

Blart and Beo looked down at Pig the Horse. He looked like any other horse to them. Bigger perhaps, but still like any other horse. And the one thing they knew for sure about horses was that they couldn't fly.

'If he can fly,' said Blart, 'then why didn't he fly off when we trapped him in the gulch?'

'By the powers,' said Beowulf, 'the boy has asked a decent question.'

'Because,' explained Capablanca, 'Pig the Horse can fly but he doesn't quite know it yet.'

'What?' cried Beo and Blart together.

'I will explain what Nimzovitsch told me,' said Capablanca patiently. 'And then all will become clear. You see, flying horses don't normally need to fly and most go through their lives ignorant of their ability. Their wings are folded away so tightly under their belly that they don't even know they're there. They only learn to fly if they are put in a situation in which they must, as a matter of urgency, and then their reflexes take over, their wings unfurl and they fly off happily into the sky … that is the theory.'

'The theory?' said Blart and Beo together.

'You see, it's all down to timing,' explained Capablanca. 'The horse must have enough time to recognise the desperate situation he is in, panic, try everything he normally tries when he's in trouble and then allow his reflexes to save him by automatically unfurling his wings.'

'And how long does that take?' asked Blart, who had been listening carefully because it had to do with his well-being.

'Ah,' said Capablanca. 'Sadly Nimzovitsch retired before he was able to establish a definitive answer to that question. However, he said a big cliff should be enough.'

'Should be?' echoed Blart.

'Indeed,' continued Capablanca. 'But horses learn at different rates. If Pig the Horse is stupid then he might not recognise the seriousness of the situation before we are all splattered on the rocks. However if we aren't splattered we will fly so fast that our chances of succeeding in our quest will be much improved.'

Blart had stopped listening after Capablanca said 'splattered'.

'I'm not carrying on,' announced Blart. 'That wizard that said Pig could fly was stuck under his own dinner until we came along and I don't believe him. Even if you put a spell on me for the rest of my life so that I can't walk and I have to stay up here and starve to death I'm not going.'

And with that he got off the horse, sat down on the grass and jutted his chin in the air.

'The boy's right,' agreed Beo surprisingly. 'I've seen many a thing in my life but I've never seen a steed fly. Steeds are for the ground and boats are for the sea. Sure let us all go back to the town and try once more to hire a boat to sail in.

That makes sense.'

And Beo allowed himself a smile of satisfaction. He had solved a problem and nobody was bleeding or dead. This was a first.

'They will not let us hire a boat and we will fall even further behind,' protested Capablanca. 'Don't you see? Zoltab's acolytes are even now making preparations to help him take control while we are squabbling. A flying horse can travel vast distances at great speed. It is our only hope. Think of the world.'

'Let's have a vote,' said Beo.

'What?' said Capablanca.

'A vote,' repeated the warrior. 'I'm against. You're for. Blart. It's up to you.'

'Against,' said Blart.

'A boat it is, then,' said Beo.

'A boat,' said Capablanca glumly.

'Yes,' said Beo. 'Don't worry, Capablanca. Things always work out all right on quests. We'll be fine. These evil-doers can never get anything done on time. They're known for it.'

'I'm not sure,' said Capablanca.

'We are,' said Beo reassuringly. 'Come on.'

'If Zoltab takes over the world it's all your fault.'

There was nothing more to be said. Blart climbed on to the horse and Capablanca turned it round and they began to trot back towards the village.

At least, they had for about a hundred paces, when the

wizard suddenly yanked hard on the reins. Pig stopped.

'Oh no,' announced Capablanca. 'I've dropped my wand.'

'When?' asked the others.

'I had it a minute ago by the cliffs and I haven't got it now. So we'd better go back.' Capablanca yanked on the reins again to turn Pig round.

'What's that?' said Blart, noticing a wand protruding from Capablanca's cowl.

The wizard looked down.

'Er, that. Oh, that. Yes, that's my wand. It's … er … not that wand I dropped. Oh, no. Er … it's my spare wand … that's it. Not this one at all. Just go back and get it quick as a flash.'

The wizard kicked. Pig started to run.

''Tis fine weather,' said Beo.

'It's too windy,' said Blart.

'That's because the horse is going so fast,' answered Beo. 'Sure, if you were sat on the ground it would be a fine day.'

'No, it's just too windy,' persisted Blart.

The thumping of Pig's hooves grew louder as he accelerated in response to a kick from Capablanca.

'Look at the sea,' shouted Beo. 'Isn't it a beautiful sight?'

'It's very blue when you get near it,' agreed Blart.

And about two seconds later they both simultaneously realised what was happening.

'Whoa!' shouted Beo.

'Help!' shouted Blart.

The horse gathered pace, urged on by repeated kicks from Capablanca. Its snorts sent gusts of steam into the air.

'Stop!' shouted Beo.

'Now!' shouted Blart.

But Pig the Horse got faster and faster. To jump off now would risk fatal injuries. They were approaching the cliff's edge.

'We had a vote!' yelled Beo indignantly.

Too late did Pig the Horse see what was coming. Too late did the horse start to disobey the urgings of the wizard. His momentum was too much for him to stop now.

'This is no time for democracy!' shouted Capablanca as the horse with its three riders sailed over the edge of the precipice.

Chapter 15

The flying horse is one of nature's great mysteries. Most creatures, you see, are born with a basic understanding of what they can and can't do. A puffin is born on the ground but somehow knows it can fly and so when the time is right it tries. A dog is also born on the ground but somehow it knows that flying and it are not compatible and so when it sees an eagle soaring in the air it doesn't think, That looks good, I'll have a go at that. For some reason it doesn't cross the flying horse's mind that he can fly even though he can.

'Heeeeeellllp,' shouted Beo, who was resolving never to have anything to do with voting ever again and to stick to violence in future.

'Noooooooo,' shouted Blart as he saw the jagged rocks racing up to meet him.

'Ooooooopps,' shouted Capablanca, who had rather less faith in his methods now he was in the air.

But what was going on in their minds doesn't matter.

What matters is what was happening in Pig the Horse's mind.

As the horse became aware of its own imminent mortality and its small brain dissolved into chaos, its reflexes took over and magically two great wings unfurled beneath its belly and began to beat.

They continued to fall.

The wings beat harder. The jagged rocks rushed up towards them. The wings beat harder still, fighting against the terrible force of gravity and fighting and fighting and winning as Pig the Horse began to rise.

Below them the jagged rocks began to grow smaller. The sea, which had seemed to be awaiting them, seethed with disappointment. The gulls, which lived on the cliffs, dive-bombed them with great cries of indignation and fear. But still they rose. Rose all the way up the side of the cliff until they were above it. They could see the place they had taken off from. They could see the harbour. They could see more than they ever had seen before.

'Capablanca!' bellowed Beo from the back of the horse. 'I hope you realise that you've destroyed my faith in democracy.'

'It doesn't work anyway!' shouted back Capablanca. 'Power always remains essentially in the same hands with only cosmetic changes. Now leave me alone. I must plot our course.'

The wizard looked at the sun, then he looked at the horizon, then he looked at the ground, then he looked at the sun again, then he shrugged his shoulders and turned Pig's head slightly to the left and the horse obligingly began to fly in that direction.

For a few minutes all was quiet except for the rush of the wind as the three comrades savoured the experience of flying high in the sky on the back of a gigantic steed. Then, for the next few minutes, they all stopped being quite so impressed by the beauty of the landscape and the wonder of their flying experience and instead began to feel queasy. Flying on a horse high above the world is an amazing sensation but it is also a disorientating one, and within five minutes each of our heroes had put his head to one side and allowed the contents of his stomach to pour down to the ocean below.

Still, once the contents of their stomachs were no longer inside them our travellers felt better, except of course they felt hungry. But they could sit back once more and enjoy the ride. At least, they thought they could. Something whizzed past Blart's head. He looked around, but there was nothing. Then something whizzed past the other side of his head. Again he looked. This time he saw. An arrow. He looked down. There were two boats underneath them. They had black sails and little men on deck. Little men who were firing arrows.

'Capablanca.' Blart tugged at the wizard's cowl.

Capablanca turned round. Blart pointed downwards with his finger. The wizard looked down and saw what was happening.

'Those ships are from Clegarn,' shouted Capablanca, recognising the sails. 'Zoltab's minions must have seen us there.'

More arrows whizzed by.

'We need more height to get out of their range,' yelled Capablanca, and he pulled back on the head of Pig the Horse.

And Pig the Horse would no doubt have begun to climb if at that moment an arrow hadn't shot into his belly. The shock sent a sudden shake through Pig. Blart and Capablanca, who were both aware of the attack, were holding on tightly when the arrow struck. But it happened too fast for Beo. He was looking upwards when the arrow struck and the horse shook.

The jerk made him lose his balance. He tilted to one side. His arms flailed in the air as he tried to right himself. For a second, it was impossible to tell whether he would fall off or hang on. He looked down at the ocean, which was a mistake. The sea was waiting far below, ready to swallow him up. He couldn't help it. He began to panic. If only he'd stayed calm then maybe he could have hung on. But he didn't and the fevered flapping of his arms and legs transferred more and more of his weight to one side of the horse. Gravity sucked at him. The jolts of the horse bounced him. And sheer terror undid him. Before he knew it he was no longer in contact with Pig the Horse and instead was embarking on the greatest dive in human history.

The first that Blart and Capablanca knew about Beo's disappearance was a sudden feeling of lightness as the horse effortlessly flew upwards. Blart looked behind him. Seeing nothing, he looked down. This time he saw Beo, with his arms and legs spread out wide, about to perform the biggest belly flop in history.

'Capablanca,' he shouted.

Capablanca looked back, and then, following Blart's finger, looked down. They both saw Beo smash into the water. There was a sickeningly huge splash where he landed, for Beo had fallen from so high up that there was a good chance that the impact had killed him.

Chapter 16

Beowulf was gone. Only the circular ripples at his point of entry suggested he had ever been there. Blart and Capablanca stared down at the sea but nothing appeared. Surely Beo could not hold his breath this long.

The ships below had stopped firing arrows as their crews looked to see what had become of the warrior. Everything was quiet and still as everybody concentrated on the place in the ocean where they had last seen him.

Each second that passed lessened the warrior's chances. And the seconds passed. Ten seconds, twenty seconds, twenty-five seconds, thirty seconds.

A head. Two arms waving frantically.

'Hurrah!' shouted Blart, forgetting for a moment that he didn't actually like Beo much. The warrior looked up towards them and then he looked towards the boats that were already reacting to his appearance. Some of the men rushed to redirect the sails whilst others placed arrows in their bows and began to loose them in the direction of the stricken warrior.

'We must go down and save him!' shouted Capablanca.

'Must we?' said Blart doubtfully. His initial enthusiasm on seeing the warrior had rapidly dissipated as he remembered that Beo was constantly attempting to cleave him in two. 'He hasn't been much help.'

'It's a matter of honour!' screeched Capablanca.

Again Blart was lost. He was still nowhere near getting the concept of honour. Honour, as far as he could work out, meant doing very stupid things for no gain whatsoever. It was not a quality Blart admired.

However, Blart could do nothing about it because Capablanca was at the front and he directed Pig the Horse to fly downwards towards the floundering Beo. Still firing arrow after arrow, the boats headed for the same place.

Soon they were so close to the sea that Blart began to worry that they might find themselves in the water as well, which wouldn't do anybody any good. But Capablanca seemed to know what he was doing, even though he'd never done anything like it before and was just guessing. When Pig the Horse got to about twenty feet above Beo he slowed Pig's descent and instead made the horse circle above him.

'I can't swim!' shouted Beo.

'Learn quickly!' Blart shouted back rather cruelly.

Beo was attempting to do just that but the jerky, desperate movements of his arms and legs were already beginning to exhaust him and their effect was becoming more and more negligible. Arrows and abuse flew at them from the rapidly approaching boats.

'We'll kill you in the name of Zoltab,' cried one voice that travelled to them on the wind.

'Help!' screeched Beo. Adding to the problem of not being able to swim was of course the fact that he was wearing a considerable amount of armour. His head disappeared for a few seconds but he fought back to the surface, his face filled with a mixture of terror and pleading. The boats were getting closer. The arrows continued to fly. The wizard was lost in thought, seemingly oblivious to everything as Pig continued to circle above the stricken warrior.

'Capablanca,' screamed Blart, ever mindful of his own safety. 'Let's get out of here.'

Capablanca didn't move.

'Help,' screamed Beo again.

An arrow whizzed past Blart's nose, missing it by the length of an eyelash. It just missed Capablanca too and seemed to jolt him back to the present.

'I've got it!' he shouted.

'Help!' repeated Beo.

'We know,' Blart told him.

A circle of fins appeared around the warrior.

'Tie this round you,' said Capablanca to Blart, pulling a rope from his cowl. 'I'll tie the other end around the horse.'

'Why?' said Blart.

'It'll keep you safe,' explained Capablanca, who knew by now that it was not always wise to tell Blart everything.

'Flying away would be safer,' countered Blart.

'Do it.'

'I can't tie knots,' pointed out Blart, who wasn't ready to give in yet. 'My grandfather wouldn't teach me because he thought I might try to hang him when I grew up.'

'Give me strength,' cried Capablanca exasperatedly. The wizard was forced to turn round and tie Blart's knot for him and trust Pig the Horse not to do anything stupid.

'What are those things around Beo?' Blart shouted as the wizard was finishing off the knot.

The wizard flicked a glance towards the warrior and stopped in horror.

'Sharks,' he exclaimed. 'Quickly.'

'What are sharks?' asked Blart.

'They're terribl—' Capablanca began, and then he thought better of it. 'Er, terribly friendly fish which are considered a sign of good luck.'

'Hurry up,' screeched Beo from below, 'or the sharks will have me!'

'Ha ha,' said Capablanca. 'Beowulf's little joke. How brave these warriors are, laughing in the face of adversity.'

Blart was confused. He knew something wasn't quite right but he wasn't quite sure what it was.

'Now –' began Capablanca.

'Get off my leg,' bellowed Beo from below.

'The plan is this,' began Capablanca, and then he hesitated. The plan was for Blart to jump into the water. The warrior

101

would hold on to Blart and Pig the Horse would fly upwards, raising them both to safety. Capablanca had considered just throwing the rope but it was too difficult to aim it precisely at Beo in the strong sea breeze. What he needed was a weight to give him more control. And the only weight he had was Blart.

'What?' urged Blart as two arrows whizzed either side of his ears. The wizard's sudden pauses were most unwelcome in a life-and-death situation.

'The plan is,' began Capablanca again. Then he changed his mind about explaining and with a sudden push he knocked Blart off the horse and sent him hurtling down towards the ocean below.

'AaaarrggghhWumph,' was the sort of sound Blart made as he plummeted through the air and then crashed into the water, smashing into Beo in the process.

'Ow,' said Beo indignantly. 'I wanted you to rescue me, not come and have a swim with me.'

'I can't swim either,' Blart spluttered as his head re-appeared above the water. Unfortunately, as Blart's head came up the warrior's head went down, making conversation difficult.

'Grab hold of Blart,' shouted Capablanca from above them, 'and I'll lift you both to safety.'

Blart fought to gain some kind of control as the sea heaved around him, but no matter how much effort he put into his movements the sea overrode them.

Beo surfaced again.

'He says hold on to me,' Blart told him before disappearing under the water again.

He fought to get to the surface, panic making his arms and legs thrash violently from side to side. *Get up to the air!* his brain screamed at his body. *Get up to the air!* And then he was back on the surface taking huge gulps.

'I can't grab on to you if you keep disappearing,' Beo said critically. 'Now stay still.'

Staying still in the ever-moving ocean was a challenge, but Blart did his best and Beo did his best to grab hold of Blart. Unfortunately, neither of their bests was much good and still the boats were bearing down on them.

'Hurry up,' Blart shouted at Beo. 'The boats are getting closer.'

'Stay still,' Beo yelled back. 'And don't worry about the boats. The sharks will have us first.'

'Sharks?' cried Blart. 'They're nice.'

'They're man-eaters, you fool,' screeched Beo. 'They haven't got me yet because of my armour, but you ...'

Blart realised that he was not ideally dressed to confront anything that ate people. All the fabrics that clothed him were cheap and thin and no barrier to teeth. Blart promised himself that the first thing he was going to do when he was back on Pig the Horse (if he ever got back on Pig the Horse) was too push Capablanca off. But it was a big if. The warrior's warning had come just in time. One of the fins that had been circling Blart suddenly turned ninety degrees and sped towards him.

'No,' said Blart, trying desperately to run away and succeeding merely in treading water.

'Stop thrashing about,' Beo told him angrily.

'Shark,' wailed Blart, his eyes held by the approaching fin and the vast grey shape that lay under the water. It was going to eat him. There was nothing he could do. He threw himself backwards and prepared for the first bite. His leg hit something. What it hit was the shark's nose. Its most sensitive part. The sudden stabbing pain distracted the great fish. Blart waited for the bite that never came.

'What are you doing lying on your back?' Beo demanded.

Blart couldn't believe he wasn't being eaten. The shark was equally surprised. It turned to attack again. This time there would be no escape.

Meanwhile, Beo had finally managed to manoeuvre himself almost close enough to Blart to be able to reach him.

'Come on,' yelled Capablanca.

The boats were getting nearer and nearer.

'We're going to kill you,' one voice cried from the ship.

'For Lord Zoltab,' shouted another.

The sails of the boats billowed as they skimmed towards the helpless pair.

'Ready?' said Beo into Blart's ear.

'What would you do if I said no?' said Blart.

Beo lunged towards Blart and grabbed hold of him as the

rope lifted them clear of the water. Beneath them an angry shark thrashed and the sailors cursed. The wizard had saved them just in time.

Chapter 17

'I'm starting to rust.'

It was two days and two nights later when the warrior uttered this doleful remark. His companions were both asleep so they answered him with nothing more than a snore. They were still flying over the sea. Beo didn't know where they were flying to. The recriminations over the water incident had been quite heated and had resulted in Blart refusing to speak to Capablanca for pushing him into the sea and nearly drowning him. Capablanca and Beo had then had a row because the wizard felt that the warrior should have kept his balance in the first place. The only questor all three of them were on good terms with was Pig the Horse. But the feeling was not reciprocated. Pig had been flying for two whole days now, and even though he'd enjoyed it at first he was beginning to feel tired and to yearn for the simple pleasures of being in a field.

'I'll never get to be a knight at this rate.'

Beo regarded his armour mournfully. There was nothing he could do about it. Once sea water has got into the minute bolts and hinges of a suit of armour there is nothing you can do. Apart from call yourself the Red Knight, of course but, as Beowulf knew, that had already been done by the White Knight of the West Country who'd drunk too much ale, fallen into his castle's moat and emerged with a new name and tadpoles in his visor. He could only hope for a new suit of armour, and these days they didn't come cheap.

Beowulf felt that in the present situation there was only one course of action open to him. He must sing a mournful ballad. He didn't know any mournful ballads about rusting suits of armour so he chose a favourite called 'My Lost Lady Love'. He cleared his throat and began to sing,

'Oh, my lost lady love is dead and gone
Cold as a stone she lies.
Oh, my lost lady love is dead and gone
And nevermore will rise.

Oh, my lost lady love is dead and gone
And I am left all alone.
Oh, my lost lady love is dead and gone
She's nothing but skin and bone.

Oh, my lost lady love is dead and gone
Live some more she will not.
Oh, my lost lady love is dead and gone
Now she's beginning to rot.

Oh, my lost lady love is dead and gone
No doctor would say she is well.
Oh, my lost lady love is dead and gone
She gives off a powerful smell.

Oh, my lost lady love is dead and gone
My mind it starts to bewilder.
Oh, my lost lady love is dead and gone
I wish now I hadn't killed her.'

By the time Beowulf had completed his mournful ballad, which at five verses was very short for him, his companions were awake. It was almost impossible to remain asleep during Beowulf's singing. He sang everything, from lusty fighting songs to mournful ballads, with exactly the same amount of noise and to the same tuneless melody.

'Shut up,' said Blart.

'Be quiet,' snapped Capablanca.

'I'm rusting,' explained Beo.

'Who cares?' demanded Capablanca.

'Not me,' said Blart.

And then a moody silence prevailed as each of them thought of their own problems and how nobody understood them and how unlucky they were to be saddled with two such horrible companions and how they were in the right about everything and everybody else was in the wrong.

Around them emerged a sight of great wonder. The sun

was rising brightly in the east. Its warm beams touched the backs of the questors and soothed their cold bones. The light changed the sea from a dark menacing swell into a playful plateau of languorous blue topped by the fleeting appearance of dancing white. The small islands below them displayed all their colours at their most magnificent. Deep browns and greens were the backdrop to the dazzling reds and gaudy pinks showing themselves joyfully to the returning yellow God. But they were all too busy feeling sorry for themselves to notice. You have to be in the mood for beauty, otherwise it simply passes you by.

'Are we nearly there?' whined Blart in a tone which he had been developing over the past two days in order to ensure that it caused maximum irritation.

'Yes,' said Capablanca.

This answer shocked Blart into silence. Repeated similar enquiries had brought answers ranging from 'No' to 'If you ask that again there'll be a croak in your voice', which was Capablanca's subtle threat to turn Blart into a toad. Too subtle for Blart, so it wasn't much use.

'Where's there?' asked Beo philosophically.

'There is Elysium, capital of Illyria in the realm of King Philidor the Happy. The most friendly kingdom in the whole world,' replied Capablanca.

'Why do we want to go there?' said Blart sulkily.

'Because,' said Capablanca, 'in the highest tower of Philidor's palace inside a locked room it is rumoured there lies the map which will lead us to the Great Tunnel of Despair.'

Blart and Beo thought about this for a second. Neither of them can be said to have quick brains, but in the race of the snail and the tortoise it was Beo who got there first.

'You mean you don't *know* where we're going?'

'I do,' said Capablanca indignantly. 'We are going to the Kingdom of King Philidor.'

'But you don't *know* where the Great Tunnel of Despair is,' persisted Beo.

'Not yet,' conceded Capablanca.

'And it's only a rumour?' continued Beo.

'A strong rumour,' asserted Capablanca.

'Sure, this is a terrible thing,' said Beo. 'Here I am brought on a quest and nobody even knows where we're going. I've been brought here under false pretences.'

'But isn't the idea of a quest that you search for something?' asked Capablanca, who felt that this was a flaw in the warrior's position.

'Don't be telling me what a quest is and what a quest isn't,' huffed Beo. 'Didn't I spend a whole term in knight school before the unfortunate incident with the lance? I'm the one who knows the rules and regulations regarding quests around here. And this is turning out to be a pretty rum one.'

'Stop moaning,' said Blart, who felt that this was his job.

'I've not forgotten my oath to cleave you in two when this is all over,' Beo reminded him.

'You're all mouth,' said Blart, who was becoming familiar with threats to his life. 'I'd be half a league away before you could get that stupid sword out.'

Beo exploded.

'I'll kill you now, you ugly little poltroon,' he promised, reaching for his sword. Unfortunately it is difficult to get a huge sword out of its massive scabbard whilst you're on a flying horse. It involves too much squirming and leaning, which can lead to a person tumbling off a horse, and Beo had no desire for an early morning swim. Therefore he had to content himself with a promise to kill Blart as soon as they got on land if he didn't withdraw his insult. Blart didn't withdraw his insult. Capablanca sighed. None of us are ever at our best towards the end of a long journey.

And in front of them they saw the end of their journey (not the end of their quest – that's something entirely different). For in front of them they saw a beach. A beach of golden sand. And on that beach there were palm trees. Palm trees that swayed easily in the warm breeze. And beyond that beach there were sand dunes. And beyond those sand dunes were fields. Lush fields in which industrious farmers threshed and scythed and ploughed and sowed and reaped. And beyond those fields were orchards. And in those orchards fruit of all kinds grew to a juicy ripeness. And beyond those orchards, shimmering in the distance, lay a silver city. And in the centre of that silver city sat a domed palace of gold. And shooting up from the centre of that palace of gold was a tower encrusted in diamonds that glistered and glimmered in the early morning sun.

'Behold,' said Capablanca. 'The most beautiful kingdom on earth.'

'I don't see any pigs,' said Blart.

Chapter 18

Capablanca decided not to try to land in the city. After all, Pig the Horse had never actually landed before and landing is the trickiest bit of flying. Therefore Capablanca spent some time picking out an appropriate field. It had to be big and it had to be flat.

'Hurry up,' said Blart, who was eager to be out of the saddle as his bottom was sore.

But the wizard was not to be rushed. His deliberations took them further and further from the city as he rejected field after field as having too many bumps. Finally he settled on one field, let Pig the Horse circle it three times so he was familiar with the ground and, pushing down Pig the Horse's head, directed him to descend.

To Blart it all seemed rather unnecessary. Pig the Horse seemed to know what he was doing. The ground was coming towards them very slowly. Well, perhaps not slowly. But gradually. Well, perhaps not gradually, but not quickly. Well, perhaps, when you came to think about it, it was quite quickly.

Maybe very quickly. Too quickly.

Thump!

Blart picked himself off the ground. The others did the same. Whilst falling off a horse is never recommended, if there was a field to do it in this was it. The grass was long so the impact of the landing was cushioned and the chances of a serious injury like breaking an arm were quite low. Blart had no more than a couple of small bruises but that wasn't going to stop him moaning.

'You're a useless rider,' he told Capablanca, 'and that's a useless horse.'

Pig the Horse did not hear the insult as he was slowing down at the other end of the field. It should be said in his defence that he had made a successful landing as far as he was concerned: one moment he was flying and the next moment he was running. It was his passengers who'd ended up on the ground.

Pig the Horse trotted back to the group. Blart approached him with the idea of giving him a good kick, but when he got close something in the horse's eye suggested that maybe it wasn't such a good idea after all.

'Come on,' said Capablanca. ''Tis no more than a five-mile walk into the city.'

'Walk?' Blart was shocked. 'We've got a horse. Why should we walk?'

'This horse,' Capablanca replied severely, 'has been flying for two days. It is in need of rest. We have been sitting for two days and are in need of exercise.'

And so saying, Capablanca set off, leading Pig the Horse with Beo behind them. Blart was obliged to follow but not until he'd made his displeasure clear by kicking off the heads of a few innocent daises.

He trailed behind the others for a while as they walked across the lush fields but he caught up quickly when he noticed that they were approaching a man who was digging a hole. Blart was not going to meet a stranger alone if he could help it.

'Welcome to my field,' shouted the stranger. 'It is a beautiful day.'

'That it be,' agreed Capablanca.

'Come hither,' he cried, stopping work and leaning on his spade.

They walked over towards the stranger, who wore a blue smock and a straw hat cocked at a jaunty angle. His face was cheerful and his eyes shone with life.

'You're a grand sight,' said the stranger. 'I love to see people walking across my fields. Many is the time that I walk across the fields and I think how lucky I am to farm these fields and how much others would enjoy it too.'

'It's a very nice field,' said Capablanca.

'Thank'ee,' said the farmer. 'That's a fine horse.'

'Thank you,' said Capablanca.

'I've just come from the orchard where I have been picking my fruit,' said the farmer. 'Nothing would make me happier than for you three to take as much of my fruit as you would like and eat it to your heart's content.'

The farmer indicated a wheelbarrow that was crammed with the most luscious of fruits. Oranges, pears, apples, strawberries, cherries, lemons, limes and a dozen other types of fruit that Blart had never seen before overflowed from the barrow.

The travellers' mouths watered at the sight of this fresh goodness. For the last few days their diet had consisted solely of stale bread and smelly cheese that Capablanca had produced from his cowl and they were ready for a change. Each took a handful of fruit and began to munch.

'Sure, this is the finest orange I've ever tasted,' said Beo.

'This be the best apple,' added Capablanca.

'The pears are a bit hard,' said Blart, but he kept eating.

The farmer laughed with pleasure at the sight of them eating so heartily and then he bade them 'Good day' and went about his business, chuckling to himself as he departed.

'See,' said Capablanca. 'The friendliest people in the world.'

They continued to walk towards the city. Though their task was urgent even the wizard could not help but feel a sense of leisurely ease as he strolled along in the delightful morning air.

They met a sturdy yeoman and a buxom matron. Then a farmer's boy. Then a young man who claimed to be a poet. Then an old couple. Then a group of children. All of these people greeted them with great friendliness and all of them insisted on giving them fruit (except for the poet, who instead insisted on reciting for their pleasure his new poem, 'Ode to a Bilberry'). They found it impossible to refuse these gracious offers – well, at least two of them did – and so in less than a mile they found themselves burdened down with fruit.

'I'm not carrying it any more,' said Blart.

'Boy, you cannot reject the friendliness and generosity of these people,' Capablanca told him.

'Yes, I can,' said Blart simply.

They met another three people and were given even more fruit. The wizard changed his mind.

'I know,' he said. 'We will dump the fruit in that shady copse over there and then the good people will not know that we have left it and we will be free of its encumbrance. Give me your fruit and I will take it.'

Beo and Blart gave Capablanca their fruit. He disappeared into a copse.

Beo and Blart continued walking, licking their fingers as they went but still never quite managing to get the stickiness completely off them.

When they reached the top of the hill, Beo came to a sudden halt.

'I forgot,' he said.

'Forgot what?' asked Blart without much interest.

'You.' Beo fumbled for his sword.

'Me?' said Blart, who was, as we know, not very good at

spotting what was going to happen next.

'You insulted me. I've got to kill you.' Beo's sword was out and pointed in Blart's direction.

Blart gulped. Until now he had relied on the defence that he was the only person who could save the world, but for that defence to work he needed Capablanca to be around to enforce it. And the wizard was nowhere to be seen.

'Now, don't be hasty –' began Blart.

'Prepare to die,' said Beo, lifting his sword. Blart told his legs to run but his legs, stricken with fear, refused to obey him. Beo's sword was poised to cleave Blart in two and with his imminent death the world was once more on the brink of doom.

And then something beyond Blart caught the warrior's eye. He remained motionless, transfixed by the sight. Puzzled by the warrior not killing him, Blart turned round too and immediately understood why he was still alive. For what Beo had seen was the chance to fulfil all of his hopes and dreams.

Chapter 19

In the field below them sat five dragons. One blue, one green, one red, one black and one multicoloured. They had huge wings and long necks and pointy tails. And out of their nostrils came fire.

And in the middle of these five dragons stood a damsel.

'Page!' cried Beo. 'My horse.'

Blart didn't move, which was fair enough when you think about it. You can't be about to kill someone one minute and give them orders the next.

But Beo had no time to discipline Blart. This was his chance. Five dragons and a damsel in distress! If he pulled this off they'd have to make him a knight. He leapt on to Pig the Horse.

'Charge!' he ordered.

Pig the Horse was essentially obliging in nature and so, despite his fatigue, he took a deep breath and charged.

From a distance what a fine sight it was. Beo in full armour, charging forward on his giant black steed with his

119

sword pointing straight out in front of him. Of course, if you were closer you'd see the rusty patches on Beo's armour and that would have taken some of the shine off the vision. Still, there was no denying the warrior's courage. A lady was in danger and his life was worth nothing in comparison.

Blart watched from above as the warrior galloped nearer and nearer to the dragons, dust rising in the wake of Pig the Horse's thundering hooves. For once, Blart wished that there was someone with him so that he could bet with them on which dragon was most likely to kill Beo. Personally, he favoured the black dragon, but it didn't really matter. He was about to see the man who was bent on murdering him killed in a new and exciting way, and for Blart that was the kind of thing that made a morning worthwhile.

Forward charged Beo and Pig.

'Hold on, fair maiden!' yelled Beo.

The maiden turned to look at the advancing warrior. Terror and panic were etched on her face. She waved her arms. Beo started thinking of which place he'd take at the round table.

'Go, black!' cheered Blart from a distance.

The dragons caught sight of the advancing warrior. They stared hard at him. They looked at each other. They returned their stare to the warrior. Steam poured from their nostrils.

'Goodbye, Beo,' shouted Blart merrily.

And then the dragons ran away.

Mythical beasts never really live up to the advance

publicity. You can blame the oral tradition for that. Stories about dragons get told time and time again and each time they are told they get exaggerated a little bit more and so when you finally meet a dragon he's got way too much to live up to. Essentially they were clumsy, shy creatures that lived in deep forests and high mountains trying not to bother anybody and keeping themselves to themselves. Unfortunately knights kept coming to kill them, which tended to annoy them, and when cornered they would breathe fire on an attacker if they had no other choice.

But they much preferred to run away, which was exactly what these dragons were trying to do. However, they are big creatures with only little legs and they take their time to get going. And Beo was on a very fast horse. The green, blue, red and black dragons all managed to escape. But the multicoloured one was less fortunate. Before it could really get going the warrior had caught up with it. A thrust of the warrior's great sword sank into the belly of the multicoloured dragon. Another thrust and blood poured from its neck. And with one final sweep of his sword the warrior removed the dragon's head. Beo could not believe it. In his excitement he leapt from his horse and began hacking at the tail of the dragon.

Now, in chivalric etiquette terms this was a mistake. He should first have gone to the damsel in distress and checked to see if her distress was gone and she was back to being simply a damsel. However, this chivalric code was overridden by dreams of future glory and that was why he began chopping off the tail. The tail, you see, is proof of a dragon kill and is required by a king before he can promote a warrior to the status of a knight.

Unfortunately, so intent was Beo on separating the tail that he overlooked a threat to his rear. Blart didn't, of course. Blart saw the threat quite plainly. After his initial disappointment that the dragons had failed to kill Beo, this at least showed some promise.

Beo knew nothing about it until there was a tremendous bang on his helmet that knocked him face forward, straight into a pile of purple dragon dung, which is a very unpleasant thing to have your face in as it smells appalling.

'Murderer!' said a shrill but strong voice behind him.

Beo turned round. His face was smeared purple and he did not look at his best. He stared up at the damsel who was, if the tears of anger and sorrow pouring down her freckled face were to be believed, definitely distressed.

'Oh, beautiful lady,' began Beo, 'though it saddens me that a gentle creature such as yourself should see such violent sights … put that rock down.'

The beautiful lady obliged. She put it down with a crash on Beo's head, which it would undoubtedly have crushed it if hadn't been for his strong helmet. But the helmet did sustain a serious dent.

'Gentle creature, has the terror of the five dragons caused you to lose your wits? Pray calm yourself, because

all danger is now gone and you are safe and … put it dow—
Ow.'

Another crash against Beo's helmet. Another dent.

'Sweet lady, I have saved thee from a fate … put it down.'

You'd think that Beo would have learnt by now, but apparently not. The giant stone smashed into his visor.

'Look, woman, they've gone. I've saved your life so you could at least show a bit of gratitude to a knight-to-be who –'

The damsel showed no desire to display any gratitude. Instead she bent down and picked up the stone again.

Beo could, if he'd wanted to, have overpowered the girl and taken the stone from her, but that would have been a serious breach of the chivalric code, which stated that on no account could a maiden be handled roughly. The knight had two options if he was going to obey the chivalric code. The first was to have his helmet continually dented; the second was to run away.

Beo picked the second.

Grabbing the tail, he sprinted towards Pig the Horse. The enraged damsel in distress pursued him. Beo leapt on to Pig the Horse and gave him a kick. The damsel in distress threw one last stone. Beo ducked. The stone flew over his head and Pig the Horse took him clear of her throwing range and back up the field towards where Blart stood watching. The damsel screamed at his retreating back. Her distress was definitely getting worse.

'What's going on?' asked Capablanca, appearing at Blart's side.

'Nothing,' said Blart.

'What's he riding that horse for?' demanded Capablanca, seeing Beo charging towards them. 'He needs rest.'

'Dunno,' said Blart. 'He said something about you being a smelly old goat and not doing what you said any more and that the next time you turn your back on him he'll cleave you in two. Perhaps we should kill him.'

'Hmmm,' said Capablanca, who felt that there might be more than a small chance that Blart wasn't telling the truth.

Beo galloped up to them.

'Come on!' he shouted.

'What are you doing on that horse?'

'Urgent bit of chivalry,' replied Beo. 'Let's ride the next bit.'

Capablanca was about to say no and point out that Pig had not been given adequate time to recover from his exertions. However, a quick glance at the sun confirmed to him that the morning was past and afternoon was now upon them. Every hour brought Zoltab's return closer. Pig was going to have to wait a little longer before he could rest.

'All right,' agreed Capablanca. He noticed something behind Beo. 'What does that damsel want?'

'Nothing,' said Beo quickly.

'She appears to be in distress.'

'She's not,' insisted Beo. 'I've just been to check. She's not distressed. She's quite happy.'

'She's waving her fist,' pointed out Blart helpfully.

'She's coming this way,' mused Capablanca.

'Coincidence,' said Beo. 'Come on. Sure Zoltab will be in charge of the world and we'll all be here looking at a damsel in distress.'

'I thought she wasn't in distress,' Blart reminded him.

Beo flashed an angry look at Blart.

'She's not in proper chivalric distress,' he replied. 'It's just that she's got an allergy to grass.'

'We could give her a lift,' offered Capablanca.

'I offered,' said Beo, 'but she's got to try and get used to it. These damsels have got to stand on their own two feet sometimes. Now come on.'

Capablanca looked at the damsel. She was running towards them as fast as she could and her long red hair streamed out behind her. He knew something wasn't right but then he also knew that he didn't have enough time to solve every problem that came along. Zoltab's minions would be ever nearer to the Great Tunnel of Despair.

So he and Blart climbed on to Pig behind Beo and they rode for the city.

They made better progress on the back of Pig but they were still hampered by people constantly stopping them to wish them good day and to say how happy they were to see them and to give them more fruit. Even the wizard's politeness was gradually eroded. He merely waited until they had ridden past the fruit-givers before dropping it directly on to the road.

Eventually they rode over the hill and saw the city laid out in front of them, the diamond tower and the golden dome at the centre surrounded by a haphazard muddle of houses and streets. Blart had never seen anything so big. Some of the buildings were so tall that he was sure it would take a day to get from the bottom to the top.

They continued down the hill until they reached the huge wooden gates that led into the city. They were shut. Capablanca climbed down off Pig the Horse and rapped on the door. A small panel within the door was opened and a guard's head popped out.

'Hello,' said the guard. 'It's good to see you.'

'Hello,' replied Capablanca.

'Would you like some fruit?' asked the guard.

'Er …' said Capablanca.

'Have an apple,' said the guard, and one was passed through the door.

'Thank you,' said Capablanca.

'It does me good to see you eating it.'

'Lovely,' said Capablanca as he fought to swallow yet more fruit.

'Now, what was it you wanted?'

Capablanca looked serious.

'I want to see the King.'

'The King?' said the guard, a little surprised. 'Have you an appointment?'

'No,' admitted Capablanca, 'but it's very important.'

'I'm sure it is,' agreed the guard. 'Well, do you know the password?'

'Er … no,' said Capablanca.

'Oh dear,' said the guard. 'I'm afraid I can't let you in if you don't know the password.'

'It really is very important.'

'It's not nice, I know,' said the guard, 'but we've had to tighten up security because of strange tidings from the east.'

'Strange tidings?' repeated Capablanca. 'What strange tidings?'

'They say,' whispered the guard, 'that there are those who have come into the east of our land who aren't nice. It's said that they won't eat fruit. They are laying waste to our land and destroying our orchards.' And then a look of horror swept across his face. 'Ooops,' he said. 'I shouldn't be telling you this. You might be one of them. But I do so like a chat.'

'I've eaten the fruit,' pointed out Capablanca.

'I know,' said the guard. 'But the new rules say if you haven't got the password you can't come in.' He lowered his voice. 'I'm not saying I agree with it, mind. It all seems very tough to me. They'll be asking us to stop people doing things next, and that's not what I, for one, came into the guards for.'

It occurred to the wizard that a trusting city like Elysium

might not opt for a very difficult password.

'This password,' he chanced. 'It wouldn't be "fruit", would it?'

The guard's face lit up.

'How did you know?' he said.

'Oh, it had just slipped my mind,' said Capablanca.

'Come in, come in,' said the guard cheerfully. 'I'm so pleased I don't have to send you away. It would spoil my day.'

Chapter 20

The mighty doors opened and the three questors and their horse walked into Elysium, capital city of Illyria. The streets were narrow but not dark. All the houses were painted in bright colours. Flowers danced on window ledges. People bustled hither and thither, all smiling and nodding and shaking hands and kissing each other. Children dashed about playing games. Everyone waved.

'My arm aches,' complained Blart, who was fed up with waving back at people.

'Keep smiling,' ordered Capablanca.

Blart kept smiling. He was too frightened not to. Never in his life had he seen so much goodwill and frankly it scared him.

They walked through streets that resounded with merry laughter, down lanes where men and women chortled together outside their houses and through thoroughfares where good-natured chatter and banter zipped all around them. Blart had thought the country was bad but this was much worse. At least in the country there were gaps between all the cheerfulness. Here it was just non-stop.

But things were to get worse. Heading for the diamond tower, they turned into a new street and gasped.

If they thought the streets before had been crowded, they were in dire need of a dictionary to come up with an adequate word to describe this street.

'I feel sick,' Blart informed his companions.

All along the side of the road were stalls. Stalls that sold everything that you could think of. Fish and meat and vegetables and cheese and spices and silk and wool and flowers and fruit. Lots of fruit.

'I want to go home,' said Blart as the heady smell of the market began to overpower him.

A man rushed from a stall and gave Capablanca a cheese.

'No thank you,' said Capablanca. 'I don't want it. I haven't got any money.'

The man gave him a strange look and rushed away, leaving the cheese behind.

A woman approached Beo and handed him some silk.

'Woman, please take this back,' said Beo, 'for we cannot pay for it.'

The woman scurried away, leaving the silk behind her.

Another woman approached Blart and handed him some bottles.

'What's this rubbish?' demanded Blart.

'These are precious spices,' replied the woman.

'I don't want them,' said Blart. 'And if you don't get out of my face I'll smash them over your head.'

Blart felt there was less danger that women would hit him back than men so he was even ruder to them. The woman's face fell but she left the bottles of spices behind her before rushing off.

They continued along the road. Each time they passed a stall someone would dash out and give them something, be it some fresh fish or some wine or some elaborate jewellery. However much they protested they could not reject the goods they were given. If a stallholder couldn't get them to take a gift directly then he just placed the object in one of Pig the Horse's saddlebags. More and more things mounted up. In their pockets, in their hands and over their shoulders.

'There's going to be a terrible bill at the end of this street,' warned Capablanca.

But they reached the end of the street and there was no bill. Nobody stopped them and nobody demanded payment.

'Sure, we'll be arrested as thieves,' said Beo.

But they weren't arrested as thieves. And the reason they weren't can only be understood by understanding the nature of the Illyrian economy.

You see, most economies work on the 'buy' idea. You want something. You go to someone who has it. You agree a price. And then you get it.

The Illyrian economy didn't work like this. Their economy, instead of being based on the idea of buying, was based on the idea of giving. Everybody gave a share of whatever he or she had to everybody else. So, a man who had grown a lot of oranges gave some to everybody he knew. A woman who made cheeses gave some to everybody she knew. And so on. Everybody ended up with all the oranges, apples, cheeses and everything else that they needed, which is all that an economy is there for in the first place. And if, for example, the man with the oranges had something go wrong like his orange trees getting a disease and dying, then it didn't mean that he had to starve because everybody carried on giving him things even though they didn't get any oranges back. They had everything else so missing out on oranges wasn't so terrible. And as soon as the man got some new orange trees he'd start growing oranges and giving them away again. This is why everybody was always trying to give Blart, Beo and Capablanca things.

Economists from all the other countries of the world had heard of this idea and said that it couldn't work because people were naturally greedy and selfish and that they liked having more things than everybody else. But Illyrians continued to make it work in complete disregard of economic theory, which was very rude of them in the opinion of the economists. And because they weren't always competing with each other and trying to make a profit, the Illyrians ended up being friendly and generous to one another and they were the happiest people in the world. It made all the economists mad.

However, Capablanca, Beo and Blart were unaware of the workings of the Illyrian economy. They just had a whole load of goods that they didn't want.

'Where's there a beggar when you want one?' asked Capablanca of nobody in particular. 'All cities have beggars. We could just give all this stuff to one of them.'

But the Illyrian economy worked so well that there weren't any beggars. Someone had once tried begging in Illyria but by the end of the second day found he'd been given so much that he was the third wealthiest person in the kingdom and had to retire.

And so the questors were forced to carry their goods because they didn't wish to offend anybody by dropping them blatantly in the street. Fortunately they didn't have to carry them far because suddenly there opened before them a grand square paved with the deepest blue marble. In the centre sat a splendid fountain. At the far side of the square stood the entrance to the golden dome, which was the palace of King Philidor and his Queen. And from the entrance to the dome a long line of people tailed back.

Capablanca approached the man who was nearest to them.

'How do I get to see the King?' he asked the man.

The man gave him a broad smile.

'I'm so glad that you asked me that question,' he replied. 'You just happen to have found the end of the queue to see the King.' The queue went right round the huge square twice.

'Surely all these people aren't waiting to see the King?' said Capablanca.

'They are,' responded the man. 'And who wouldn't want to see the King? He does an excellent job and he's a fine man and we all like to pop in and tell him how well he's doing.'

'And how long do people stay?' asked Capablanca.

'Oh, as long as they like,' replied the man. 'The King never throws anybody out.'

The wizard did a small mathematical calculation. He multiplied the number of people in the queue (lots) by the time they could stay with the King (as long as they liked) and came to the conclusion that he could be waiting for ever. This is not a good thing to discover when you have only limited time left to save the world.

'Still,' said the man, 'I'm in no rush. You go in front of me.'

'Thank you,' said Capablanca.

But he knew that moving one place further forward in the queue wasn't going to change the fact that it was going to take far too long to get to the front. By that time Zoltab could have triumphed.

The woman in front of Capablanca turned round.

'I haven't quite worked out what I'm going to say yet,' she told him. 'Why don't you and your friends go in front of me?'

This didn't make much sense to Capablanca as she had a great deal of time to make up her mind, but there was the future of the world at stake and so he didn't point out her error but instead changed places, accompanied by his two companions.

'They're all doing it,' said Blart, who was younger and had the best eyesight.

Looking closely, Capablanca saw that it was true. The queue was not a stationary patient mass but a line of people constantly changing positions and swapping places forward and backward.

The reason for this movement is the friendliness and generosity of the Illyrian people, which shows itself in its highest form when it comes to queues. Being so polite, they find it almost intolerable to get something before someone else and therefore are prepared to go to almost any lengths to get the person behind them to take their place. Which explains why only an hour after joining the longest queue in the world Capablanca, Blart and Beo found themselves at the front of it. They had been ushered there with much polite encouragement. The most impressive reason for swapping – an old man who claimed that he could feel a heart attack coming on and didn't want the wizard to trip over his corpse – actually drew applause from onlookers.

Between them and a visit to the King was only one courtier. He sat behind a desk on which rested a large book and a bowl of rather mouldy-looking fruit. Unlike the other Illyrians he didn't smile when they approached him. Instead he gave them a sour look and said, 'Names?'

Capablanca gave their names, including that of Pig the Horse.

The clerk wrote down their names and then said, 'The horse can't go in. Guard, take it to the stables. The rest of you can go through there.' The clerk indicated a large golden door behind him. 'The King and Queen are the ones sitting on thrones.'

The questors walked towards the large golden door, which swung open as they approached to reveal a vast, rectangular room with a gold ceiling, silver walls and a bronze floor. In front of them, sitting on two jewelled thrones, sat the King and Queen of Illyria. Both were wearing golden crowns and dark purple ceremonial robes. Indeed, the grandeur of the sight was initially daunting but any nerves the questors may have had were eased by the jovial smile on the King's bearded face and the welcoming expression of the Queen.

Encouraged, the questors approached the throne.

'Your Majesty, we have –' began Capablanca.

'Sssh,' replied the King.

Capablanca stopped speaking. From behind him came a raucous brass fanfare. All three turned round to see five trumpeters standing in the far corner, blowing with all the energy they could muster and turning their faces very red in the process.

'Thank you,' said the King loudly. And then, in a quieter voice, he said to his guests, 'All a bit unnecessary, I know. I don't like to stand on ceremony here, but they do so like playing that I can't bring myself to stop them. Now, what can I do for you good people?'

The wizard began his tale. Blart, who had heard it all before, yawned rather conspicuously until Beo accidentally stood on his foot. Beo wanted to create a good impression because he was well aware that the only person who can turn a common warrior into a knight was a king and it wasn't every day you got the chance to impress a king.

The wizard continued his tale. When he got to the bit about Zoltab's return the King shook his head and the Queen tutted. When he got to the bit about the fight in the tavern the King said, 'Well, I never,' and the Queen said, 'Oh dear.' And when he described the attempt to murder them over the sea the King was shocked and the Queen covered her ears. Finally, the wizard finished his tale by explaining that if his quest to save the world was to be successful then he must humbly beg the King and Queen to allow him access to the diamond tower and the map which lay within which would reveal the location of the Great Tunnel of Despair.

The royal couple sat a while in thought after the wizard's story and request.

'There do seem to be some bad people about,' remarked the King eventually.

'Perhaps they didn't mean it,' said the Queen.

'Yes, my dear,' agreed the King. 'You're right. I was too quick to judge.' He turned to Capablanca. 'Have you tried offering them fruit?'

'No, we haven't,' admitted Capablanca. 'We think it's

gone beyond fruit.'

'We mustn't be too hasty,' said the Queen. 'Give these people some fresh fruit and they may stop all this silly digging for Zoltab.'

'With respect, Your Majesty,' said Capablanca, 'these minions are servants of the most evil lord this world had ever seen. The only way to stop them spreading their contagion throughout the world and destroying everything including your beautiful kingdom is to fight. To get to the top of the Great Tunnel of Despair and cover it with the Cap of Eternal Doom. And to do that I must have the map.'

'Surely you're overreacting,' said the King.

'I wish I were, Your Majesty,' replied Capablanca.

'Have you considered counselling?' asked the Queen. 'I've heard it can work wonders. Many of these people have had unfortunate childhoods marred by parental break-up and consequently lack self-esteem.'

'That's true,' said the King.

'Try fruit and counselling,' said the Queen.

'Yes,' said the King, 'fruit and counselling. But,' he added kindly, 'if that doesn't work feel free to come back and we can all discuss it some more.'

'But there's no time,' said Capablanca urgently. 'Zoltab will soon be free and his evil reign will spread through the world and there will be no more fruit and no more counselling.'

Capablanca was trying hard to remain calm but he was not succeeding. The anger and frustration was there for all to hear, except Blart, who was so used to being spoken to with anger and frustration that it sounded normal to him.

'Now you're getting emotional,' said the Queen soothingly. 'It's been a long journey for you and I'm sure you and your friends are very tired. Why don't you go to one of our guest suites? Have a little rest and I'm sure it will all seem better in the morning. We will ask our clerk to show you the way and bring you some fruit.'

'No,' said Blart firmly, before Beo could stop him. 'No fruit.'

'Please trust me,' Capablanca begged. 'Please let me have the map.'

'We're sorry,' said the King, 'but if we give you the map then somewhere there will be violence and destruction and as King of Illyria I cannot permit it.'

'But ...' spluttered Capablanca in desperation.

'We're sorry,' said the Queen. And with that the royal couple stood up to end the questors' audience.

And so the world once more looked destined to fall to Zoltab and his ministers and minions. Famine, disease, pestilence and death would cover the earth for ever.

'Your Majesty hasn't got any vacancies for a knight, has he?' asked Beo.

Chapter 21

But before the questors could leave there was a bang as the throne room door was booted open.

'I don't believe it!' shouted a very angry female voice. 'There I am feeding my pets and some big fat oaf charges up on a horse and kills one of them. Unbelievable. All the rest of them have run off and now I'll never get them back.'

Blart, Capablanca and Beo turned round. It would perhaps have been best if Beo hadn't. For he recognised the furious girl and she recognised him.

'You!' she yelled at Beo.

'Him!' she yelled at the King and Queen. 'That fat ugly lump killed Gumbo. Arrest him!'

For the first time since they had landed in Illyria, Blart began to feel at home.

'May I present my daughter, Princess Lois?' said the King. 'I think she may be a little upset.'

Upset was somewhat of an understatement. What stood in front of the questors was five-foot-two-and-a-half-inches of freckled red fury – otherwise known as Princess Lois. Her long red hair was bedraggled, her eyes were red with tears and her red dress was torn – all caused by her hot pursuit of Beo across the fields earlier in the day.

'Calm down and have some fruit,' said the Queen.

'I don't want your filthy, horrible, disgusting fruit,' said Princess Lois. 'I want him thrown in jail. And then I want him killed. In exactly the way that he killed Gumbo.'

'Who's Gumbo?' asked a very puzzled Capablanca.

'My pet dragon, if you must know, you dried-up old corpse. And all the others have gone. They were the only things that I liked about this whole crummy place.'

'You don't mean that, dear,' said the Queen.

'I do. This is such a hole. Everybody's always nodding at you and being nice to you and giving you stupid, smelly, nasty fruit.'

'Yeah,' said Blart, who couldn't help supporting someone who actually knew what they were talking about.

The Princess turned on him.

'Who asked you, you nasty little weasel?'

Blart warmed to her even more.

'Now arrest the fat one.'

'Well, Lois,' said the King, 'I'd like to. But we don't have a jail. You see, crime is unknown in Illyria so there's never really been a need.'

'Well, build one, then.'

'That would take a little time, darling,' said the Queen.

'Well, do something. He killed my dragon.'

The King and Queen conferred quietly for a second and seemed to reach an agreement.

The King looked severely at Beo. Well, as severely as he could manage, which meant not smiling.

'Now, sir,' he began. 'You have been accused of a cri— an offen— an action which is perhaps not what some people would call nice. Now, you may have had your reasons. I for one don't know, and I certainly don't propose to say harsh words to you now that in time we may all come to regret. But an accusati— er … a suggestion has been made, and as the King I must investigate this suggestion. So, if you wouldn't mind just going to stand in the corner whilst I investigate –'

'Stand in the corner?' screeched Princess Lois. 'That's the best you can do? Making him stand in the corner?'

'I'm not making him do anything, my dear,' said the King. 'I was just asking him if he'd mind.'

'Guards!' yelled Princess Lois.

Two guards entered the throne room.

'Hi,' said one.

'Er …' said the King, who felt he was having his hand forced a little, 'would you mind escorting the good warrior to the corner?'

'Shall we give him some fruit?' asked the other guard.

'No. Just escort him to the corner,' said the King.

The two guards approached Beo.

'Would you mind coming with us to the corner?' said one.

'If you don't want to go we'll understand,' said the other.

But Beo was beyond arguing or resisting. Damsels keeping dragons as pets. His whole world view had been shattered.

'All right,' said Princess Lois. 'Forget about the jail. Put him to death straight away.'

'My dear,' said the King, 'we don't have the death penalty in Illyria.'

'Well, we should have.'

'And,' pointed out the Queen, 'there isn't really any evidence against the warrior, is there?'

'Yes, there is,' said Blart, seeing his chance to be revenged upon Beo for all his death threats. 'I saw the whole thing. He killed the dragon for no reason at all.'

'I was trying to rescue her,' shouted Beo from the corner.

'There you are,' said Princess Lois triumphantly. 'Ferret-face over there saw that lump of lard kill Gumbo. Now you can kill him.'

There was a pause.

'Well, you see, my dear, things aren't really that simple,' said the King.

'Wouldn't it be better if we were to try and reform him?' suggested the Queen. 'To show him that it wasn't really a good thing to kill other people's pets?'

'Oooh, I hate you,' said Princess Lois to the Queen. 'And you,' she added to the King. 'I'm going to bed.'

And with that the Princess stormed out of the throne room, slamming the door behind her.

There was an embarrassed silence.

After a while the King coughed.

'Sorry about that,' he said.

'Puberty,' added his wife. Everyone in the room nodded wisely, except for Blart, who didn't know what puberty was, which was a shame really as he was going through it.

'Come out of the corner,' said the King.

Obediently Beo came back across the room.

'We haven't traumatised you, have we?' asked the Queen anxiously.

Beo assured her that he was all right.

'I'm sure you didn't mean to kill our daughter's pet,' said the King.

'He did,' insisted Blart, who was unwilling to let this go. 'He charged across a whole field and stabbed it and then he chopped off its tail. Search his armour, it'll be there some-where.'

The King and Queen chose to ignore Blart and instead began to talk about their daughter to Capablanca, for they were great believers that a problem shared was a problem halved.

'We worry about her, you see. She's so full of anger and violence,' said the King.

'What will happen after we're gone?' asked the Queen.

'Exactly,' said the King. 'We can't leave Illyria to be ruled by someone who isn't nice.'

'If only she'd seen some of the rest of the world,' sighed the Queen.

'Exactly,' agreed the King. 'Then she'd realise that anger and violence are terrible things, and when she came to rule Illyria she would do so wisely and preserve the friendliness and generosity that is so characteristic of our people.'

'We've talked to her and talked to her about it,' said the Queen, 'but we just can't get through.'

'She's always slamming doors,' added the King.

'What can we do?' both of them implored the wizard.

'You could put Beo to death,' suggested Blart eagerly. 'She'd like that.'

'Or …' announced Capablanca, who had been listening intently to the royal couple. He paused dramatically to make sure he'd got everyone's attention. 'You could let her go with us. We are on our way to face and defeat the forces of evil. She would no doubt see terrible things and return with a sober appreciation of the awfulness of anger and violence, a great love for her country, and a resolve to rule as you have done when her time comes.'

'Do you think so?' asked the King.

'What a fantastic idea,' said the Queen.

'But alas,' said Capablanca, his face suddenly falling, 'we cannot, for we do not know where we are to go without the map which you have denied us. Unless we have the map we will be unable to take your daughter to experience the educative force of encountering pure evil.'

'Perhaps we've been a bit hasty,' added the Queen.

'Yes,' said the King. 'If this Zoltab is as bad as you say he is then perhaps fruit and counselling won't be enough.'

'After all,' said the Queen, 'we don't really know much about this Zoltab character and you do so perhaps we should trust you to deal with him as you think fit.'

'Yes, yes,' nodded the King. 'That seems to be the right idea. Call in the clerk. He's got the key to the tower. It has never been opened in my lifetime, you know.'

A guard went out to fetch the clerk.

'Won't it be exciting to see a key again, dear?' said the Queen.

'Why?' said Blart bluntly, who thought keys were not much to get excited about.

'In Illyria,' explained the King, 'we don't believe in keys and locks. They encourage secrecy and mistrust. The door to the tower is the only one in the whole kingdom that can be locked.'

'But, what about …' said Beo, and then he stopped. His chivalric sensibility had instantly alerted him to a problem.

'Yes?' said the Queen.

'What about …' Beo blushed a deep red. 'What about intimate moments?'

'Intimate moments?' repeated the Queen, arching her eyebrows.

'Personal functions,' elaborated Beo as the red on his face turned purple.

'Personal functions?' repeated the Queen again as her eyebrows climbed higher.

'He means when you go for a –' began Blart.

'A visit to the Queen's little room,' interrupted Capablanca, who feared quite rightly that Blart was on the point of using a term that would not sit well in the royal ears.

'Yes,' said Beo, whose face was now a colour that has yet to be given a name.

'The women of Illyria,' said the Queen firmly, 'are renowned for their whistling.'

Everybody looked at their feet, apart from Blart who saw no reason to be embarrassed. He had after all spent his formative years on a pig farm.

Fortunately, the awkward atmosphere was broken by the arrival of the clerk.

'Aha,' said the King. 'Tal. Good. Could you furnish us with the key?'

'What key?' said the clerk, who seemed to go a little paler as he said it.

'Ha, ha, ha,' laughed the King. 'I like a good joke as well as the next monarch. What key? You know what key. The only key. The key to the tower.'

'Right,' said the clerk. 'It's just that I can't quite remember where it is.'

'Oh,' said the King. 'That's unfortunate.'

'You mean it's lost?' said the Queen.

'Not quite,' said the clerk, looking awkward.

'I'll break down the door, then,' said Beo, who was pleased to be able to say something macho after the debacle of the toilet conversation. 'I'm good at doors,' he added. 'You get lots of practice when you're collecting debts.'

'I fear not,' said Capablanca. 'That door was built by the six lords and it is indestructible. They wanted to guard Zoltab's whereabouts well in case people tried to dig him up.' Capablanca turned back to the clerk. 'Are you sure you can't remember? It's very important.'

'Yes,' said the King. 'It's most unlike you, Tal. That's why we gave you the key to look after in the first place. Now, I'll tell you what helps me when I get a bit forgetful. How about a nice juicy pear? Does wonders for the memory.'

The King took a pear from the golden bowl that sat beside his throne.

'No, thank you, your Majesty,' replied the clerk.

'It helps,' the King assured him.

'Go on,' urged the Queen.

Aware that the eyes of everyone in the room were on him, the clerk gulped, 'Well, if you're sure.'

He took the pear and bit into it. It was very ripe and the juice flowed down the sides of his chin in two rivulets. But the flesh of the pear did not stay in his mouth long. He cupped his hands to his mouth and spat it out.

'Uuurggh!' said the clerk as he shook the pear off his hands and on to the floor, which wasn't very polite.

'Grab him, Beo!' shouted Capablanca immediately. 'He's a minion of Zoltab.'

Things in the room happened very fast indeed after that.

The Queen's hands flew to her mouth in horror. The King opened his mouth to speak but found he couldn't. Beo lumbered towards the clerk with his massive hands outstretched. But the clerk was nimbler than the warrior. He evaded his grasp and rushed to the window. As he stuck his hand outside, the sunlight flashed off something gripped in his palm. A key.

'Damn you, wizard,' said the clerk in a voice which sounded entirely different. 'Why can't you leave well alone? Yes, I'm a minion of Zoltab and proud of it. You may have caught me but I am not important. My last act for my master will be to throw this key into the river that lies below. It is deep and fast flowing and it will carry this key far from you. You will never find Zoltab's tunnel and he will rise in triumph. Master, your servant has served you well.'

And with that the clerk opened his hand. Beo threw himself at the clerk. Everyone else held their breath. But Beo was too far away and the key would slip out of the clerk's hand, fall into the river and be lost for ever, and with it would go the last hope of saving the world.

Chapter 22

Except that there was one factor that no one, not Capablanca, not Beo, not the King, not the Queen, not the clerk and certainly not Blart had taken into consideration.

Pear juice.

It's sticky.

The key didn't move.

Gravity pulled with all its might but the juice held on.

The clerk's smug smile of triumph vanished. But one shake of his hand and the key would be dislodged. His brain screamed at his nerves; his nerves yelled at his muscles; his muscles twitched; and at that moment a diving warrior hit him headfirst in the stomach and took all decision-making power away from him.

But the eyes of the others did not follow the two men as they collapsed in a heap. Instead they watched the key. Knocked from the clerk's grasp it flew up into the air, hung for a microsecond that seemed like a whole second and then began to fall. It tumbled over itself in an easy somersault, added a twirl for good measure and came to rest with a tinkle on the ledge that jutted out from the window.

'Damn,' said the clerk.

Everybody breathed again. The wizard hastened over to the ledge and retrieved the key.

The Queen collapsed back into her chair, sobbing uncontrollably. She'd never seen anybody hit anybody before and was in no way desensitised to violence. It was all too much.

'There, there, my dear,' said the King soothingly whilst patting her on the head.

Beo got to his feet and pulled the clerk up with him.

'Check behind his ear,' instructed Capablanca.

Beo did.

'It's grubby,' revealed Beo.

'Is there a tattoo of an "m"?' demanded Capablanca irritably.

'I don't know,' said Beo. 'I can't read, can I?'

'Do I have to do everything?' said Capablanca, and he went up to examine the ear himself whilst the clerk hung helplessly in Beo's bearlike grip.

'An "m",' exclaimed Capablanca somewhat theatrically. 'The conclusive proof that this is definitely a minion of Zoltab.'

'He told us that ages ago,' pointed out Blart, which rather punctured the wizard's grand moment.

'You can't trust the word of a minion,' said Capablanca.

'But …' began Blart and then he stopped. There was

something wrong with what the wizard was saying but he was far too stupid to be able to work out what it was.

'Imagine,' said the King. 'A minion of Zoltab. In our palace. And we didn't even know. How did you work it out so quickly?'

'I have my methods,' said Capablanca with more than a hint of self-satisfaction.

'Lucky guess,' suggested Blart.

'It was not!' snapped Capablanca. 'There were two vital clues which led to my detection of the minion. First, he didn't smile and he wasn't friendly like everybody else in Illyria, and second, he couldn't eat fruit. During my researches in the Cavernous Library of Ping I unearthed a rare text that revealed Zoltab's minions and Ministers can't eat fresh food. It needs to have gone off before their evil stomachs can tolerate it. When the minion spat out the pear the conclusion was obvious.'

'Astounding, sir,' commented the King.

'All in a day's work,' Capablanca assured him with what he thought sounded like modesty.

'And now,' said Beo, 'we'll torture him and find out all he knows about Zoltab's return.'

At the word 'torture' the Queen, who, as we know, was rather sensitive on the subject of violence, fainted dead away and banged her head with a nasty thump on the back of her throne. Her crown fell off and clattered on to the bronze floor.

It was an unfortunate occurrence. Perhaps an even more unfortunate occurrence was that Beo, shocked at having caused another damsel's distress, momentarily released his grip on the clerk. Perhaps even more unfortunate than that was the fact that the Queen liked to eat her fruit sliced. Perhaps even more unfortunate than that was that her sharp fruit knife was within reach of Zoltab's minion.

In a second, the knife was in his hand, his tongue was stuck out and the knife was slicing through it. A tiny plop and another tongue lay on the floor twitching with the reflexes of its newly severed nerves.

'They're always doing that,' observed Blart.

Chapter 23

The early morning sun caught the dew in the long grass and made it sparkle. The air was fresh and light. A cool breeze swished through the leaves of the trees and in the fields young rabbits lolloped in play.

''Tis a fine day,' said Beo.

'Indeed,' agreed Capablanca.

'I'm tired,' yawned Blart, who would have much preferred to stay in bed.

The three questors sat astride Pig the Horse in a field outside the walls of the great city of Elysium. They were joined by the King, the Queen, Princess Lois and a large number of Illyrians, who all queued up politely to watch this state occasion and continually swapped positions in order to give each other a better view. They had all been nervous about whether the Princess would agree to come but she had leapt at the chance. Little did they realise that she had her own reasons for coming that she kept firmly to herself – for the time being, at least.

'We must go,' said Capablanca. After retrieving the map from the tower he had spent much of the night examining it and had discovered that the location of the Great Tunnel of Despair was even further away than he'd feared. He knew that every moment counted if they were not to arrive too late.

Princess Lois approached the great horse. She was wearing a leather jerkin and stout boots and her long red hair was pinned up in preparation for the journey. It was the first time Blart had seen the Princess when she wasn't throwing a tantrum and being nasty to people, and yet he still found her attractive. There was something about the spark in her brown eyes when she looked at him that made him think that they somehow understood each other. The Princess caught sight of his open-mouthed gaze.

'Stop staring at me, spotty,' she told him. 'I want to see the world. I don't want to see your ugly face.'

Blart turned away. Maybe they didn't understand each other.

The King and Queen went over to their daughter.

'Now, dear,' said the Queen. 'Promise me you'll wear a vest every day. I've heard that the big wide world is full of draughts.'

'Yes, mother,' said Princess Lois.

'And don't talk to strange men,' advised the Queen.

Princess Lois nodded towards the three comrades already sitting astride Pig the Horse.

'I'm going with strange men,' she pointed out.

'Well, don't talk to strange women, then, dear.'

'Oh, *Mother*,' said Princess Lois.

'Give your old dad a kiss goodbye, then,' said the King, offering his cheek.

'*Dad.*' Princess Lois raised her eyes to heaven, but she could think of no way out and gave her father a very quick kiss.

The watching Illyrians didn't miss the kiss, though, and, being supportive of all forms of positive affection, burst into loud applause. Princess Lois rounded on them.

'Shut up!' she yelled at the assembled crowd. 'I only did it because he made me.'

The crowd was shocked into silence. Then there were mutterings among them as, in traditional Illyrian fashion, they tried to see the best in it. Within a few seconds it was agreed among the crowd that Princess Lois was suffering from nerves at the thought of leaving their wonderful country. They all looked at her sympathetically.

'Aaaaaah,' they said together.

'Don't do that!' shouted Princess Lois. 'Don't you dare start aaahing me. That's even worse than when you smile and clap.'

Unfortunately, the more abusive Princess Lois became, the more convinced the crowd became of her nervousness, the more they sympathised with her and the more they went 'aaah'.

'Stop it!' said Princess Lois.

'Aaaah,' said the crowd.

'I hate you!' she screamed at them. 'I hate all of you and I hope I never see any of you ever again!'

And with that Princess Lois climbed on to the back of Pig the Horse, the three questors became four and they set off to meet their destiny.

'Three cheers for Princess Lois.'

'Hip hip hurrah! Hip hip hurrah! Hip hip hurrah!' obliged the crowd.

'If anybody else is nice to me today, I'm going to kill them,' said Princess Lois grimly.

Chapter 24

And so they flew east. Over the other half of Illyria with the green fields and the abundant orchards. All the people they flew over waved. Capablanca waved back. Beo waved back. Princess Lois made rude gestures. Blart thought this was a rather good idea and made rude gestures too. Princess Lois hit him hard on the back of the head and said that she was the only one who was allowed to make rude gestures on this horse and that if Blart did it any more she'd push him off. She was sitting behind Blart in what is undoubtedly the position of power on a flying horse so Blart stopped.

And then they were flying over a different land. The grass was no longer as green and the orchards were no longer as full. As they flew overhead the people below made rude gestures. Capablanca ignored the rude gestures. Beo waved his fist. Blart did nothing for fear of being pushed to his death and Princess Lois waved happily to the people below.

'This is what I've always wanted to see,' she commented enthusiastically. 'The big wide world where total strangers make rude gestures at you for no apparent reason. Travel really does broaden the mind.'

'They're rubbish rude gestures,' shouted back Blart, who was something of an expert in the field. 'I can make far better rude gestures than that.'

'Shut up, you ugly little toad,' said Princess Lois. 'Let me enjoy the moment.'

And so they flew on. After a while the grass disappeared below them entirely and there was sea. But it was not a deep, calm, blue sea like the last one Blart had seen. It was grey and angry, and mysterious black objects bobbed up and down in it. Even though they flew high above it a terrible stench reached their nostrils.

'That is the Sea of Corpses,' Capablanca shouted back to them. 'Any living thing that enters it dies immediately. The black objects you see bobbing up and down are the dead bodies of unfortunate creatures who have swum in here by mistake.'

'He's always showing off about all the stuff he knows,' Blart whispered to Princess Lois.

'Don't talk to me, you little worm,' replied Princess Lois.

Blart began to think there were signs that they were getting on better.

The silence above the Sea of Corpses was eerie. When they had crossed the sea before there had always been birds flying around them. But here there were no birds. Just the questors and the vastness of the ever-darkening sky.

And the sky did not darken because of approaching night. It was dark in the middle of the day. Even Pig the Horse sensed the oppressive atmosphere and stopped making the cheerful neighs that often punctuated his breathing whilst he was flying.

Finally they sighted land. Each of them secretly cheered but not for long. For replacing the Sea of Corpses below them was the Land of Harsh Parch. A land made up of sand and scrub grass where strange thin-looking beasts burrowed and searched hopelessly for water. The sun's power was diminished in the semi-darkness, but as the dark thinned to the light of dawn the temperature slowly began to rise and sweat began to run from their bodies. Beo suffered worst of all as he insisted on travelling in full battle armour. Capablanca began to feel his old bones aching inside him. Blart felt like a sponge that had been wrung out. It was even more difficult for Princess Lois as royalty was not supposed to sweat. Fortunately her companions were much smellier than she was and no one else noticed this unfortunate departure from royal protocol.

But much worse than the sweaty smell was the incredible thirst. Blart's throat felt harsh and rough and hurt each time he swallowed. His lips were chapped and raw from the sun and his tongue was no longer wet enough to moisten them. His fellow questors suffered similarly – nobody spoke for a long time as each concentrated on preserving the water in their bodies.

Most worrying of all was the condition of Pig the Horse. Unlike those sitting on his back, he was working, which was causing him to lose water quickly. It poured out of him. The heat caught the rivulets that travelled down his neck and flanks and converted them to steam. So it seemed as though they were travelling through a thick fog. Pig's breathing became noisier and more rapid.

'We must land soon,' croaked Capablanca. 'Pig is exhausted.'

'I don't want to stop here,' said Blart, who didn't like the look of the land below.

'We must save the horse,' said Beo.

'Why?' demanded Blart. 'We'll just carry on until he dies and then find another one.'

A tremendous blow crashed on to Blart's back from behind, which nearly sent him tumbling off the horse and down to his death in the endless wastelands of the Land of Harsh Parch. He had forgotten that Princess Lois, who had little time for the human race, was a confirmed animal lover.

'Careful!' Blart shouted at her. 'I'm the only one round here who can save the world, you know. You ought to be nicer to me or I might decide not to.'

'Don't talk to me, you mouldy runt,' shot back Princess Lois, 'or I'll push harder next time.'

She was good. Blart had to admit it. She was good.

'Look for an oasis!' shouted Capablanca. 'We'll stop there.'

They all looked. However, only three of them actually knew what they were looking for. Blart didn't know what an oasis was but there was no way he was going to ask with Princess Lois sitting behind him ready to laugh at his ignorance. So he looked just as hard as the others. But the ever-darkening sky and the steam rising from the sweat on Pig's flanks meant that visibility was limited. Blart had the best eyesight, as we know, and so spotted quite a number of oases without recognising them before finally Princess Lois shouted out, 'There!'

'Where?' asked Capablanca, scanning the ground below.

'*There*,' repeated Princess Lois with added emphasis but no added assistance to Capablanca in finding it.

'Oh, yes, there. Well done,' said Capablanca.

Blart looked down and saw that what they were heading for was just a big puddle with a couple of scruffy trees next to it.

'I've seen loads of those,' he boasted proudly but stupidly.

'Shut up, Blart,' said his three companions as one.

'That's not fair,' Blart continued. 'She sees one puddle and everybody says "Well done" and I see five and everybody says "Shut up".'

'But you didn't tell us about them,' explained Capablanca through gritted teeth.

'You're just biased,' sulked Blart.

Pig the Horse circled down towards the oasis. Blart closed his eyes as he saw the ground rushing up to meet them. However, Pig the Horse had learnt from his last landing and, even though they came down with a bump, none of them fell off. Without waiting for them to dismount Pig made straight for the pool in the middle of the oasis where he began to drink greedily. None of the others was far behind him. They threw themselves down and drank in great gulps of the clear, cold water. For a time there was nothing but the sound of slurping and swallowing.

Blart had never thought that water could taste so wonderful. He could feel it trickling through his body, reviving his parched insides. He drank until he could drink no more and finally lay back on the sandy bank and smiled.

'Don't pull faces at me,' said Princess Lois.

'I wasn't –'

'You're ugly enough without pulling faces.'

'But –'

'When I get to be Queen I'm going to introduce the death penalty especially so I can kill you.'

'I'll feed you to my pigs,' snapped back Blart. He was relieved. Finally he was able to insult her. He felt a huge wave of relief.

'You are a pig,' responded Princess Lois.

At this point the argument ended. Princess Lois was satisfied because she thought that she'd had the last word, and Blart was satisfied because he'd been called a pig, which to Blart was a compliment. So they both thought they'd won.

'We must build a fire,' said Capablanca, 'and then consult

the map in order to decide what we will do tomorrow. I believe that we may be only a day's flight away from the Great Tunnel of Despair and our great battle with Zoltab and his Ministers and minions.'

Despite the heat, Blart shivered. He had not forgotten that he was going to have to face Zoltab when the time came, and the nearer the time came the less he fancied it. But he had no option. He was lost. If he did not follow the wizard he would die in this terrible desert. If he did he would die at the hands of Zoltab. It wasn't much of a choice, when you came to think about it.

'I can't wait to be a-cleaving and a-smiting,' announced Beo, flexing his huge bicep. 'My arm is out of practice. It aches for the lack of a good killing.'

'Will there be many Ministers and minions?' asked Blart.

'Sissy,' said Princess Lois.

'Legion,' said Capablanca. 'For tomorrow we fly towards Crathis, Land of Storms and Terror where lies the Great Tunnel of Despair.'

Blart sighed and turned his back on the other questors. He was feeling very sorry for himself. He didn't want to save the world. After all, it had never done anything for him.

Chapter 25

They were sitting round the fire listening to Beo's stomach make noises. They had eaten a dinner of fruit, bread and sand. Something had gone wrong with Beo's guts and they were filling the night air with their unpleasant rumblings.

'I apologise, Princess,' said Beo, who was very much aware that it was considered unchivalric to make noises in front of a damsel, however uncontrollable they were. 'I have not eaten meat all day and a warrior needs his meat.'

'That's disgusting,' said Princess Lois as another noise escaped from Beo.

'Please don't tell anybody about them,' pleaded Beo. 'Especially your father.'

'Why shouldn't I?' demanded Princess Lois sharply.

'Because he'll never make me a knight then,' explained Beo pathetically.

'Why should I care?' said Princess Lois. 'Who wants a big fat lump like you as a knight anyway?'

'There are more important things to worry about than your promotion,' Capablanca told Beo irritably. 'We must examine the map and decide on a plan of action.'

Capablanca pulled out the map and spread it out on the sand.

'That doesn't look much like a map to me,' said Beo.

'That's the back,' said Capablanca testily. 'I'll just turn it –'

'What's that writing?' said Princess Lois.

'What writing?' asked Capablanca.

'There.' Princess Lois pointed at some very small, very faded script in the bottom left-hand corner of the back of the map.

'I didn't notice that before,' admitted Capablanca, 'but my eyes are not what they used to be. Read it to me please, Princess.'

Princess Lois put her face close to the unrolled parchment and read:

'Know ye, men who hold this map
This prediction is not pap
Zoltab may rise and then worse be wed
To a noble woman back from the dead
Why he'll do this I don't see
He never seemed the marrying type to me.'

'What does that mean?' asked Beo.

'Whoever wrote the prediction wasn't sure,' answered

Capablanca, carefully avoiding admitting that he wasn't sure either. 'But it will be entirely irrelevant if we can prevent Zoltab rising, which is what we intend to do. We can't waste time trying to solve ancient puzzles. Turn the paper over.'

Princess Lois did so to reveal the map.

'Now, I think that this is where we are now.' Capablanca pointed to a picture of a blue pool on the map with an 'S' by it.

'What does that mark mean?' asked Blart.

'It has a number of possible meanings,' said Capablanca, which was his way of avoiding saying 'I don't know'. 'But whatever meaning it has will probably start with an "S" sound.'

'Sea,' suggested Blart.

'It's not the sea, is it?' said Capablanca irritably.

'Sand,' suggested Beo.

'There's sand everywhere,' pointed out Capablanca. 'Why would they just mark it here?'

'Stupid men,' suggested Princess Lois, looking meaning-fully at Blart and Beo.

'It's probably not important,' snapped Capablanca, who reasoned that if he didn't know something then it couldn't possibly matter. 'Now here is the Great Tunnel of Despair.' He pointed to a picture of a large, gaping black hole. 'That is our destination.'

'What's that?' said Princess Lois, indicating a different symbol on the map.

'That's not relevant,' said Capablanca.

'Please tell me, Capablanca. You are so wise and clever,' said Princess Lois in a tone so unlike the one she usually used that Blart could hardly believe it. It was sweet and melodious and it made Blart feel sick.

'Well, all right then,' said Capablanca with fake reluctance. For all his great knowledge and experience, he was not above being flattered by a young princess. 'This symbol means that the area is home to a great colony of dragons.'

'Dragons!' said Princess Lois excitedly.

'Dragons,' said Beo dolefully. He had hoped that the whole dragon episode could be forgotten.

'Yes, dragons,' snapped Capablanca, who wanted to focus on more important things. 'But they are in totally the opposite direction to our journey and aren't at all important.'

'No,' agreed Beo quickly, thankful that the subject of dragons could be dropped.

'No,' agreed Princess Lois. This surprised Blart, considering she'd been going on about how attached she was to them all the time that they'd been in Illyria.

'We should be able to reach the Great Tunnel of Despair by tomorrow. Let us hope we are not too late.'

'What happens if we are?' asked Blart hopefully.

'We'll improvise,' said Capablanca and he gathered up the map and stalked off.

'He should tell us, shouldn't he?' Blart appealed to Princess Lois and Beo.

'You've got a huge spot growing on your nose, ugly boy,' replied Princess Lois, which was hardly to the point.

'If you weren't always moaning on we'd do a lot better,' growled Beo. 'If it was up to me we'd have cleaved you in two days ago.'

'Then you wouldn't have to worry about that big spot,' added Princess Lois, 'and I wouldn't have to look at it.'

Blart was abused into silence. They were all mad, he decided. None of them seemed to care whether Zoltab killed them or not. Blart was beginning to realise that it is very dangerous to hang around with brave people.

'I think I shall go for a brief stroll,' said Princess Lois in the sweet voice Blart hated. 'Beowulf. Would you care to escort me and provide me with protection?'

'Protection from what?' asked Blart scornfully. All around them as far as the eye could see was nothing but sand. And sand is not renowned for its aggressive qualities.

'Quiet,' said Beo, standing up. 'If a damsel asks for an escort then any man worth his salt will give her one. A man should be prepared to sacrifice his whole life to give a fair damsel an extra moment of tranquility and peace of mind.'

'But she doesn't need protection,' pointed out Blart. 'She's scarier than you ... Ow.'

Beo cuffed Blart across the head.

'Never call a damsel scary,' Beo told him.

And with that Beo escorted Princess Lois off on her stroll. Blart sat alone and watched Beo and Princess Lois walk towards the setting sun. As they got further away they turned into two silhouettes – one big and fat and the other small and thin. Even from a distance Blart could tell that the small and thin one seemed to be doing all the talking. He felt very lonely. Here he was in a wasteland with three people who didn't like him and tomorrow he was probably going to get killed trying to save a world that had never done anything for him. Blart was feeling something he had never felt before. It was simply the need for another human being just to sit and be with.

But Blart didn't know this so he thought he might be getting ill. He put his hand to his forehead. It was very hot but then again he was in the middle of a desert and most things tend to be. Even if I was ill, he thought, nobody would care. And then he thought that if he had a really bad disease then perhaps he'd die in the night and then they'd all feel sorry for being so nasty to him. Except he'd be dead, and that was the outcome he'd spent most of the quest trying to avoid so it wouldn't do him any good. Blart's brain protested at this point. It had been doing far too much thinking, it told him, and it wanted to stop now.

Blart, with no other companion available to him, stood up and walked over to say hello to Pig the Horse. But when he tried to stroke the great horse it immediately moved away. Perhaps Pig remembered some of the nasty comments Blart had made about him; perhaps Pig remembered some of the kicks Blart had given him; perhaps Blart simply smelled bad.

Whatever the reason Blart felt rejected all over again. Too depressed even to call Pig the Horse names, he stumped back to the fire and sat down.

By now the wizard had returned but he still ignored Blart and continued studying the map. Princess Lois and Beo came back. Even though they had been talking non-stop on their walk they had nothing to say now. Capablanca yawned, folded up the map and told everyone that they should get a good night's sleep as they might well be saving the world tomorrow. He lay down, placing the folded-up map under his head in place of a pillow, and was soon asleep. Princess Lois and Beo nodded to one another and moved to different sides of the fire, where they too lay down and were soon asleep.

Blart lay on his back staring up at the stars. He remembered his grandfather and his favourite pigs. It seemed so long ago since he'd left them. He wasn't too bothered about his grandfather but he'd really missed his pigs. And so, with thoughts of feeding Wattle and Daub apples floating round his mind, Blart fell asleep. Would he be able to rise to the challenges that the next day was sure to bring?

Chapter 26

Blart was leaning over the side of a large pen. In the pen were ten glorious pigs. They were eating. Then they stopped eating and began running about. Suddenly – Blart didn't know how – he was in the pen with them. He and the pigs were running around in the mud. Faster and faster they ran, but all at the same pace so that he never banged into the pig in front or got hit by the pig behind. He was laughing. On the outside of the pen he could see Princess Lois, Beo, Capablanca and Pig the Horse. They all looked miserable. They wanted to be in the pen running round in the mud with the pigs but they had to stay outside.

'Serves you right for being so nasty to me,' Blart shouted at them.

But then there was a flash of blue light from the wizard's eyes and Blart felt himself stumble and fall into the mud. He tried to get up, but the mud clung on to him and pulled him down. He wanted to run with the pigs but the mud wouldn't let him. The Princess, Beo and Capablanca started laughing at him. Behind them he could see Pig the Horse and even he was laughing at him. He struggled violently but still the mud wouldn't let him go. And then one of the pigs that was hurtling towards him stumbled, tripped over and landed smack bang on Blart's chest.

He couldn't breathe.

He opened his eyes. Above him the stars were dotted around the clear night sky. It was all a dream. Except …

He still couldn't breathe.

'Euch,' said Blart, which is the kind of noise you make when you are attempting to breathe but not really succeeding.

Then Blart noticed something else. He couldn't move his arms. They were bound tightly to his sides. He tried hard to push them outwards. Whatever was holding them tightened. Blart managed to suck a little air into his cramped chest. He tried to work out what was holding him. It felt like rope. Thick rope. Thick rope with a pulse. Thick rope which was alive.

'Euch,' euched Blart again. It was supposed to be a scream of fear but was instead more like the croak of a modest toad. Blart felt himself begin to move. Whatever was holding him wanted to put him somewhere else.

'Blart.' Capablanca's voice was inside his head.

Blart would have jumped in shock if he had been able to. He'd never had anybody inside his head and frankly this was not the ideal time for it to happen.

'Blart,' repeated Capablanca, 'I am unable to speak at the

moment and so am using my magic power to communicate directly from my brain to your brain. It's not easy.'

'Oh,' said Blart but predictably it came out as, 'Euch.'

'I have made an error,' continued Capablanca in Blart's head. 'I was under the impression that on the map there was an 'S' by this lake. I now realise that this was in fact a mistake.'

'Stupid old man,' thought Blart.

'I heard that,' said Capablanca. 'This is no time for recriminations. We have a practical problem on our hands. As I was saying, what I thought was an "S" was in fact nothing of the sort. It was actually a picture of a serpent.'

'What's a serpent?' thought Blart, who, as we know, was not particularly well-endowed in the vocabulary department.

'I thought you might be wondering about that,' said Capablanca. 'Serpents are big snakes. They slither out of pools at night and coil themselves around any living thing that is nearby. Unfortunately they have coiled themselves around you and me. They will then pull us underwater, where we will drown. Then they will wait for us to rot and then eat us. Any other questions?'

'Big snakes. Drown. Rot. Eaten,' screamed Blart inside his head.

'That's hardly a question,' said Capablanca sternly. 'Don't panic. I know a spell that will get the serpent to release me. All I need to say is "*Shanti*" three times and the serpent will be forced to let go.'

'Say it, then,' yelled Blart in his head.

'I was about to,' replied Capablanca. 'I was just letting you know what the situation was because I thought you might be concerned. Consideration costs nothing.'

'Say it,' screeched Blart in his head as he felt his feet being pulled into the water.

'Don't rush me,' said Capablanca. 'You have to do these things right.'

The serpent holding Blart gave a sudden twist and Blart was tugged further down the side of the pool. He felt his calves slide into the cold black water.

'Eeeek,' squeaked Blart in his head.

'Keep quiet, can't you?' ordered Capablanca. 'You're destroying my concentration.'

Blart tried his best to keep quiet. The serpent produced another lunge and pulled Blart into the water up to his waist.

'*Shanti, Shanti, Shanti.*' Blart heard Capablanca in his head and there was a sudden flash of crackling blue light that whizzed across the night sky.

'That seems to have done the trick,' said Capablanca. But he said it in his normal outside voice. To Blart, it sounded very loud and strange.

The spell, which had managed to get rid of Capablanca's serpent, didn't seem to have had any effect on the one gripping Blart. Instead it produced another shuddering convulsion and pulled him into the pool up to his chest.

'The spell hasn't worked,' screamed Blart in his head. 'Get this thing off me.'

'The spell has worked,' insisted Capablanca indignantly. 'The serpent that was dragging me to my doom has released its vice-like grip and slithered back into the murky depths from whence it came.'

'Mine hasn't,' pointed out Blart.

'It wasn't supposed to,' replied Capablanca patiently. 'The spell is only designed to remove a serpent from the person who utters the spell. To get a serpent off someone else is a different spell entirely.'

'Say that one, then,' screeched Blart in his head as the serpent, with another burst of energy, dragged him into the pool up to his neck.

'There's a slight problem there,' began Capablanca. 'You see, I don't know it.'

'Well, kill it then,' demanded Blart in his head.

'Not really practical, I'm afraid. Serpents have impenetrable skin and are two hundred times stronger than me.' By now Capablanca was standing on the edge of the pool right next to Blart's head. He crouched down and spoke directly into his ear. 'The only way to get it off you is for you to say, *Shanti, Shanti, Shanti,* and the magic words will release you from the serpent's dreaded coils.'

'*Shanti, Shanti, Shanti,*' said Blart straight away. But the coils didn't vanish. Instead they flexed even more sharply around Blart, pulling him further into the pool. Water lapped around the corners of his mouth.

'You had to rush it, didn't you?' said Capablanca irritably.

'It's *Shanti, Shanti, Shanti*. Not *Shante, Shante, Shante*. Thanks to that slip of the tongue some poor woman will wake up tomorrow to discover that her husband's been turned into a dragon. Now concentrate. Try and get that sharp "*i*" sound at the end.'

Blart concentrated as well as he could manage in the circumstances. But he found he was continually distracted by an image of a huge serpent eating his rotting body.

'*Shanti, Shanti, Shanti*,' he said.

'No, no, no,' shouted Capablanca in frustration. 'That was *Shantii, Shantii, Shantii*. You're making the "*i*" last too long. With that mistake, you've just made some poor innocent man's nose turn into a root vegetable. Now get it right!'

Blart forced himself to focus on exactly how the wizard had said the words. This time I'll get it right, he promised himself. This time I'll get it right.

And then before he had time to think anything else he felt a huge tug and the serpent dragged him under the water. Without thinking he opened his mouth. Water poured into it and rushed straight down into his lungs. Blart felt horribly full of water and horribly empty of air at the same time. It had happened so fast. He felt as if he was going to explode.

'*Shanti, Shanti, Shanti*,' he screamed inside his head. Then there was nothing but blackness.

Chapter 27

There was a huge weight on his back. It was pressing up and down. Something was oozing from the side of his mouth. There was another bang on his back. He felt sick. This was it. His grandfather had always told him that he would rot in hell. And here he was. Doomed for eternity to feel sick and be for ever hit on the back with no hope of any escape.

Except Blart wasn't in hell. Instead, he was lying face down in the sand by the pool from which Capablanca had pulled him after Blart had said *Shanti, Shanti, Shanti* correctly and succeeded in freeing himself from the coils of the serpent before falling into unconsciousness. The banging on his back was simply Capablanca trying to force the water out of Blart's lungs, and the oozing from the side of his mouth was the water gradually escaping. But it was typical of Blart to look at things from their worst possible angle.

There was another bang on Blart's back. A particularly hefty one.

'Erp,' said Blart as more liquid oozed out of him.

'Aha,' said Capablanca. 'So you're alive, are you?'

'Yerp,' said Blart.

'I hope you learnt your lesson,' said Capablanca, giving another bang to Blart's back.

'Werp?' said Blart.

'Pronunciation is very important,' continued Capablanca severely. 'Slangy lazy speech can condemn you to a watery grave.' And with a final slap Capablanca released Blart.

Blart raised his head. He was deathly pale and his clothes were sodden and dirty. Sand and spit dribbled down the side of his mouth. The night in the desert was cold and Blart shivered uncontrollably.

'I want to go home,' he said miserably.

'Stop moaning,' ordered the wizard. 'And clean yourself up. You can't save the world in that state.'

The darkness was beginning to thin. Dunes invisible in the night were formed once more.

'Where are the others?' asked Blart.

'What?' said Capablanca.

'The others.'

'Others?' replied Capablanca. 'Oh, the others. They're …' He looked around. 'They were there last night.'

'What about when the serpents attacked?'

'I don't remember. I was too busy being attacked and then saving your life. Did you see them?'

'I was too busy nearly being killed,' pointed out Blart.

'Oh,' said Capablanca. 'I don't know. If they're not here then I don't know where they can be.'

Capablanca and Blart stood up and looked from left to right for as far as they could see, but there was nothing. No sign of Princess Lois, no sign of Beo and no sign of Pig the Horse. Just endless sand dunes slowly turning from grey to brown in the weak dawn light. Where could their companions be? They both found themselves staring at the inky black water of the oasis.

'Oh dear,' said Capablanca.

There was no other conclusion to reach. Princess Lois, Beo and Pig the Horse had all been dragged to a watery grave by the remorseless writhing of the serpents and even now their corpses lay in some foul den slowly rotting.

'If only,' said Capablanca, breaking the silence, 'if only I hadn't misread the map. None of this would have happened.'

The silence continued.

'Mind you,' continued Capablanca, 'a picture of a serpent does look a lot like an "S" when you think about it. Whoever drew up that map really should have been a bit more specific. It's a mistake anyone could have made.'

The silence continued.

'If I could get my hands on the man who drew that map,' continued Capablanca, 'I'd give him a piece of my –' Capablanca broke off. Blart looked at him. His face, which had been a mask of calm control, was suddenly creased with panic. 'The map. The map. The map. Where's the map?'

Capablanca rushed over to where he'd been sleeping. Nothing. He rushed to the edge of the oasis. Nothing. He rushed back and forth between the two places. Still nothing. He rushed round and round in a circle. Not very surprisingly, there was still nothing, as this is hardly the most sensible way to look for something.

'This is awful, terrible, horrible, miserable,' Capablanca shouted in despair.

Blart, however, was not concerned. He saw the death of his companions and the loss of the map in a positive light.

'Can I go home now?' he asked Capablanca.

'What?' shouted the enraged wizard.

'Can I go home now?' Blart repeated patiently. 'The Princess, Beo and Pig the Horse are all dead and we've lost the map. There's no point going on if we don't know where we're going so I think I should go home.'

People say every cloud has a silver lining, and the silver lining for Blart was that the quest was now surely at an end.

'Go home?' said Capablanca. 'Don't you understand, boy, that if we go home there won't be a home to go home to? Zoltab will destroy everything. Haven't you listened to anything I've been saying?'

'Not much,' admitted Blart.

'We'll just have to think of another plan.'

'Oh,' said Blart.

'And the map has not been lost. It has been spirited away by evil forces whilst I was distracted.'

'Like the wind,' suggested Blart.

'A wind under the control of evil forces is a possibility,' conceded Capablanca. 'Now shut up and let me think of another plan.'

The wizard sat down cross-legged, put his head in his hands and proceeded to think very visibly. But it was not the wizard who came up with a new plan. It was Blart.

'Couldn't we ask Zoltab to leave our homes alone?' he suggested.

Capablanca didn't even bother to look up. Wizards are not like humans. Normal humans can think for about a minute before they want to do something else, and that's if they're clever. Wizards can think for hours. And Capablanca did just that. The sky lightened, the desert began to heat up and the oasis pool became a deep and inviting blue that would have tempted anybody to jump in for a swim if they didn't happen to know about the serpents that lurked in its depths.

The sun climbed steadily up the sky and the heat rose accordingly. Blart began to imagine he could actually feel his body beginning to burn, and sought what shelter there was under the two scruffy trees. The sun was directly above them when the wizard suddenly uncrossed his legs, stood up and spoke one word.

'Dwarves.'

It didn't sound much of a plan to Blart. But Capablanca seemed perfectly happy with it. He looked up at the sun, studied the dunes that surrounded them and then pointed purposefully at a mound of sand that to Blart looked exactly like any other lump of sand and said, 'That way.'

Immediately he set off. Blart watched the wizard depart, wishing more than anything that he didn't have to follow him. But he was in the middle of a desert miles from home. And when you're in that situation and the only other person says 'That way' and sets off, your options are strictly limited.

For three days they struggled across the desert. Their faces were burnt, their lips dried and cracked, and their throats parched, but still they walked. The cruel sun shone red hot during the day, but at night the empty sky lost all warmth and they shivered their way through the dark hours until the sun returned. But soon the sun's welcome light became searing heat and they cursed its boiling rage as much as they had cursed its absence in the night. Each unfolding hour was walked more slowly than the last. The sand slipped and slid below them, grit lodged in their eyes which became red and sore with rubbing. And then, just as they thought they could go on no more, they would find a small pool of water to save them.

They would set out again and soon their throats would be dry once more. It was as though the desert was playing with them. Keeping them going just a little bit longer. But the end must come eventually. Sooner or later one of them would fall and would not get up.

And during all this time did they think of their lost

companions, of the fiery princess, the brave warrior and the amazing horse? They did not. They thought only of the next step and then the step after it. All that they knew was that they must keep going. They had no idea why.

And then, on the third day, as the sun was at its highest and most unforgiving, Capablanca was walking down a dune when the sand slid away from under him as it had done time and again in the last two days. On the first day Capablanca's reactions would have allowed him to balance himself. On the second day he would have attempted to balance himself, but would have been too slow and would have fallen. But now he did nothing but fall. Down the dune he rolled, until he landed in a heap at the bottom. A heap that did not move.

Blart saw Capablanca roll past him. He continued to plod down the dune. He passed the heap that was the wizard but he did not stop. The wizard had fallen over many times. Blart had fallen over many times. They got up and carried on. Blart continued to walk. Another dune lay in front of him. He began to climb. The sand slipped away from his feet. He struggled upwards. He was no longer Blart. He was no longer a person. He was simply a thing that moved.

Beneath him the sand gave way. Now his face was pressed into the sand and its gritty particles invaded his mouth. He had fallen over. He should get up. His arms refused to lift him. The sun burnt his eyes but he was too dazed to look away. He stared at it for a while. And then he remembered that he should be doing something. What was it that he should be doing? He wasn't sure. He should be moving. His body didn't want to move but his brain kept saying he should. Move, his brain told him. Leave me alone, he said to himself. Move, his brain repeated.

Blart began to crawl. Slowly, ever so slowly, he moved up the dune. He slipped back and then crawled up and then slipped back some more. He was moving so slowly now that it was almost impossible to tell that he was moving at all. The sun, which had been at its highest point when he began, was now dropping into the west, but its harsh unyielding heat remained. Still Blart inched up the dune. He could not stop now because he no longer knew how to. Only death could end his crawling now. But death did not come. The top of the dune came instead. Blart raised his head and saw colours. Colours whose names he could hardly remember. Greens and blues and other ones frazzling his brain with their sudden difference.

And Blart felt angry. Angry at these new colours. Angry that they weren't sand. Angry that he could not lie down and die, when that was all he wanted to do. Angry that he had been saved.

And the new colours made him think. Made him remember. Capablanca. He looked behind him. There at the bottom of the dune was the wizard, where Blart had passed him an age ago. He had to go and get him. He'd know what to do about all these new colours. Blart began to crawl back down the dune towards the blot in the sand that was Capablanca.

Chapter 20

'I saved your life,' said Blart.

'Shut up,' replied Capablanca.

'But you'd be dead if it wasn't for me,' pointed out Blart.

'You'll be dead in a minute because of me,' grumbled Capablanca.

'I came back for you. I could have gone on. But I didn't.'

'I know. You've told me a million times.'

'I'm a hero,' concluded Blart proudly.

Now, this is a difficult thing to judge, as there are no hard and fast rules about how you become a hero. Can you rightly claim to be a hero based on only one courageous action or must there be a number of courageous actions one after the other and an absence of cowardly ones? History has never given us a definite answer to this question. Blart, however, had already promoted himself to heroic status.

'You're not a hero,' said Capablanca, who obviously hadn't. 'Now pass me some bread for this is our last meal before we depart.'

They were eating at a table in a deserted two-roomed cottage that sat on the edge of the desert next to a babbling river. Three days previously, Blart had dragged Capablanca to it and knocked on its solid door with all that remained of his strength. There was no answer. Blart had pushed open the door and found a tidy kitchen with an immense jug of water on the table and a fresh loaf of bread by its side. He had drunk greedily, feeling life return to his body as the water rushed through it. Then he had forced some water down the wizard's throat that made him cough and spit at first but soon brought him back to consciousness. In the other room they had found two freshly made beds and, without a word to one another, had collapsed on to them and slept for many hours.

Quickly, they had recovered. They had eaten and drunk. They had rested. They had caught fish in the river that ran past the cottage and built a fire to cook them. Then they began to wonder whose cottage it was and why they hadn't returned. They looked out across the fields for a sign of an owner but they saw nobody. In the end they gave up. If somebody appeared then they'd explain what had happened, apologise for eating the person's bread and sleeping in his bed and hope that he didn't have a short temper.

But nobody did appear and now the wizard pronounced them ready to leave. Blart had another point of view.

'I'm still tired,' he said. 'I need more time to get better.'

'We're going now,' said Capablanca grimly. 'The chances of us arriving before Zoltab has been released are getting smaller all the time. We must go now.'

'Uuugghh,' said Blart.

But he stood up and headed for the door. The world still had a chance.

They had been walking for a while when they saw a figure coming towards them. Blart, who had by now come to the conclusion, based on his experience during the quest, that it was best to regard any stranger as a potential murderer, was all for hiding behind a bush until the figure had passed, but Capablanca insisted that you couldn't decide someone was a potential murderer until they did something which gave you evidence of their homicidal intentions. The problem with this theory is, of course, that you may only become aware of their homicidal intentions a moment before you are murdered, which means that the time available to change your behaviour is severely limited. But fortunately for Capablanca, Blart wasn't really clever enough to understand this and so Capablanca had his way.

As the figure got nearer it became a tall strong farmer. But it was not until he got right up to them that they discovered the surprising thing about him. His nose was a carrot.

'Look at him – his nose is a carrot,' said Blart, who, as he had recovered his strength, had also recovered his marvellous ability to say exactly the wrong thing at the wrong time. The man was obviously embarrassed by his nose because his face flushed red.

'Woe is me,' he said. 'I have a carrot for a nose.'

'How did that happen?' said Capablanca.

'I don't know. But three days ago, I woke up feeling completely normal and was just preparing for a day's farming when my wife woke and began to scream.'

'Oh dear,' said the wizard rather uncomfortably, because he strongly suspected that he knew the cause of the man's nose becoming a carrot – Blart's mispronounced spell as he fought to free himself from the serpent's clutches.

'What happens when you sneeze?' asked Blart.

'Now, now, Blart,' said Capablanca. 'The man doesn't want us prying into his problems. Let's get going. Good day to you, sir.'

'I've been to the doctor,' continued the man, who seemed eager to talk of his troubles. 'I walked for two days to his house. My wife came with me. The doctor said there was nothing he could do. My wife said she couldn't live with a man with a carrot for a nose, and so she refused to return to our little cottage and has gone back to her parents. I've been a good man and yet my life has been ruined. I will spend the rest of my life living quietly in my cottage hiding my shameful hooter from the eyes of the world. All I have to look forward to is the last loaf of my wife's bread that is waiting for me on the kitchen table. It is all I have left of her now.'

Capablanca looked at his feet. He could not help the man. The carrot would revert to a nose eventually, for all spells wore off in time, but he did not know how long it would take. Also, he felt that by demonstrating any knowledge of the subject he would be bound to attract unwelcome suspicion. The man might have neighbours and the neighbours might have wood and before you knew it he'd be burning at the stake.

'We had some nice bread yesterday,' said Blart, who had no idea that he was responsible for the man's new appendage and the consequent destruction of his marriage.

'Not as nice as my wife's,' said the man with the carrot for a nose.

'How do you know?' argued back Blart. 'You weren't there. It was in this —'

'We must be going,' said Capablanca quickly.

The wizard's nervousness aroused the suspicion of the man, and his expression became one of distrust.

'The one strange thing that the doctor said to me was that it could have been caused by magic. You wouldn't know anything about magic, would you?'

'Me?' Capablanca looked incredulous. 'Magic? No. I'm just an old man going about my business with my young grandson.'

'Funny I've never seen you in these parts before,' persisted the man, who was now scrutinising Capablanca's clothes.

'Just passing through on our way to market,' said Capablanca.

'Which market?' asked the man.

'Er … any market. We like markets. All the hustle and bustle. So many spells … er smells.'

'You look like a wizard.'

'Do I? Ha Ha.' Capablanca laughed unconvincingly. 'You look like a vegetable patch, but it doesn't mean you are one.'

'That cloak and your beard . . . and what's that in your hand?' The man indicated Capablanca's wand, which he had forgotten he was holding.

'Oh, that,' said Capablanca, looking at it as though he was seeing it for the first time. 'That's my walking stick.'

'It's not very long for a walking stick.' The man looked more and more suspicious.

'I have a terrible stoop.'

The man paused and looked Capablanca up and down once more. Capablanca tried to look as little like a wizard as possible.

'Are you sure you're not a wizard?' he asked again.

Blart was biding his time and enjoying Capablanca's discomfort. He decided enough time had been bided.

'He is a wizard,' he announced.

'What?' said the man with a carrot for a nose.

'Ha! Ha! Ha!' laughed Capablanca. 'The boy will have his jokes.'

'No,' persisted Blart. 'He honestly is a wizard. He put a spell on my legs so I can't run away from him, and he's made me travel all over the place and do loads of dangerous things because he says I've got to save the world.'

The man stared open-mouthed at Blart and then at Capablanca. And then he burst out laughing.

'What a tale,' he roared. 'There was me thinking you were a wizard until your boy comes out with all that nonsense. Saving the world indeed. Hahahahaha. Spells on legs. Hahahahaha. I didn't think I'd ever laugh again now that my nose is a carrot, but you've proved me wrong, young lad.'

'But he is a wizard,' repeated Blart indignantly.

The man slapped his thigh and laughed some more.

'Now, now, grandson,' said Capablanca. 'Don't overdo it.'

But Blart was not to be stopped. He had never seen the wizard so worried, and it occurred to him that now was the time to escape. Now, before he had to meet any dwarves or face the wrath of Zoltab. He could go back with the man and live in his cottage. He could make him get some pigs. This was his chance.

'Look,' Blart cried. And he proceeded to run away from Capablanca. Before Capablanca had time to react, Blart had run for ten paces and his legs had tripped him up.

'Did you see?' shouted Blart from the ground. 'My legs tripped me up.'

But the man was unable to respond. He was laughing so much that he was gripping Capablanca to stop himself falling over.

'What are you laughing at?' yelled Blart. 'I'm being taken to save the world against my will.'

The man wiped tears from his eyes.

Blart got up and stomped back to the other two.

'There's nothing funny about it,' he said angrily.

'Oh, there is, my boy,' said the man with the carrot for a nose. 'What a fool I've been – accosting perfect strangers and accusing them of being wizards. I see now that it's just a reaction caused by the shock of discovering that my nose has become a carrot. Still, at least I can laugh about it. If you can't laugh at yourself then who can you laugh at?'

'But you're right,' insisted Blart.

'Enough joking, grandson,' said Capablanca sharply. 'We have delayed this man too long. He needs to get home to his wife's loaf.'

'He shouldn't bother,' said Blart sulkily.

'Why?' asked the man with a carrot for a nose. 'No, don't tell me. It's because you've eaten it, isn't it?' And a great snort of laughter issued from him which made his carrot wobble up and down precariously.

'Yes,' said Blart.

'You're too much,' said the man, laughing once more. 'I must be going, but I'll tell you what, old man. Your grandson has a great future as a fool.'

And so saying, the man with a carrot for a nose nodded amiably and walked off in the direction of his cottage. What he said when he got home and found that his wife's loaf had indeed been eaten we will never know but we can guess that it was probably rude.

Blart and Capablanca set off in the opposite direction, Capablanca almost doubled up in order to use his wand as a walking stick. It was not until the man with the carrot for a nose was out of sight that he could rise to his full height and shout at Blart.

'Have I taught you nothing on this great quest?' shouted Capablanca. 'Don't you realise that your welfare is less important than that of the whole world? Have you learnt nothing of sacrifice? Would you condemn me to a burning at the stake to preserve your own miserable hide? Have you learnt nothing of sacrifice and loyalty and friendship and honour?'

Blart didn't say anything. He trudged along with his head bowed down as the wizard abused him. He hadn't learned anything about sacrifice and loyalty and friendship and honour. What he had learned mainly on this quest was that saving the world wasn't anything like what it was cracked up to be and that the best thing to do with a quest was not go on it.

Chapter 29

'I believe that we must begin to look for the dwarves around here,' Capablanca announced.

Blart immediately began darting nervous glances about him. The quest had taught him that it was safe to assume that every new thing he met along the way might well try to kill him so he had no desire to meet dwarves.

'You don't find dwarves out in the open,' scoffed Capablanca. 'Dwarves live underground. Don't you even know that?'

Blart didn't.

'First,' continued Capablanca, 'you must look for large stones. They must be at least three feet high and at least two feet wide. Like that one.'

The wizard pointed at a big stone that sat in a field next to their rough path. A moment ago Blart would not have said that there was any difference between that rock and any other. However, as soon as Capablanca had picked it out the rock seemed to be different. It was lighter than all the other stones and it didn't seem to have got where it was naturally. They left the path and approached the rock.

'Now we push,' said Capablanca.

'Couldn't you magic it away?' asked Blart.

'I could not,' said Capablanca. 'If you started using magic for everything you'd become casual, your spells would become sloppy and then they'd stop working. So, as we can move this stone with a bit of physical effort, then we should.'

Capablanca put his shoulder to the stone and pushed. Reluctantly, Blart joined him. The stone moved. They pushed harder. The stone resisted and then suddenly gave. It tumbled over and landed in the grass with a muffled crash to reveal some flattened yellow grass.

'This is always happening,' said Capablanca in annoyance.

Suddenly the stone didn't seem to be quite as out of place in the field as Blart had originally thought. In fact, if you looked around you could see a number of other stones which looked quite similar.

'Oh, well,' said Capablanca. 'Let's carry on.'

Three fields later they saw another stone.

'That is definitely a dwarf stone,' observed Capablanca.

Blart looked at it. It did seem to be out of place and standing at an awkward angle, but then the last one had seemed like that too and nothing had been under that one.

'Are you sure?' he asked.

'Yes. Come on.'

'What are dwarves like?' asked Blart.

'They're short,' said Capablanca briefly.

I think even I would forgive Blart a scornful glance at the wizard here.

'But the thing about dwarves,' continued Capablanca, 'is that they don't like people being bigger than them.'

'Oh,' said Blart. 'It's a shame they're called dwarves, then, isn't it, because that makes everybody think that they're small.'

'Which they are,' agreed Capablanca. 'But they're very sensitive about it. You must on no account give a dwarf the impression that you think he is short. They are liable to become violent. In tense situations it is always best to keep an eye on your shins. When attacked by a dwarf, the shins are the most vulnerable area. The kicks from their boots will only bruise, but real injuries can be sustained if they use their axes.'

'But aren't they on our side?' said Blart. 'Why should we be worried about them attacking us?'

'Dwarves are on nobody's side,' explained Capablanca. 'They are the most unreliable and unpredictable of creatures. But they may be on our side once they know about Zoltab, for the dwarves have reason to hate him. At least, as much on our side as a dwarf can be, but until then they might be a little hostile. We will after all be breaking into their homes.'

'Can't we do without a dwarf?' asked Blart.

'No,' replied Capablanca firmly. 'Now we have lost the map a dwarf is absolutely necessary. They are now our only hope of finding the Great Tunnel of Despair. There is nobody in the world who knows more about tunnels than dwarves do. That's where they spend their lives – underground, digging tunnels and mining precious metals and jewels. Come on, push.'

The stone was a little bigger than the previous one. By the time they finally got it to roll to one side, both Blart and the wizard were very red in the face.

'Blast,' said Capablanca. For under this stone was nothing except more grass and a large collection of surprised insects.

They continued walking and the wizard would exclaim when he saw a dwarf stone. He saw six more dwarf stones, each of which turned out to have nothing more than moss underneath it. By the time that Capablanca pointed out his ninth dwarf stone Blart, whose patience levels were not high, was becoming distinctly unhappy.

'There's no such thing as dwarves,' he told the wizard. 'You've made them up.' And then a greater doubt bubbled up in his head. 'I bet there's no such thing as Zoltab and there's no such thing as the Great Tunnel of Despair either. You are just a mad old man who makes up stories and keeps people from their pigs.'

It was late afternoon and the sun was sinking and reddening as Blart spoke these unpleasant words. It should be said in his defence that this was a particularly difficult time for him, as this was the hour of the day he used to feed the pigs, and in his mind was the happy image of them munching away on their swill. And here he was pushing over stones.

Capablanca didn't appreciate Blart's sensitivity so all he said was, 'Heave.'

They pushed the latest stone as hard as they could and then, when it didn't move, discovered that they could push a little bit harder after all, and the stone wobbled a little and then a little more and then finally tumbled over. Blart had seen enough in the way of flattened grass and surprised insects that day, so he didn't even bother looking at the ground that had been exposed.

He changed his mind, however, when Capablanca shouted, 'Eureka!'

For there, under the stone, was a trapdoor.

The wizard pulled the door open and both of them looked into the hole that was exposed. It was dark.

'Right,' said Capablanca. 'What are we waiting for?'

It was at this moment that Blart realised he suffered from claustrophobia.

Chapter 30

Claustrophobia is the fear of enclosed spaces. Blart explained to Capablanca that he was suffering from it. Capablanca explained to Blart that he didn't care, and threatened him with dire consequences if he didn't get in the hole immediately. After a few reluctant moans, Blart obeyed.

'Remember not to mention the word "small",' Capablanca reminded him.

Blart eased himself further down into the hole and then he stopped.

'I can't touch anything with my feet,' said Blart. 'I don't want to go any further.'

'Let me help you,' said Capablanca kindly, bending down and pushing Blart's head with all the strength he could muster.

Blart was forced to let go.

'Aaaaarraarrgghh!' he screeched as he dropped into the hole and accelerated towards the centre of the earth. He kept screeching until he landed with a thud.

Blart checked his body to see if any of it was broken or missing. It all seemed to still be there. Then he felt something sticky underneath him, and he was just wondering what it was when he realised that there was an awful smell and the sound of something breathing. Looking up, he saw a pair of gleaming diamond-shaped eyes fixed upon him.

'Murderer!' accused the owner of the eyes.

'Guuh,' said Blart incomprehensibly.

'You have killed my daughter Acrid.'

'No, I haven't,' said Blart.

'I just watched you jump on her,' said the voice, 'and now she's dead.'

Blart began to get an uneasy sensation about what the gooey-feeling thing was underneath him.

'It wasn't me,' he said hopelessly.

'Wasn't you?' said whatever it was indignantly. 'My daughter Acrid, granddaughter of Noxious, great-granddaughter of Obnoxious, lies beneath you dead. Tears well up in the very soul of my being as I remember her. A young and beautiful dwarf. A dwarf with a wonderful future. A daughter with a luxuriant beard who attracted suitors from every one of the Seven Gargantuan Mines.'

'A beard?' said Blart. 'Your daughter had a beard? Nobody wants a daughter with a beard.'

Blart was certainly in error on this point. Both male and female dwarves grow beards, and it is the prime factor in determining their sexual attractiveness. A male dwarf will

201

travel for many miles to find a female dwarf with a fine fluffy beard.

Still, Acrid certainly wasn't attractive any more. She was mainly goo seeping out from under Blart's bottom.

'Vengeance shall be mine. Oh, Acrid, daughter of Yucky, granddaughter of Noxious, great-granddaughter of Obnoxious ...'

Dwarves are very keen on their family trees, which means that whenever a person is mentioned by name at least three of their ancestors (four on special occasions) have to be mentioned too.

'... your killer shall perish.'

Gradually Blart's eyes became accustomed to the dark. Very dim lights revealed a room decorated almost entirely in silver — a silver ceiling, a silver floor, a silver carpet, a silver chair and a silver axe! A silver axe that Yucky the dwarf was raising above his head and obviously intending to bring down with great force on the top of Blart's skull.

Blart squirmed backwards. Yucky seemed much bigger and more menacing than the three feet that he actually stood.

'Prepare to die,' said Yucky. 'I, Yucky, son of Noxious, grandson of Ob—neeeeeeeeeagh!'

Capablanca landed with a splat right on Yucky's head, turning him instantly from a vengeful wronged father into a smelly and sticky goo just like his daughter. If only he hadn't insisted on reciting the names of his ancestors he might well have had just enough time to cleave Blart's skull in two, which goes to show that you should never boast about your family.

'You just killed a dwarf,' said Blart.

'Did I?' asked the wizard, rather surprised.

'Yes,' answered Blart. 'You're a murderer.'

'Oh dear,' said Capablanca, feeling the goo under his bottom and experiencing the sickening feeling of sitting on a dead dwarf.

Blart shook his head in disgust.

'I didn't mean to kill him,' insisted Capablanca. 'And just at the moment we've got the whole world to save. This is no time for sentimentality.'

'I would like to stand in silence for a minute to remember him,' protested Blart, who had never seen the wizard so discomfited and was determined to extract the maximum amount of embarrassment from the situation.

'Oh, all right,' said Capablanca.

And so the two questors stood in respectful silence over the goo that used to be dwarves. Actually, due to the low ceiling, it was more of a respectful stoop.

'Don't mention this to anyone,' ordered Capablanca when the minute had elapsed. 'It won't go down well. Now follow me and head towards the sound of digging.'

'Ow,' said Blart as he banged his head on the roof.

Blart and Capablanca passed through the silver tunnel, down the silver steps, across a silver river and over some silver boulders. They banged their heads so often that after a while the bumps on their head developed bumps of their own.

And all the while the sound of digging grew louder and louder.

Presently a dwarf appeared out of the murky gloom, trudging along with a sack on his back which he dropped in surprise on catching sight of the questors.

'Greetings to you, oh dwarf,' said the wizard quickly, 'from Capablanca, Grand Master Wizard of the Order of Caissa. I come to seek your leader on a matter of great importance. Know ye only that this matter regards Lord Zoltab.'

The dwarf's eyes bulged and his nose flared.

'D-d-d-don't s-s-say that n-n-name,' he eventually stammered out.

'I do not say it lightly,' said Capablanca. 'I know what Zoltab did to the dwarves many years ago and –'

'Y-y-you s-s-said it ag-ag-ag-ain,' pointed out the dwarf.

'But I do for a reason,' insisted Capablanca. 'For I know what was done to you and I have come to ask for your assistance in preventing the return of Zo— er … the evil one who is even now on the verge of being freed by his Ministers and minions. Take us to your leader, then we can get on with saving the world.'

The dwarf made a head movement which might have been a nod of agreement or a shake of refusal or indeed the beginning of a quaint dwarf folk dance. It was impossible to tell.

'Look,' snapped Capablanca, 'I haven't got time for all this shaking. If you don't pull yourself together then we might as well all go home, put our feet up and let the world be doomed.'

'What did Zoltab do to the dwarves?' Blart whispered to Capablanca.

'N-n-no,' cried the dwarf as yet again the dread name was mentioned. His shaking began all over again.

'Look what you've done,' Capablanca said to Blart in exasperation. 'Let us move out of earshot until he has calmed down.'

They both moved a little down the tunnel to where they could still see the dwarf but he could no longer hear them.

'What did Zoltab do to the dwarves?' repeated Blart as soon as they were at a safe distance. Whatever it was, reasoned Blart, if his name had an effect like that then what he did must have been incredibly evil and well worth knowing about.

'Do to them?' replied Capablanca. 'He shrank them, of course.'

'Shrank them?' said Blart. 'But they're dwarves.'

'Yes,' said Capablanca, 'but dwarf didn't always mean small. A long time ago it meant tall.'

'What?' said Blart, who really wasn't getting this bit.

Capablanca glanced at the dwarf. He wasn't shaking quite as much but he was still not able to talk.

'Before Zoltab's brief reign,' continued Capablanca, 'there lived a race of extremely tall men called dwarves. Some of them stood up to eight feet high. They sided against Zoltab when he attempted to take power, but before he could be encased in his underground prison he managed to unleash some infernal power to shrink every dwarf and all their offspring by half. Nobody could work out how he'd done it, not even the other lords, so the effect couldn't be reversed. Now the dwarves had always been extremely proud of their height and were deeply ashamed to have become so small. It was then that they left the surface of the earth to hide their shame in the gargantuan mines. Over time everyone else stopped using dwarf as a term for tall and elegant and instead used it as a word meaning short and stubby.'

'Oh,' said Blart, his forehead creasing in the attempt to understand. 'So dwarf used to mean tall but now it means small.'

'Exactly,' said Capablanca, 'unless you are talking to a dwarf in which case the whole question of size shouldn't be mentioned.'

Blart was really doing very well here, as he was getting to grips with two of the fundamental laws of linguistics: that language is arbitrary and that meaning changes over time.

'I don't get it,' said Blart.

Or perhaps not.

Blart and Capablanca relapsed into silence and bump-rubbing whilst they waited for the dwarf to calm down.

Eventually, the dwarf regained control of himself. He approached Blart and Capablanca warily.

'I am Porg, son of Stench,' he said. 'Follow me. And don't utter that word again.'

'What word?' said Blart, displaying once again his superb memory skills. 'Oh you mean Zo— ow.'

Capablanca hit Blart smartly over the head.

The dwarf picked up his bag and led them back the way he had come. They continued walking through silver tunnels and caverns, passing increasing numbers of dwarves who stared at them open-mouthed. However, Blart noticed that Porg tugged three times at his beard on entering each new cavern and this sign seemed to reassure the other dwarves that things were all right, though it presumably didn't do his chin much good.

Blart now felt very tired and hungry. He had not eaten since breakfast and he had been walking non-stop. Between stomach rumbles he produced a series of loud yawns and sighs. It may have been to hide these repulsive noises that the dwarf embarked on a song.

'I'm Porg, the dwarf son of Stench the dwarf
And I dig all day for silver.
I'm Porg, the dwarf grandson of Pong the dwarf
And I dig all day for silver.
I'm Porg, the dwarf great-grandson of Gag the dwarf
And I dig all day for silver.
I'm Porg, the dwarf great-great-grandson of Sour the dwarf
And I dig all day for silver.'

Neither Blart nor Capablanca had ever heard a worse song. Blart had regularly been exposed to that well-known tear-jerking ballad, 'The Piglet and the Cleaver', as sung by his grandfather, but this was far worse. Blart was contemplating clubbing Porg the dwarf to death with his own axe when the tunnel suddenly widened, the damp air suddenly lightened and they came upon a silver door. In front of it stood two guards with extra-large axes.

'Halt in the name of Squat, Emperor of the Silver Dwarves. Who goes there?' both dwarves said at exactly the same time without even looking at each other. A particularly useless skill that must nevertheless have taken ages to practise.

Porg explained why Blart and Capablanca wanted to see Emperor Squat.

'I'll see if he's in,' said one of the guards, and he turned the doorknob. The door didn't move.

'Haven't they oiled it yet?' the second guard asked. 'They're a law unto themselves in Repairs.'

The second guard added his weight and then Porg joined in. Finally Blart and Capablanca put their shoulders against it too and, after one huge heave, the door gave way. Predictably, the force they had all applied could not be withdrawn, and they tumbled into the room, landing together in a big heap.

'Uuuummmooorrrrppppuuuummmmppppphhh,' is the most accurate rendering that I can manage of the noise they made.

Emperor Squat woke up.

'What? What?' he said.

The dwarves and Blart and Capablanca untangled themselves and stood up to face the emperor.

Emperor Squat studied his visitors and in response they studied him. What Blart and Capablanca saw was a very fat dwarf indeed with an extraordinarily bushy beard. Indeed, so fat was Emperor Squat that his throne was a wide as it was tall. What was more the Emperor was on the point of bursting out of his silver robes – his legs bulged through his stockings, his belly protruded through his shirt and even his crown seemed a tight fit.

'Are you in to visitors, Your Bulkiness?' asked one of the guards.

'No,' said Squat.

'Yes, you are,' said Blart.

'Who dares contradict me in my own throne room?' demanded Squat, who had a deep voice and was fond of using it.

'Me,' said Blart.

'Kill him,' ordered Squat.

'Sorry, it wasn't me. It was him,' Blart added, pointing at Capablanca. 'I got muddled.'

'Kill them both,' decreed Squat. 'Just to make sure.'

The guard indicated a door marked 'EXECUTION WITHOUT TRIAL' at the side of the room. Blart stared at it in horror, and gained a belated understanding of the importance of the thoroughness of judicial process.

And so once again it seemed as though the whole world lay at the mercy of the infernal Zoltab and his Ministers and minions as the last hope of humanity faced extinction.

Chapter 31

'Ex-ex-excuse me, Emperor Squat,' began Porg nervously. 'B-b-begging your pardon, I did bring the strangers here for a reason, and loath though I am to intervene on behalf of anybody who has insulted Your Bulkiness, I must tell you that they have come about ...' And here Porg twitched his beard in that particular way which indicated Zoltab.

'What about him?' the Emperor demanded.

'They think he's coming back.'

'Coming back? He can't come back. He's in an underground prison at the bottom of the Great Tunnel of Despair. Don't you know anything?'

'But not for much longer,' interrupted the wizard. 'I am Capablanca, First-Class Wizard and Bar. I have travelled far and wide and studied for many years at the Cavernous Library of Ping. I —'

'Enough,' cried Squat, holding up his hand. 'I will hear your story, Wizard, even though wizards are not always welcome in these parts, but I will not hear it without my court. It is beneath my dignity. Guards, tell the court to come in. And bring the Ambassador too.'

'But the fewer people who know about this the better,' protested Capablanca.

'I have spoken,' decreed Squat, pointing out the obvious.

'Can I have something to eat?' said Blart. 'I'm starving.'

Squat looked a little taken aback by this request. Nobody had ever asked the Emperor of Dwarves to feed them before.

'And order this one some food. I don't know. One minute you're sentencing them to death, next minute you're giving them tea. And they call me a tyrant.'

The wizard would have liked to order some food too but he felt it would show weakness at a time when he was supposed to look strong so he resolved to eat some of Blart's later.

The guards departed to get the court and the Ambassador and Blart's tea. There was an awkward silence. The wizard couldn't tell his story until the court came and nobody else felt much like speaking. When one person has the power to order the execution of all the others it tends to put a stop to the free flow of conversation and the lively exchange of ideas.

The silence was broken by a muffled cry of 'Heave', and the sticky door suddenly shot open, tumbling the Court of His Imperial Bulkiness Squat into the room. There were only three of them, because Emperor Squat needed most of the silver dwarves to work so he could tax them heavily and continue living in the manner to which he had become accustomed.

'Greetings, Your Bulkiness,' said the three courtiers from the floor.

'Shut up,' said Squat, 'and nod supportively when I say things.'

'Yes, Your Bulkiness.' They rushed to stand beside Squat's throne, pushing and pulling at each other to try to be nearest to the Emperor.

'Now,' declaimed Emperor Squat. 'Our ears will hear your story.'

The three courtiers nodded violently in agreement.

The wizard opened his mouth but, before the first word could emerge, through the sticky door that the guards had sensibly avoided closing came an additional dwarf. He was different from the other dwarves. Whereas all their beards were a silvery grey, his was a rusty red and his expression was open and friendly.

'Welcome, Ambassador,' said the Emperor. 'This,' he informed Capablanca and Blart, 'is Tungsten, Ambassador from the Iron Dwarves. He is the first person for many years to travel down the silver and iron link –'

'The iron and silver link,' interjected the Ambassador.

'The silver and iron link,' insisted the Emperor, 'which connects our two gargantuan mines. He hopes to re-establish the trade that was broken off due to his own leader's unreasonable attitude concerning exchange rates. How do you find

213

our mines, Ambassador? Too rich for your taste, I assume.'

'I wouldn't say rich,' said the Ambassador.

'Wouldn't you?' said the Emperor. 'But is not silver a much more precious metal than iron?'

'More precious,' said the Ambassador, 'but less useful.'

'Nonsense!' shouted the Emperor, reducing the room to silence once again.

Capablanca took the opportunity to launch into his story. Soon he had the dwarves gripped by his narrative. He told them about all his research and travels and all about the Cult of Zoltab even though he only referred indirectly to the name and concluded with a request.

'I beg the use of a capable dwarf to assist us on our quest to cover the Great Tunnel of Despair with a Cap of Eternal Doom.'

The Emperor paused to consult his first courtier, who nodded. He debated it with the second courtier, who nodded harder than the first. He asked the opinion of the third courtier, who nodded so hard his head nearly fell off.

It was whilst the third courtier was nodding that Blart's dinner arrived. A guard brought it over to him and he received it as the Emperor cleared his throat and offered his conclusion.

'Capablanca, First Class Wizard and Bar, we are minded to look favourably on your appeal for a dwarf. We have decided to send –'

'Call this a dinner?' said Blart. 'This is the smallest

portion I've ever seen in my life.'

All the dwarves' eyes swung round to stare at Blart.

'No wonder you're all small if you only eat this much.'

Everybody in the room, apart from Blart, stopped breathing.

'What did you say?' demanded Squat. 'Did you say the "s" word?'

'Yes. You're small. He said I shouldn't mention it, but I'm fed up. Low ceilings, narrow tunnels and stupid beards. And now this food. It's all too small.'

Everybody who'd stopped breathing realised that this was going to take a little longer than they'd expected, took a sneaky breath and then stopped again.

Emperor Squat leapt to his feet.

'I was,' he announced, 'about to use my power to grant your request but I have never been so insulted in my own throne room. There are some things that once said to a dwarf can never be forgiven. I sentence you to death. Guards, take him away.'

The guards pulled out their axes and approached Blart.

'You don't want me,' he shouted at Squat. 'You want him.' Blart pointed at the wizard. 'He murdered Yucky and Acrid.'

'What?' shouted Squat.

Which is how Blart and Capablanca both found themselves sitting in a spellproof cell with a week to live.

Chapter 32

The Third Law of Magic, as proposed by Znosko-Borovsky in his seminal paper delivered at the University of Theoretical Wizardry five centuries ago, states that to be successful a spell must not only be based upon the correct incantation but have accurate direction, and what is more it cannot disappear until it has engaged. This law, which is seen as common sense now by most wizards, revolutionised the whole process of magic. Until its proposal wizards had been mystified by the unpredictability of their results. Trying to turn a table into a pig, for example, they were surprised to discover that they turned their assistant into a pig instead. For centuries wizards felt that the way to greater reliability lay in finding a slightly different incantation. The breakthrough discovery of direction increased wizards' reliability but paradoxically reduced their power. For directly related to the discovery of the necessity of direction in spells was the invention of the spellproof cell, which meant that wizards could be locked away for ever with no need for a large guarding force to recapture the wizard whenever he made one of the walls collapse and made a run for it.

A spellproof cell is made entirely of small mirrors all placed at irregular angles to one another, with the result that any spell that is cast is automatically reflected to another mirror that reflects it once more to another mirror and so on for ever. The wizard's magic power is thus rendered useless. Historically, mirrors have always been a problem for wizards, demonstrating the limitations of their powers whilst also reminding them that they aren't very good-looking.

'Ow!' said Blart as another irregularly angled small mirror grazed his behind.

'Shut up,' growled Capablanca. They had been in the cell for approximately five days now and relations between them had steadily worsened.

'Do you think it hurts?' asked Blart.

'What?' snapped Capablanca.

'Being put to death.'

'It depends how it's done.'

'How do dwarves do it?'

'They cleave your skull in two with a ceremonial silver axe.'

'Does that hurt?' asked Blart.

'Only the first time.'

There was a silence while Blart pondered his immediate future.

'What happens after you're dead?' he asked.

It is perhaps a pity that at this precise moment the ceiling of the cell was smashed open, showering glass everywhere. A pity because, had the wizard known, he could have answered the most fundamental question of man's existence and saved us all a lot of worry.

A rope was let down into the cell and a familiar face with a rusty-red beard appeared.

'Hurry,' said Tungsten, the Ambassador from the Iron Dwarves, 'we haven't got much time.'

Capablanca immediately shinned up the rope with an agility that you wouldn't have expected in a wizard of his years.

'Come on!' he shouted to Blart.

Blart leapt on to the rope and wound his legs round it exactly as he had observed the wizard do. Then he tried to pull himself up. Unfortunately, he didn't move.

'Come on!' shouted Capablanca and Tungsten.

Blart tried several times without success. Eventually he could hold on no longer and fell back to the mirrored floor.

'Tie it round you,' hissed Tungsten. 'We'll pull you up.'

Blart grabbed the rope, pulled it down and attempted to tie a knot around his middle. In his panic, he forgot that nobody had ever taught him how.

'Ready?' demanded Tungsten.

'Yes,' said Blart.

'Heave!' ordered Tungsten.

The Ambassador and the wizard strained hard. The

rope flew up to them. Unfortunately it was no longer attached to Blart.

'Someone's coming,' whispered Capablanca, who could hear the sounds of approaching footsteps.

'Silver dwarves,' said Tungsten. 'We must go.'

'Don't leave me,' squeaked Blart.

'I can't leave him,' said Capablanca reluctantly.

'We haven't got time,' insisted Tungsten.

'Delay them,' said Capablanca.

'How?'

'Do I have to think of everything?'

Tungsten stomped off.

'Blart,' whispered Capablanca, 'take the rope,' and he threw the rope into the cell.

'Greetings, guards,' Tungsten said at the end of the corridor.

'Place the rope around your stomach and then take one end in each hand,' instructed Capablanca.

'Musty sort of day, isn't it?' observed Tungsten.

'Place the left end over the right end.'

'Do you know, I don't think we've been properly introduced,' said Tungsten.

'Left? Right?' repeated Blart blankly.

'I'm Tungsten.'

'Give me strength,' said Capablanca.

'Son of Gravel.'

'Put one over the other, bring the top one round and

underneath the bottom one and pull up into the gap,' directed Capablanca.

'Grandson of Slab.'

'And repeat,' finished Capablanca.

'Great-grandson of Hurry Up,' shouted Tungsten.

'Hurry Up?' said one of the guards. 'That's a strange name.'

'Done,' said Blart.

Capablanca heaved. Blart began to rise.

'Well, if you'll excuse us,' said the guard, 'we have to go and carry out the execution.'

'You mean you haven't heard?' said Tungsten.

'Heard what?' said the guard.

'About the reprieve.'

'Reprieve?'

'The cancellation of the execution announced by Emperor Squat to celebrate the new trade agreement.'

'That doesn't sound like the Emperor,' said the guard doubtfully.

'He issued it only moments ago,' insisted Tungsten.

The guards muttered to each other.

'I wonder what His Bulkiness would do to two guards who disobeyed his orders,' asked Tungsten hypothetically.

'He'd kill them,' the guards told him immediately.

'Would he really?' said Tungsten.

'Yes,' said one of the guards, and then he paused and said, 'Oh.'

The guards muttered to each other some more.

'I suppose we'd better check.'

Their footsteps retreated down the passage as Blart emerged from the cell.

'Come on,' said Tungsten. 'Our only hope is to reach the iron and silver link before they find out you've escaped.'

They ran behind Tungsten through the tunnels of the silver dwarves until they finally reached another tunnel where Tungsten stopped.

'Behold the Iron and Silver link,' he announced.

To Blart and Capablanca, who lacked the expert eye of a dwarf, the Iron and Silver link looked exactly like any other tunnel and unworthy of this grand introduction. Still, Tungsten had rescued them and saved their lives, so they tried to be respectful.

'Very nice,' observed Capablanca.

'So what?' said Blart.

At least Capablanca tried to be respectful.

Tungsten gave Blart a hostile glare.

'He is a mere boy. He doesn't appreciate these things,' Capablanca urgently reassured Tungsten. The wizard was well aware that all dwarves have fierce tempers and are very proud. The last thing he wanted was for the situation to escalate before they had reached safety. 'Let us enter this great tunnel.'

'Hmmm,' said Tungsten, considering. 'I don't know if he's worthy.'

'It's only a hole in the ground,' pointed out Blart unhelpfully. Blart lacked the sensitivity to appreciate that those from different cultures valued different things.

'How dare –' began Tungsten, but he was silenced by the sound of running feet behind them. The silver dwarves were coming.

'Come on,' said Capablanca.

'I will remember this insult,' replied Tungsten. 'And I will have my revenge.'

And so, yet again, Blart had managed to turn a potential friend into an enemy.

'We must hurry,' insisted Capablanca.

Grim-faced Tungsten led them into the Iron and Silver link.

'They will not follow us here,' he informed the others.

Once inside Blart and Capablanca understood why. The tunnel was in a state of advanced dilapidation – the timbers that shored up the roof were buckled and in many places the roof had partially collapsed, leaving mounds of earth that they could only climb over with difficulty. And all the while the creaking of the beams hinted that another collapse could be imminent.

'This tunnel is rubbish,' observed Blart after they had been walking and clambering for a while. 'Not like the ones the silver dwarves mine. You can't be very good dwarves if this –'

'Tell me, Tungsten,' Capablanca decided to distract the

dwarf before Blart could make their situation any worse, 'why did you rescue us?'

'What do you mean?' said Tungsten. 'I have the natural repugnance of all right-thinking dwarves towards the abuse of judicial process.'

'Hmmm,' replied Capablanca, who wasn't convinced.

'What do you mean, hmmmm?' demanded Tungsten. 'I save your life and all you can do is hmmmm at me. There's no gratitude there.'

'I apologise,' said Capablanca hastily. 'Blart and I thank you.'

'I don't,' said Blart.

Tungsten led the way through the link. It was only wide enough for them to proceed in single file.

'What I meant when I asked why you rescued us,' panted Capablanca, who still believed that there was more to Tungsten's rescue than merely the wish to see justice done, 'is whether you wanted us to do something for you in return.'

'There might be something you can do,' conceded Tungsten.

Finally, thought Capablanca. If only other beings were more like wizards there'd be none of this beating about the bush.

'What is it?' asked Capablanca.

'Know ye,' said Tungsten importantly, 'that the tunnel of the iron dwarves lies closer to the Great Tunnel of Despair than that of the silver dwarves. We have heard noises coming from that direction. When I heard you speak in the hall of Emperor Squat of names that we dwarves had hoped never to hear again, I knew that you spoke the truth. And so I resolved to rescue you.'

'What do you want?' cajoled Capablanca, increasingly aware that if Tungsten didn't get to the point soon then it wouldn't be so much a case of stopping Zoltab as of being the first tourists to visit his empty dungeon.

'Know ye, Wizard, that my people have suffered for centuries. All dwarves look down on iron dwarves and regard us as their social inferiors. We would like to become top dwarves. We have the breeding, we have the deportment, we have the beards. What we lack is the metal. Iron is regarded as less rare than platinum, gold and silver. Therefore what I request of you in return for my assistance is that you create more platinum, gold and silver, making iron the rarest and therefore the most valuable. Dwarf society would change and we, the iron dwarves, would be the greatest of dwarves.'

'Is that all?' said Capablanca sarcastically. 'Just alter the entire metal balance of the earth? That would require the work of many wizards for years to achieve.'

'Dwarves are patient,' said Tungsten. 'We will wait. But I demand your word that if I help you then one day you'll help me.'

'I give you my word,' replied Capablanca.

'You give him your what?' said Blart, who didn't want to miss out if there were gifts being handed out.

'My word,' said Capablanca.

'What's that?' said Blart.

'It's like my promise,' said Capablanca.

'Can you eat it?' demanded Blart.

'Shut up, Blart,' snapped Capablanca. Not only did he have to save the world from Zoltab, he had to start on the laborious business of altering the earth's constituent parts. All in all he felt it was a bit much.

And so yet again we discover a hero with an agenda. First, Blart has to be forced to try to save the world and now, Tungsten only agrees to help on condition he is repaid with social advancement. Ah, for the stout-hearted zeal of yester-year.

'Waaaaaaaaaaaaah!' shouted Blart, Capablanca and Tungsten in unison as the ground gave way beneath them and they fell even nearer to the centre of the earth.

Poetic justice, some might say.

Chapter 33

'Doomed,' wailed Tungsten. 'Doomed.'

'Uh,' said Blart, recovering consciousness. Nothing seemed to be in focus and he felt as if he was spinning.

What does 'doomed' mean? Blart wondered. And why was it so hot? He was definitely spinning. His arms wouldn't move. Heat intensified on his back. Things were getting clearer. He was in a cave. But the cave was moving. No, that couldn't be right. He was moving. He felt the heat again. There was a fire below him. Now it had gone. Now it was back again, searing his forehead.

He was being cooked.

'No!' screeched Blart. 'No!'

When a being has assumed that he is top of the food chain it is always a sobering moment when he discovers he isn't. Humans who for centuries have been roasting, boiling and grilling every animal that they can get their hands on get notoriously uppity when someone starts cooking them.

'Doomed,' repeated Tungsten.

'Help!' yelped Blart as a particularly sensitive part of his anatomy began to singe.

'Farewell,' responded Tungsten, which wasn't much use in the circumstances.

Blart squirmed until he managed to loosen slightly whatever was gripping his head. He turned his neck to one side and what he saw made his entrails turn cold with fear. However, little stays cold with fear for long when it is being heated powerfully from below. Instead his entrails became hot with fear, which doesn't sound right, but that was what happened.

For the sight that met Blart's eyes was indeed terrible. Next to him was Capablanca and further away was Tungsten. They were naked and tied on to spits under which burned fires. Below them, their clothes lay in untidy piles on the ground. But terrible as this sight was, it was as nothing to what Blart saw next. Hordes of thin spindly creatures surrounded the spits, their grey bodies standing out from the gloom of the cave. Their eyes bulged as they gazed rapt at the three captives with famished glee. Greasy globules dripped from their chins.

'Goblins!' screeched Tungsten. 'Doomed!'

Dwarves have only one natural predator, the goblins, so-called for their habit of gobbling any dwarf they catch. They live deep in the bowels of the earth and catch dwarves by digging holes under their tunnels. Dwarves falling through these holes are spirited away to the great fires of the deep where they become the goblins' breakfast, lunch or dinner depending on the time of day. Breakfast is generally thought to be the worst fate, as goblins like their first meal to be raw and alive.

What with dwarf holes and goblin holes, not to mention moles, it's quite surprising that the earth manages to stay up at all, but it does and we should all be thankful for that. Thankful, though, was not the most dominant feeling in the heart of either Blart or Tungsten as they revolved steadily. The wizard was unconscious so his feelings were a mystery.

'Doomed!' cried Tungsten once more. 'The shame! That I, Tungsten, son of Gravel, grandson of Slab, great-grandson of Tar, should be eaten by foul goblins.'

For his part, Blart had no ancestors' names to recite. Instead he watched the goblins. They stared hypnotically back at him, salivating at the sight of their barbecue. A curious slapping noise came from their mouths as they opened and closed them in anticipation of the feast that was to come.

Blart decided to take the situation in hand.

'I'll tell you what!' he shouted out. 'Let me go and eat the other two. I'm poisonous.'

The goblins showed no sign of having heard what Blart had said. Their mouths slapped louder as the moment for them to feast grew closer.

'Traitor!' screeched Tungsten. 'Die like a dwarf with honour!'

Blart tried again.

'If you let me go,' he shouted to the goblins, 'I'll bring back my pigs for you to eat. And I'll throw in my granddad as well.'

This was truly shocking for, despite all the disgraceful acts we have witnessed from Blart, we have never seen him stoop to the level of betraying his pigs.

But even this astonishing betrayal had no effect. The goblins continued to slobber and slather expectantly and Blart, Tungsten and the unconscious wizard continued to rotate.

Blart watched Capablanca revolve. And, as he stared at him, a huge well of anger and bile rose inside his chest like a bubbling volcano, or it might just have been that the fire had made his gastric juices boil. He felt a tremendous sense of hostility towards Capablanca. He was, after all, the reason that Blart was being cooked alive and would soon be consumed by goblins with their starved slathering faces.

And what was worse, whilst Blart was experiencing all this horror, Capablanca was happily unconscious.

'Oi!' yelled Blart.

'Wizard!' he shouted.

'Capablanca!' he bellowed.

There was no response. Capablanca's eyes stayed shut. Unless Blart did something soon the wizard was going to die peacefully, never knowing the torment of his fellow questors. The thought of Capablanca having it easy whilst he himself suffered was more than Blart could bear.

Blart was not a boy with a vast array of talents. But he was capable of producing a piercing whistle. It's not much of a talent and the quest has managed quite well without it up to now. But now its moment had come. Blart pursed his lips and blew.

In the enclosed space the noise was ear-splitting. The walls shrieked with its echoes. Tungsten felt the sound shoot through him. Even the goblins, who do not have very good hearing, took a step back. Two bats hanging innocently off the roof of the cave doing nobody any harm were instantly deafened and the wizard woke up.

'This is all your fault,' yelled Blart immediately.

'What?' stammered Capablanca.

'We're being cooked, thanks to you.'

'Cooked?' repeated Capablanca, whose incredulity was swiftly undermined by the searing pain in his bottom.

'I wish I'd never met you.'

'Be quiet,' screamed Capablanca, 'and I might just get us out of here.'

This shut Blart up fast. When you are being steadily roasted and someone offers you an alternative you tend to jump at it.

Luckily for our three questors the goblins did not think anything unusual was going on. They were quite used to their dinners shouting during preparation. Normally, of course, it was merely dwarves reciting the names of their ancestors but as the goblins couldn't understand a word of what was going on they couldn't tell the difference.

The wizard closed his eyes and searched his brain for a spell that would save them. It had been many decades since Capablanca had studied spells as all of his time recently had been dedicated to research in the Cavernous Library of Ping. Spells are like foreign languages and musical instruments. If you don't use them, you lose them.

'Come on,' said Blart, unhelpfully breaking the wizard's concentration.

'Sssh. He's thinking,' hissed Tungsten.

'Don't tell me to ssshh, shorty.'

There was a blue flash from the wizard's eyes. The knots that held them to the spits began to unravel. The ropes loosened. They were free.

If you were being choosy about the method adopted to release you from being barbecued this would not be the one you would pick, for as soon as the ropes were undone each of them dropped like a stone into the fires below. Luckily the fires weren't too big as the goblins preferred their dinner slow-cooked to keep more of the juices in. Still, each of them uttered a high-pitched squeal as they dropped into the burning coals, and a moment later the three were standing facing the circle of goblins, their posteriors gently steaming behind them.

'Aaargh,' uttered Blart, raising his fists and baring his teeth at the goblins.

'Grrrrr,' rumbled Tungsten, grabbing his axe that had been left near the fire and brandishing it in the faces of the goblins.

'Where is it?' asked Capablanca, fumbling in his pile of clothes for his staff.

Now for the goblins this was a new experience. Their dinner had never made a bid for freedom before and they were shocked. Being creatures with few physical skills, their reaction to this was to open and close their mouths some more.

The wizard searched frantically through his coat for his staff while Tungsten gripped his axe tighter. The goblins with their bulging eyes and dagger-like teeth got closer. Blart felt a mixture of fear and embarrassment. Not only were the goblins about to kill him they were also seeing him naked which, as he was a teenage boy, felt worse. He turned away from the goblins, grabbed his trousers and pulled them on. Unfortunately, this turning away was the sign of weakness that spurred the primitive goblins to attack. They surged forward in a slavering mass.

'Aha,' said Capablanca as he finally found his staff and then 'Ouch' as a goblin sank his teeth into his leg. The first goblin's bite was the sign for a general attack. From all sides the goblins dived at the three questors, hoping to bite chunks from their bodies. Tungsten's axe rose and fell as he twisted and turned, chopping to his left and to his right. Blart, newly confident now he was dressed, smashed his fists into the

232

advancing grey shapes. Capablanca whirled his staff in a great circle, smiting the attackers that came his way, but still the goblins and their teeth got through. Flesh was bitten, blood ran down their legs and arms and still the famished figures flung themselves at their bodies, each desperate for another mouthful. It seemed as though at any moment the goblins would overwhelm their prey and that Blart, Capablanca and Tungsten would be overpowered and forced to the floor where, in a frenzied attack, their flesh would be torn from their bones.

And yet, desperate as the goblins were to eat, there was a greater force working within their intended prey – the desire to live. Blart, Capablanca and Tungsten found extra reserves of strength. When it seemed all was lost, they fought on. Forced on to the defensive, they now stood back to back in a rough triangle as the goblins leapt at them with even greater ferocity.

'Aaarrggghh!' yelled Blart as his fist smashed into the face of an attacking goblin.

'Yeeeaarrgghh!' yelled Tungsten as he swung his axe in a horizontal arc, separating an approaching goblin's upper half from his lower half with one sickening squelch.

'Huummph,' grunted Capablanca as he raised his staff with such precision timing that two advancing goblins snapped their necks on it.

More goblins attacked. More were killed or repelled and yet still they came. Sooner or later this wild savagery was destined to overpower the three fighters. They could not resist the irresistible for ever.

Except that suddenly the assault seemed different. The goblins still leapt towards the triangle of defenders but they did not seem to be reaching them. In the panic of flying goblins it took a little time for Capablanca to realise that they themselves were no longer being attacked.

'Cease the combat!' he bellowed, and the others were so surprised by the order they obeyed it. Nothing happened to them. The goblins had forgotten they were there and were leaping in to feast on the corpses of their own dead. The jagged teeth tore at the soft pulpy flesh and the feverish slapping of mouths grew quieter as the starving goblins satisfied themselves.

'We must get as far away as possible before they are finished eating,' urged Tungsten. 'For if we are still nearby they will come after us once more.'

The three picked up their clothes and ran for the nearest tunnel. It was completely dark and they could have no confidence in their footing but still they ran. Anything to escape the awful sight of the goblins devouring each other. They ran until they could run no more.

Chapter 34

'I want to go home. I'm fed up,' said Blart.

Now there had been many occasions when Blart had announced he wanted to go home, but this was undoubtedly the least appropriate. None of them had the faintest idea where they were and their chances of returning to the earth's surface were remote. No creature venturing into the goblins' passages came out alive.

'Doomed,' announced Tungsten, presumably to confirm that his prediction of their future hadn't changed.

'Oh, grow up!' snapped Capablanca.

'Oh, outrage!' shouted Tungsten. 'That I, Tungsten of the iron dwarves, should be so insulted!'

'I didn't mean it like that,' explained Capablanca. 'I meant it like –'

'I don't want to know,' said Tungsten.

And there was silence.

Which was a good thing because otherwise they might not have heard the noise above them. At first it was a scratching noise. Then a scraping noise. And then a digging noise. And then the roof fell in on top of them.

There are remarkable similarities between drowning in water and being covered in earth. Both events have the same effect – the removal of air. Unsurprisingly, humans behave similarly in these situations. They keep their mouths tightly shut and wave their hands wildly, trying to push the water/earth away so that they can reach the air. Blart, who had now experienced both these life-threatening situations, could have reflected upon this if he hadn't been so busy panicking. He felt the earth rise up his chest, over his face, his eyes and above his head. He was being buried alive. Frantically, he flailed his arms from side to side. A wild urge to survive beat inside him. However much human beings moan about what a miserable life they lead and how they'd be better off dead they are always unwilling to go when their time comes.

Blart pushed away the earth closest to his face. More fell in its place. Again he fought to dig out a space but again it was filled. Sick with fear, he thrashed out one final time. He must have air. He scraped a gap around his face. The pocket of air did not disappear. Blart breathed in. He was safe.

Except, of course, he wasn't. Air that goes in is filled with oxygen, which is good, whereas the air that comes out is filled with carbon dioxide, which is very bad. Blart had only succeeded in making a tiny space around his head. Each breath was bringing death closer. Luckily for Blart, death was not the only thing getting closer.

There were voices.

'What happened?'

'Don't know, Chief.'

'What do you mean, you don't know? I'll whip the skin from your back, you scum.'

'It's collapsed, Chief. The sides have collapsed.'

'Shore it up, then, you dolt. Have we lost any workers?'

'The earth has covered some of them.'

'How long will it take to dig them out?'

'I don't –'

There was a crack followed by a scream.

'I told you what would happen if you said that again. Get them out. We have lost too many already and we need them. But any more mistakes and I'll flay you alive. Do you understand?'

'Yes, Chief.'

'Get moving. We must be very near Lord Zoltab now.'

Blart's heart skipped a beat. What he'd just heard could only mean one thing. They were in the Great Tunnel of Despair. Zoltab's minions were all around him. He felt very lonely and very afraid.

Above him came the noise of frantic digging.

Blart's oxygen was rapidly disappearing. What would happen if they didn't find him? The answer was becoming all too obvious. He choked and coughed. He fought to make his air pocket bigger but the faster he scratched the faster earth slipped in. He could hear the digging coming closer but he could feel death coming closer too. Which would get there first?

Chapter 35

Suddenly there was light. After so long in the darkness it made Blart squint.

Precious air rushed into his lungs.

'I've got one, Chief.'

Blart's eyes adjusted to the lanterns. Above him was a figure covered entirely in earth. Behind him stood a cleaner figure holding a more powerful lantern and a whip. Blart gulped. These were minions of Zoltab. There was no sign of Capablanca or of Tungsten.

'Don't stand there gawking at each other,' said the man with the whip. 'Pull him out.'

Two hulking figures grasped Blart around the shoulders and dragged him free of the earth. Blart lay panting for air on the ground.

'Get up,' yelled the man with the whip and a crack by Blart's nose showed that he was prepared to use it. Hurriedly Blart got to his feet. He stood, head bowed, waiting for his punishment. If Capablanca was right, then to be found in the

Great Tunnel of Despair by Zoltab's minions could mean only one thing – death.

Therefore, the next words of the figure with the whip came as a great surprise.

'Where's his shovel?'

'He must have lost it in the landslide, Chief,' said one of the figures that had pulled Blart free.

'Give him another one,' ordered the Chief. 'And do it fast.'

The figure scurried off and swiftly returned with a shovel that he thrust into Blart's hand.

'Get digging,' he said.

'What?' said Blart, finally finding himself able to speak.

'Dig,' ordered the man.

'Oh,' said Blart.

But he didn't start digging. He couldn't understand what was happening to him. These were the dreaded minions of Zoltab. Why weren't they killing him?

'Aaaarrrggghhh!' screeched Blart as a terrible pain cracked across his back. Maybe they weren't killing him but they were certainly whipping him. Blart started to dig.

'That's right, you worm!' bellowed the Chief's voice behind him. 'And don't let me see you slacking or we'll bury you again!'

'Found another two, Chief!' yelled a voice nearby.

Blart sneaked a glance while making sure he continued to dig. From the rubble there appeared two figures caked in mud and earth. Their faces were totally unrecognisable. Now he understood why he had not been killed. Zoltab's minions had simply assumed that he was one of the workers buried in the landslide. The lanterns in the tunnel were not strong and one figure covered in mud looked very much like another.

The two figures clambered into the tunnel. One was tall and thin and one was short and sturdy and Blart knew that they were Capablanca and Tungsten. He felt a curious feeling he had never felt before. He didn't know it, but in this terrible tunnel at the mercy of Zoltab's minions he was suddenly happy.

'Get them digging!' yelled the Chief. 'They'd better work hard after wasting our time or they'll suffer tortures that will make them wish we'd left them to die.'

'Shall we keep looking for the others?'

'No,' said the Chief. 'We can't afford the time. Leave them to choke. They deserve nothing better. Now, all of you dig. Straight down. Faster than you've ever dug before.'

And so they dug. Blart did not dare look towards the mud-caked figures of Capablanca and Tungsten, for the Chief prowled so closely behind them that Blart could smell his foul breath. Any slowing was punished with a slash of the whip. The cry of anguish from the recipient echoed through the tunnel and proved a great incentive to the others. As they worked, a tuneless dirge rose from the minions, the beat provided by the thump of the shovels into the earth.

'Dig, dig, dig
Don't stop, don't flag.
Dig, dig, dig
Don't slow, don't drag.

Dig, dig, dig
Don't talk, don't blab.
Dig, dig, dig
For the Lord Zoltab.

It was repeated endlessly. Behind the diggers other figures wheeled away the earth in giant barrows. Blart's muscles ached and his body cried for rest and water. But the thought of the cruel knotted lash kept him working.

Only once did he stop, when the digger next to him slumped over his shovel and collapsed on the ground.

Immediately the Chief's whip snapped on his back.

'Get up, you dog!'

Again the whip cracked.

'Up and dig, you idle scum!'

But there was no response from the digger. He had gone to the only place where the pain of the lash could never touch him again. The Chief kicked the dead body.

'What are you looking at?' he yelled at Blart. 'Get back to work before you get worse.'

Blart began to dig frantically. When the barrows returned to remove the earth they took the corpse away.

The dirge returned. The digging continued. Blart found himself chanting. It was the only way to keep going. The only way not to be whipped. But a way that was helping to free Zoltab and bring disaster to the world.

Chapter 36

'Cease!'

The voice behind Blart was not the Chief's but it was nevertheless a voice that he felt compelled to obey instantly. He turned round. Behind the Chief stood a tall black cloak. Blart could see neither face nor feet. All this thing amounted to was a voice. But it was a voice that had an effect on the Chief.

'Master,' he said, 'they have not stopped. We have made much progress.'

The Master did not respond.

'Nobody could have done more in the time, Master. Nobody.'

Still the Master remained silent.

'Soon the Lord Zoltab will be free,' said the Chief.

'Do not speak of the Lord Zoltab,' ordered the Master. 'You are unworthy to utter his name. You know the rules. Your work rate is compared to that in the nearest sector. I have visited your nearest sector. They have dug further than you. You know what the punishment is for idleness.'

'No!' shrieked the Chief, falling to his knees. 'We had a landslide and one of the men died. I cannot be held responsible for that. Have mercy, Master. I tried my best.'

'Bury him alive,' commanded the Master.

Four of the diggers who had been whipped all day leapt forward.

'No, Master, no,' begged the terrified Chief. But his pleas for mercy were wasted. The four men dragged him off down a side tunnel and his cries were silenced.

The Master did not wait for them to return. His hand shot out. It was the bony hand of an old man but it did not shake. One finger pointed straight at Blart.

'You will be the new Chief of this section. Make sure you do a better job or tomorrow the same fate awaits you. Now, all of you return to the surface and eat and sleep.'

And with that the Master was gone.

The diggers began to shuffle to the back of the tunnel. Blart, Capablanca and Tungsten joined the line. None of them uttered a word, for anything they said could be overheard. Instead they began the slow climb up the roughly hewn steps that led to the surface.

What met their eyes when they emerged from the tunnel would have turned a brave man's entrails cold. Blart was not a brave man so there was a danger that his entrails might freeze entirely.

The sky was like no sky that any man had ever seen

before. One moment darkest black, the next a harsh orange as a fireball streaked across it. The angry light revealed hundreds of tents. Around each tent there were men, dwarves and other creatures. Zoltab had a vast army of followers. Behind loomed the shadow of a huge amphitheatre. It was the biggest thing Blart had ever seen. Built into it were four immense towers and at the top of these towers great fires burned. A minion saw him looking in awe at the terrifying structure.

'The Terrorsium,' said the minion with a mixture of fear and pride. 'When Lord Zoltab comes it will be opened. And he will rule from there.'

Capablanca and Tungsten were also gazing at the awful sight. What terrible deeds would take place when it was finally opened?

All around them minions were streaming out of various entrances to the tunnels. Work was obviously over for the day. The minions made their way to a large tent. Blart, Capablanca and Tungsten followed them. They queued up and eventually reached a table where they were given a bowl, and then another table where an unappetising grey mixture was poured into it. Imitating those in front of them they thanked Zoltab for the food. No sooner was it received than the minions rushed outside the tent to gobble it down. This was the opportunity the questors had been waiting for and they managed to seat themselves some distance from the crowd where they could speak privately.

'Why didn't you do something?' hissed Blart at Capablanca. 'It was horrible down there.'

'Zoltab's Ministers are everywhere. If I'd used any magic they would have sensed it straight away. I must prepare myself for tomorrow. I will get only one chance and that will be in the morning when I will cast the greatest spell of my life to create the Cap of Eternal Doom which will seal Zoltab in for ever.'

'But they'll kill us,' said Blart.

'There are worse things thing than death,' replied Capablanca. 'If Zoltab's minions tear us to pieces in anger after we have created the Cap of Eternal Doom then we have given our lives in a good cause.'

'You never said I'd have to die,' protested Blart.

'Keep your voice down,' ordered Capablanca.

'But why am I here?' demanded Blart. 'I don't have to do anything.'

'I brought you here in case Zoltab had already been freed,' said Capablanca. 'Only you have the power to stand up to him. But as he hasn't, then I may be able to deal with it myself.'

'You mean I didn't need to come?' said Blart.

'Well … er …' Capablanca looked a little embarrassed. 'That is how it looks like it's going to turn out. But I wasn't to know that when I began, was I?'

'You mean I'm not going to be a hero?' asked Blart.

'Probably not,' admitted Capablanca.

It's funny. However much you say you don't want something as soon as someone says you can't have it you find out that you always wanted it after all.

'But you promised,' insisted Blart. He felt that after all he'd been through he was entitled to be a hero. He conveniently forgot about all the times that he had tried to run away or get his companions caught. It seemed to him that the world had behaved very badly towards him.

'Boy,' said Capablanca, 'did you not think it strange that I did not tell you what it was that had to be done by you to defeat Zoltab?'

Blart thought about it. It did seem strange. But then everything that had happened to him lately seemed strange.

'I will tell you because it will not now be necessary,' continued Capablanca. 'To defeat Zoltab and rob him of his powers blood directly from your heart would have to spill on to him. He would be defeated but you would die in the process.'

Blart decided that maybe he didn't want to be a hero after all. Then another thought occurred to him.

'You mean you would have killed me to get rid of Zoltab?'

'I've told you to keep your voice down,' Capablanca reminded him, 'or we'll all perish. And when I stabbed you I wouldn't have meant it personally.'

'Oh, thanks.'

Tungsten, who had been silent up to this point, suddenly

shook himself and spoke.

'You know,' he told them, 'I know that Zoltab's minions are our enemies, but you've got to hand it to them. They can dig a decent tunnel. It could have been the work of dwarves.'

And then Tungsten returned to silent contemplation, which was perhaps for the best.

'Now,' said Capablanca, 'I need to sleep because at the moment I'm too tired to conjure the greatest spell that a wizard has ever produced. I will have to use so much power that I may exhaust myself to the point of death in creating it. But you won't hear me complaining.'

Capablanca looked significantly at Blart but the look was lost on him as he had his mind on something else.

'Are you going to cast your spell first thing in the morning?' he asked Capablanca.

'Of course. We cannot allow any more digging or Zoltab may be freed.'

'Oh,' said Blart, looking rather sad.

'What?' said Capablanca, who was still feeling a little bit bad that he had dragged Blart on a quest and that he wasn't going to get to be a hero after all.

'It's just that I get to be Chief tomorrow. And I've never been a Chief before.'

'But, boy, did you not see how a Chief is forced to act?' asked Capablanca. 'He must scourge his diggers until they work themselves to death. It is a horrific thing to do.'

'I could still have a go,' said Blart.

'I wonder which tent we're supposed to sleep in,' Capablanca asked. 'I must get a good night's rest if I am to –'

There was the sound of cheering around them. The diggers were getting up off the ground and half-walking, half-running towards something. Curiosity overcame the three companions and they joined the crowd. The sky was no lighter than it had been when they emerged from the tunnel and there was no clue as to what was causing all the excitement, but the momentum of the diggers carried them. They found themselves lining a crude, recently made road that led to the door of the Terrorsium. The diggers were cheering wildly. But there appeared to be nothing to cheer.

Then they saw it. A wagon pulled by two horses. It made slow progress over the rough road but gradually it came closer to them. They could see two figures on the wagon but they could not make out anything more. As it passed, the diggers directly alongside cheered more loudly and waved their hands in the air. Capablanca tapped one on the shoulder.

'What is it?' he asked. 'What's going on?'

'A great day. A great day. They have found Lord Zoltab's bride-to-be.'

'His bride-to-be?' said Capablanca, astonished.

'Indeed. After Lord Zoltab was buried deep in the Great Tunnel of Despair there was nobody to carry on his good work. It has taken many millennia for us to find and raise him. Zoltab will marry as soon as he is free and his wife will have child after child so that the seed of Zoltab spreads throughout the world and its glorious light can never be extinguished as it once was.'

'Oh, I see,' said Capablanca.

'The Ministers have searched the world for a woman who would be suitable to bear the children of Zoltab. And now they have found her and brought her here and when Zoltab is released they will be married in the Terrorsium and there will be much rejoicing.'

'Hurrah!' said Capablanca, remembering that he ought to be enthusiastic.

'Hurrah, indeed,' replied the digger. 'Now, hush, for here she comes.'

The wagon was indeed getting closer, but just at that moment the sky darkened and it was impossible to see who was in the wagon. But they were not to be disappointed for long. There was a tremendous crack and a huge bolt of lightning shot out of the sky and smashed into the ground behind the Terrorsium. It lit up the whole area and revealed Zoltab's future wife to be …

Princess Lois of Illyria.

Chapter 37

*S*he stood in the wagon, glaring hatred at the cheering crowds. Her head was held high and her chin jutted out aggressively. Her eyes were a challenge to anyone who met her gaze.

The wagon wobbled past towards the Terrorsium, leaving Blart and Capablanca open-mouthed. Tungsten the dwarf, who had, of course, never met her before, was unmoved.

'By the bones of my grandmother,' he said, 'I wouldn't want to marry a woman who didn't have a beard. Look at that girl. Hardly a hair on her chin and someone's going to marry her. Still, it takes all sorts, I suppose.'

'*Zoltab may rise and then worse be wed/To a noble woman back from the dead,*' said Capablanca. The prediction that they had read on the back of the map by the oasis so long ago began to make horrible sense. Princess Lois must have been pulled to a watery death and now, by some foul and terrible magic beyond even Capablanca's comprehension, Zoltab's Ministers had brought her back to life. And her terrible fate was now to be Zoltab's bride.

'G-g-g-g-ghost,' said Blart.

'What?' enquired Tungsten.

'Be quiet,' ordered Capablanca desperately.

'B-b-but she was p-p-pulled into the pool by the s-s-serpents,' jabbered Blart.

'Shut up,' urged Capablanca. 'You're attracting attention.'

Blart was. The crowd of minions, having lost sight of the wagon, was transferring its attention to the nearest thing of interest. And it was Blart.

'B-b-but she's dead!' shouted Blart.

'Who's dead?' demanded a minion.

'Yes, who?' asked another.

'What happening?' shouted a different voice.

A crowd was beginning to form. Capablanca and Tungsten grabbed Blart and began to pull him away from the group.

'Where are you taking him?'

'He said they were dead.'

'Who's dead?'

'What's going on?'

'Send for a Minister.'

'No,' said Capablanca, holding up his hand. He could fool the minions of Zoltab but a Minister was a different matter. A Minister might spot something strange. And a Minister could do magic. But the crowd continued to swell.

The minions of Zoltab lived in constant fear and anything out of the ordinary upset them.

'Who do you think you are?'

'Let me see.'

'Who's dead?'

'Fellow minions,' shouted Capablanca, 'nobody is dead. We were just looking forward to the death of Zoltab's enemies. My friend cried out in anticipation of the great day when Zoltab shall rule and those that oppose him shall be crushed underfoot.'

The mood of the crowd changed with the words of the wizard. There were cheers and shouts.

'Death to the enemies of Zoltab!'

'Praise Lord Zoltab!'

'Let Zoltab come!'

And the chant of 'Let Zoltab come!' was taken up by the crowd and spread to the other minions, and soon the whole camp was chanting 'Let Zoltab come!' The sky exploded into bellows of thunder and sent down streak after streak of savagely forked lightning.

The crisis had passed. The crowd's interest had swung away from Blart. Aware that it could swing back, Capablanca ushered him away.

'She's dead,' Blart insisted to Capablanca. 'She was killed by serpents. Things that are dead and come back must be ghosts. What else could she be?'

Now, Capablanca was, as he frequently reminded

everybody, a very knowledgeable wizard. But all that learning in the Cavernous Library of Ping could not explain the reappearance of the Princess. She couldn't be a ghost. But what other explanation was there? He realised he was going to have to use three words that he hated above all others.

'I don't know,' he told Blart grumpily.

Tungsten yawned.

'Tungsten's right,' said Capablanca, surprising Tungsten, who was not aware that he had offered a suggestion. 'We cannot be worrying about the Princess. We must get some sleep. Tomorrow I will rise early and cast the greatest spell in the history of wizardry.'

'But –' protested Blart.

'Enough,' ordered Capablanca. 'There will be no more talk. Now is the time for action.'

Having declared that now was the time for action, Capablanca started looking for somewhere to sleep. After pulling back the flaps of a few tents and finding them filled with sleeping minions, they eventually came to one which had a number of empty beds. The beds were made of nothing more than straw, and straw that had not been changed for many days. But they lay down anyway.

'Capablanca,' whispered Blart.

'What?' hissed back a plainly irritated wizard. 'I'm trying to get some sleep.'

'You know after you've cast the spell and rid the world of Zoltab for ever?'

'Yes.'

'And then you've been captured by Zoltab's angry Ministers and minions?'

'Yes.'

'And they torture you and cut pieces off you and burn you and stretch you and beat you?'

'Yes.'

'Will you try not to tell them about me?'

'If you don't say another thing then I won't mention your name,' Capablanca told Blart.

This silenced Blart. But it did not ease his mind. He lay in bed wondering how he was going to escape and where he would go once out of the reach of Zoltab's minions. He had travelled great distances over land and sea and through many tunnels to get where he was. He had no idea how to get back to his grandfather's farm. Even if he got away from the Terrorsium there would be much arduous travelling if he was ever to see his pigs again. He thought about his grandfather. His grandfather was old. He might have died while Blart had been away. Blart felt worried about this. Not, it has to be said, because of any great concern about his grandfather's welfare but because there would be nobody left to look after his pigs.

But no matter how great the worries of the mind eventually the body must have its rest. And after a time Blart slept.

Chapter 38

DONG!

Blart's eyes snapped open. He could hear cheering and yelling.

DONG!

All the minions were leaping out of bed and pulling on their boots as fast as they could. It was just another day's digging. Why were they all so excited?

DONG!

Blart sat up. Capablanca and Tungsten looked as perplexed as he did.

DONG!

'Zoltab has come! Zoltab has come! Zoltab has come!'

DONG!

'Make haste, brother!' a minion shouted to him. 'Why do you lie in bed on this great day? The thing that we have waited for so long has come to pass. Zoltab has returned.'

'But –' protested Capablanca.

'If I have one regret, my brother,' continued the minion

as he tied his belt rapidly around his jerkin, 'it is that I was on the day shift. Oh, to have been on the night shift and to have been there when the Dungeon was opened and Lord Zoltab was freed. Make haste! Make haste! The bell calls us all to the Terrorsium where Lord Zoltab will accept our homage.'

The minion finished tightening his belt, pulled back the tent flap and rushed outside to join the throng. Behind him he left Capablanca open-mouthed. For, great wizard that he was, skilled in the arts of magic and learned from many years' hard study in the Cavernous Library of Ping, he had overlooked one thing:

There was a night shift.

While Capablanca, Blart and Tungsten were leaving the Great Tunnel by one set of passages, another set of passages was full of minions descending to start work at the tunnel face. What a simple mistake. And yet what a terrible effect it could have.

All that hard work. All the time spent studying, searching, travelling, learning. To come so close to defeating Zoltab and then to fail. No wonder Capablanca sat in stunned silence.

DONG!

The bell continued to toll the news of Zoltab's return.

With Capablanca still stupefied by his mistake it was left to Blart to rouse him to some action.

'Come on,' Blart urged Capablanca. 'If we don't go they'll know we're fakes.'

'A night shift,' said Capablanca. 'How could I have been

so stupid? I, Capablanca, have failed. Zoltab has returned and we are doomed.'

'I thought we were doomed before,' Tungsten reminded them.

'Come on,' said Blart, who was hoping to remain undoomed for as long as possible.

'Mind you,' continued Tungsten, suddenly seeing one of those silver linings, 'my grandfather used to say that it's not over until the fat dwarf sings. And I don't see a fat dwarf singing.'

'What?' said Blart. 'What kind of a stupid thing is that to say? Dwarfs never shut up singing. And they're all fat.'

'Mock, if you choose,' said Tungsten, 'but there is wisdom in these words.'

'Come on,' said Capablanca, shaking himself back into action. 'There is still hope. We must go to the Terrorsium. What are you waiting for?'

'You,' answered Blart and Tungsten together.

The three of them pulled on their boots as fast as they could and rushed out of the tent.

The sky was no longer black. It was orange. But it was not the light orange which precedes a calm, sunny day. Instead it was an angry, burning orange presaging storms and tempests. A steady rain was falling. The three companions rushed across the barren blasted wasteland to join the chanting line thronging outside the Terrorsium.

'Zoltab has come! Zoltab has come!'

The Terrorsium was even more awesome in the light of day. It was easily the largest building ever constructed – a huge oval made entirely of black stone. And at four regular points in the oval were the huge square towers. They were fiercely fortified. Cannons projected at all points and along the turreted walls archers stood on watch with longbows. Around it was a vast moat filled with voracious fish and deadly snakes engaged in a constant life or death struggle with one another that made the water boil with blood.

'Zoltab has come! Zoltab has come!'

The rain grew more insistent but it did not dampen the enthusiasm of the minions. Blart felt rivulets dribbling uncomfortably down his back. He wiped his hands over his face. There had been no chance for anybody to wash since they emerged from the tunnels the night before. Indeed, to the minions washing seemed pointless because all day, every day was spent digging, and no sooner were you clean than you were dirty again. But the heavy rain was beginning to clean them up, leaving them smeared but individual. Blart saw that the minions were not just men but women as well. And some dwarves. People who looked as if they came from the land where he was born. People who resembled Illyrians. People who looked like no people that Blart had ever seen before. All of them brought to this desolate place to build the Terrorsium and to dig for Zoltab.

'Zoltab has come! Zoltab has come!'

The crowd moved forward, the chanting growing louder

and more intense. As they approached the bridge that crossed the moat there was a crush. But the momentum of the crowd was too great to stop and some of the minions were forced over the side of the bridge into the moat where they were devoured by the hideous swimming creatures. But this did not slow the crowd. All that mattered was to get inside, to be where Zoltab was.

'Zoltab has come! Zoltab has come!'

Prisoners of the crowd and its relentless advance, Blart, Capablanca and Tungsten were pushed on to the bridge. Minions piled up against them from behind and forced them tight up against minions in front. They gasped for air.

'Zoltab has come! Zoltab has come!'

Suddenly the front shot forward. The pressure from behind was still as intense and there was a stampede to get across the bridge. Those who were taken by surprise by the surge fell forward and anybody who hit the ground did not rise again. Blart fought to stay on his feet as he was hurled forward, but the weight behind was too great and he felt himself lose control, stagger and fall.

But almost immediately he was held. He looked down to see Tungsten supporting him, his arms strengthened by years of digging. They were swept through the mouth of the Terrorsium and into the gate house. Here guards slowed the tide of minions by pointing spears directly at them. There was more space. Blart righted himself and took a deep breath. He looked around for Capablanca, but there was no sign of him. Had he fallen in one of the great surges and was he even now screaming his last as the manic hordes rushed over him? Blart had not realised how much he depended on the wizard until he was without him. What would he do if Capablanca was gone?

Just as Blart began to despair, he spotted Capablanca being pushed into the gate house. He seemed lost and confused in the tide of minions. But by the time Blart had struggled over to him, Capablanca was straightening up. He still looked frail but there was fire in his eyes.

Blart opened his mouth and was about to say something he had never said before. He was about to say that he was glad to see Capablanca, that he had worried about him and that he was pleased he was all right.

But before he could speak, a hysterical voice behind him screeched, 'He has no brand!'

All people have some ability to know, even in a chaotic crowd, when they are being talked about. Blart knew that the words were aimed at him without understanding what they meant. But Capablanca's face showed him that it was serious.

The voice behind him screamed louder than before. 'He has no brand!'

Chapter 39

$f$or the heavy rain which cleaned Blart had also betrayed him. It had revealed that there was no 'm' tattooed behind his ear. And in the crowded gatehouse with everybody squeezed so closely together it had been spotted. Blart was exposed.

The first cry of the minion had gone unnoticed, but the second attracted the attention of those nearby. Fingers pointed and a circle formed instantly around Blart and the wizard.

'No brand!'

'An impostor!'

Blart's accusers screamed from every side.

'Kill him!'

'Torture him!'

'Turn him over to the Master!'

'Bury him alive!'

The shouts swiftly led to violence. Hands reached out to tear at Blart's hair. Punches thumped into his stomach and kicks crashed into his legs.

'Kill the traitor! Kill the traitor!'

Blart crouched in a hopeless attempt to ward off the blows. Clumps of hair were torn from his head. The kicks intensified.

And then there was a huge explosion. The kicks stopped. Blart fell back. Above his head stood a tall thin figure dressed entirely in red.

'Brothers!' it shouted. 'Control your anger! I, Maroczy, Minister of Zoltab, command it!' The mob seemed cowed by the Minister and was reduced to mutterings. 'Your thirst for vengeance at this vile intrusion is admirable but we cannot allow it to distract us. We have found one impostor. There may be others.'

A gasp of horror rose from the crowd.

'Check all ears for the brand of Zoltab,' ordered the Minister.

Pandemonium ensued as the mob was given a new target of attack – their neighbours' ears. Cries resounded as ears were examined. Minions who had had their ears pulled responded by pulling the pullers' ears more aggressively. Just when it seemed that a riot was inevitable news of another traitor spread. And then another. The mob surged forward to catch a glimpse of these new infidels and was rewarded by the sight of Capablanca and Tungsten alongside Blart.

The traitors were encircled by a Minister of Zoltab and

six guards armed with spears, but still the mob wailed for blood.

'Give them to us!'

'Traitors!'

'Murderers!'

'Deniers of Zoltab!'

'Kill! Kill! Kill!'

Blart's whole body shook. The Minister of Zoltab held up his hand. Slowly, the cries of anger and the demands for vengeance tailed off.

'Brothers!' cried Maroczy, Minister of Zoltab. 'Allow me to compliment you on your thorough search. It shows us once again that we should all be constantly vigilant against those evil forces that seek to prevent Zoltab's return.'

The mob hissed and booed

'Brothers,' continued Maroczy, 'we are now truly fortunate. For today we no longer need to decide the fate of these traitors ourselves. We can pass the decision to a higher power. For the first time in an age we are able to raise our hands in the air and cry, 'Let Zoltab judge!''

A roar reverberated through the gatehouse. The Minister pointed to the entrance to the Terrorsium and the mob turned and marched into the amphitheatre.

'Let Zoltab judge! Let Zoltab judge!'

Maroczy made a sign to the guards, who dragged Blart, Capablanca and Tungsten through a door and down stone steps that spiralled round and round. At the bottom was a passage and on one side a row of doors with barred windows. The Minister stepped forward and opened one of them.

'In!' he ordered Tungsten.

He opened the door of the next cell. Capablanca walked in without being told. He opened the next cell and looked at Blart. Blart didn't move.

'In!' said Maroczy.

'I'm claustrophobic,' said Blart, proud of having remembered this word.

'In!' repeated Maroczy.

'How do I join?' asked Blart, who had always doubted he was on the right side.

'What?' said Maroczy.

'How do I join?' repeated Blart. 'I'd like to become a minion. I've always wanted a tattoo behind my ear.'

'Show some dignity, boy!' shouted Capablanca from his cell.

But Blart could only show cowardice and he continued to show it rather well.

'Zoltab must judge!' he began to shout.

'You shame your ancestors!' called Tungsten from his cell.

'Zoltab is going to judge,' pointed out Maroczy.

'Yes, but I don't want him to judge me,' explained Blart. 'He can judge those two.'

'Guards!' demanded Maroczy, deciding that the best way

to treat Blart was to ignore him.

'Please,' begged Blart. 'I'm happy to be just a minion.'

But entreaties were hopeless. Two guards dragged him into the cell and threw him roughly to the floor.

'Traitors to the cause of Zoltab,' announced Maroczy, 'very soon you will appear before Lord Zoltab to answer for your crimes. It would be best for you if you spent your few remaining moments dwelling on your past errors and preparing yourselves to face the awesome power of true justice. Banish any thoughts of escape. The dungeons of Zoltab are subject to a terrible curse. Should any prisoner attempt to escape from his cell it will immediately collapse inward, crushing his bones and squeezing all life from him. The only escape from these dungeons is death. Guards, close and lock the doors.'

The doors slammed shut. Keys turned. Marching feet receded. The prisoners were left with nothing but their own thoughts.

Which meant that Blart was soon bored. He looked around his cell but there was little to see. A board covered in straw to serve as a bed, a plate of stale bread and a foul-smelling bowl. Water trickled down the cold stone walls. There was a squeak and a scuffling and two rats scuttled across the dungeon floor

'Yaahhh!' shouted Blart, and they disappeared through a tiny gap in the wall. But their disappearance did not make him feel any better. He knew they would be back. He vowed never to sleep again for fear that he should wake to find one rushing across his face or gnawing at his toes.

Things could not be any worse.

And then, from another cell, there came the sound of singing.

Chapter 40

Harsh, tuneless, unpleasant singing.

'Oh, I'll tell you a story of a warrior brave
Sing hey ho, hey ho ho
They threw him into jail like the basest knave
And he never has felt so low, low, low
No, he never has felt so low.

His dungeon had naught that would do for a bed
Sing hey ho, hey ho ho
There was lice in his hair and weevils in his bread
And a corn on his big toe, oh, oh
And a corn on his big toe.

They branded him with irons and they stretched him on the rack
Sing hey ho, hey ho ho
He suffered chronic pain in his lower back
At the hands of his evil foe, oh, oh
At the hands of his evil foe.

They dragged out his nails and they pulled his teeth
Sing hey ho, hey ho ho
He longed for a mouthful of the River Lethe
For his death it was so slow, oh, oh
Yes, his death it was so slow.

They robbed his jewels and they stole his clothes
Sing hey ho, hey ho ho
They stamped on his vitals and they squashed his nose
With a very nasty blow, oh, oh
With a very nasty blow.

So, if you're jailed by a man bad and wrong
Sing hey ho, hey ho ho
There's not much comfort in this song
And your life it soon will go, oh, oh
Yes, your life it soon will go.'

Blart realised it was indeed possible for things to be worse.

'Beowulf?' he heard Capablanca shout.

The singing stopped.

'Who wants to know?'

'It is I, Capablanca.'

'I didn't know it was visiting time.'

'We're not visitors, you fool,' Capablanca responded. 'We've been captured as well.'

'Oh.' Beowulf sounded a little hurt.

'How did you get here?' demanded Capablanca. 'We thought you and Princess Lois and Pig the Horse had been pulled into the oasis by serpents and killed.'

'Why did you think that?' asked Beo, who felt this was rather a wild guess.

'You mean you weren't killed?' said Capablanca.

'Do I sound like I've been killed, Wizard?' responded Beo.

'Your singing does!' shouted Blart.

'Has nobody cleaved that boy in two yet?' enquired Beo.

'Not yet,' replied Capablanca, 'but I have been sorely tempted. However, it is you and Princess Lois not dying that is of more concern to me at the moment.'

'That's nice, I'm sure.' Beo sounded offended. 'Old comrades-in-arms meet up after a time apart and all you can say is that you wish I was dead.'

'Not you so much as the Princess,' explained Capablanca.

'That's worse. Nobody can wish death upon a damsel.'

'I'm not wishing her dead,' said Capablanca exasperatedly. 'I'm wishing her back from the dead because then she would fulfil the prophecy we found on the back of the map.'

'Sure isn't her safety more important than a prophecy?'

'Don't underestimate the importance of prophecies,' warned Capablanca. 'If a quest is to make proper sense then all the prophecies must be fulfilled.'

That silenced Beo, who liked his quests to be in good order.

'Still,' observed Capablanca, 'we did think she was dead.'

'I wished she was dead,' added Blart somewhat unnecessarily.

'And you always have to be prepared to be a bit flexible when it comes to prophecies,' continued Capablanca.

'What do you mean?' shouted Beo.

'I mean that, taking everything into account and with a little give and take on all sides, I think I can conclude that the prophecy has come to pass.'

'Hurrah!' shouted Beo.

'It is not a matter for rejoicing.' said the wizard sternly. 'A more appropriate reaction would be a scholarly nod at the implacable forces of fate and destiny. Now tell me what really happened to you.'

'Oh … er … not much.'

'What do you mean, not much?' demanded Capablanca. 'You vanish in the middle of a desert and reappear as a prisoner of Lord Zoltab. Something must have happened in between.'

'Oh,' said Beo. And then there was a pause. 'Well, all right, then. But only as long as you understand that it wasn't my idea.'

'What wasn't your idea?'

'The … er … thing that … er … happened. That … er … idea.'

'What idea?'

'Going dragon catching.'

'Dragon catching?' yelled Capablanca.

'Sure, I knew you'd take it all out on me. Didn't I tell you that it wasn't my idea?'

'Whose idea was it then, Pig the Horse's?' Capablanca suggested sarcastically.

'No, indeed. 'T'was all that spalpeen Princess Lois's idea. We went for a walk by the pool, and didn't she say that if she stole the map then it would tell us where the dragons were and we could ride there on Pig the Horse and catch a multi-coloured dragon to replace the one that I slew and we could take it back to Illyria and she'd make sure her father made me a knight.'

'So,' Capablanca's voice echoed down the corridor. 'You were prepared to betray your friends and abandon the quest and sacrifice the future of the world just so you could be a knight?'

'Sure, it sounds very bad when you put it like that,' lamented Beo.

'How would you put it?' demanded Capablanca.

'I'd have come back for you,' insisted Beo. 'And I wasn't really abandoning the quest, I was just having a few days off. I knew you'd be all right.'

'Hardly all right,' pointed out Capablanca. 'We are in Zoltab's cells awaiting our doom.'

'Exactly,' said Beo rather confusingly. 'And that proves why I was right all along. I got to thinking that if Zoltab did succeed in winning I was going to die a warrior, and what a fool I would have been to turn down my last chance to die a knight instead. If we hadn't been captured by one of Zoltab's Ministers with a whole group of his minions then I'd be a knight this very day.'

'You fool,' shouted Capablanca. 'If you hadn't run off we'd have got here in time to place a Cap of Eternal Doom on the Great Tunnel of Despair and the world would have been saved.'

'It's all ifs and buts and maybes with you, isn't it, Wizard?' responded Beo. 'A damsel was in distress and I did what any other man would have done who had an ounce of chivalry in his bones. My conscience is clear.'

'Unlike your arguments,' retorted Capablanca. 'What happened to Pig?'

'They took him off to work, dragging dirt away from the tunnel,' said Beo. 'They don't know that he can fly.'

'He is the only one of you I'm glad is still alive,' said Capablanca viciously. 'You are the ... '

But his words tailed off, for there was the sound of footsteps coming down the spiral steps. Had Zoltab decreed they should be put to death in their cells? If so, none of them had any hope of escape. Each of them steeled himself to face the fate he had been allocated. Each of them except Blart, of course, who was wondering whether he could talk his way out of it.

'Open!'

Simultaneously, keys were turned in the locks and doors were thrown open.

'Out!'

Each of them walked out into the passage. An armed guard, face covered by a black visor, stood by each of their cells. At the head of the passageway stood Maroczy.

'You are most fortunate,' he told them. 'Zoltab has decreed that he will hear your case personally and immediately. Even if he condemns you to death it will be a great honour. Guards!'

They were marched up the spiral steps. Maroczy led the way, followed by Tungsten, Capablanca, Blart and finally Beowulf. The guards walked fast and the spears encouraged their captives to do the same. Blart wished it could be slower. He had no wish to face Zoltab. He did not want to be judged. Surely, he thought, Zoltab would understand. He'd been taken against his will from the pigs he loved. He hadn't wanted to do Zoltab any harm. He'd have been quite happy for Zoltab to take control of the world if that was what he wanted. Zoltab would be bound to let him go because he hadn't done anything wrong. Little did Blart realise that he was thinking the thoughts of countless small men down the ages who became embroiled in events bigger than themselves and had suffered the consequences whether they deserved to or not.

At the top of the steps Maroczy led them into a passage. There was daylight at its end and from it came an angry roar.

'Guards!' ordered Maroczy. 'Keep a close eye on our prisoners and march in perfect formation. For any moment now you will be under the gaze of Zoltab. Any mistake we make will be punished for Lord Zoltab rightfully demands nothing but the best from those who serve him.'

The guards quickened their pace and Blart had to half run to keep up with them. As he struggled to maintain the pace he realised his body was close to exhaustion but he had no choice but to keep going.

Now Blart could see that the passage led out into the Terrorsium. Fear gripped him and he felt as though he was about to be sick as the roar grew louder. The guards, eager to impress their leader, marched even faster. Blart tried to think of a way to escape but even his mind had switched itself off and offered no ideas. He was doomed. And then they were out in the open.

The roars turned to boos instantly. Blart felt as if he was no longer a person. He was just a thing to be abused. All this noise. All these minions. Thousands and thousands of them, filling every space in the vast Terrorsium, going back in row upon row until they reached the sky. Blart had never seen so many in one place and this was too much for him. His mind refused to accept what his eyes were telling him. And so he was led to the centre of the Terrorsium like an empty shell, a body from which all the insides had been torn.

And then Maroczy and the guards stopped, turned to one side and bowed. Blart turned too and what he saw shocked his brain into action again. For Blart was facing Zoltab.

Chapter 41

Zoltab was a huge, terrifying figure clad in armour of cold, grey steel and holding a giant sword in his hand. He stood immobile in front of a black throne adorned with fierce gargoyles and raving demons while all around him his minions roared their homage. Suddenly he reached up and, snatching off his helmet, dashed it to the floor, revealing his shaven head and a face twisted with hate. The hysterical cries of the minions grew louder. Zoltab slowly surveyed his acolytes with arrogant satisfaction and then finally allowed his gaze to rest on the four questors. They stood alone in the centre of the Terrorsium and awaited their fate.

'Silence!'

His voice filled the whole amphitheatre. Blart's mouth hung open in disbelief.

Instantly the minions fell silent. Zoltab stood, his giant sword raised. Not one minion breathed, such was their fear of breaking the eerie calm. Zoltab's gaze halted on the four questors. Though he was a great distance away, Blart could feel his eyes burning into him.

'Ministers and minions.'

That voice. Gigantic, arrogant, dominating everything.

'Today is a great day. Thanks to your efforts I am free. A wrong has been put right. I, Zoltab, who was banished from the world, have returned.'

Cheers and roars burst from the crowd. Zoltab held up his hand. The noise vanished as swiftly as it had erupted.

'Yet today is only the beginning. Tomorrow you will set off in great armies to conquer the world, to cleanse it of the weakness of human will, to replace all with one mighty right. The worship of Zoltab.'

Again the crowd could not be restrained. Minister and minion cheered madly and wildly. Zoltab held up his hand.

'But today we rest, for much hard work has been done and much remains to be done. Today you will be richly honoured for you will see Zoltab married. Bring forth the bride.'

Princess Lois, wearing a simple white dress, was dragged out from behind Zoltab's massive throne by two black-vizored guards.

'Get off me!' she yelled. 'I don't want to get married!'

But her struggles were in vain. The guards pulled her forward until she was standing in front of Zoltab. He stared at her. A terrible, cruel stare that would have reduced a normal girl to a quivering wreck. But Princess Lois was not a normal girl. She jutted her chin in the air and stared at Zoltab.

'I'll never say "I do",' she said. Though her head was held

high, her body trembled.

Zoltab ignored her and turned to address the crowd.

'This is the woman chosen to bear Zoltab's children. His line shall never again be banished from the world.'

The crowd exploded with applause. This time Zoltab allowed the applause to continue as he turned to his bride-to-be. Princess Lois met his eyes and her face remained hard and resentful. But Zoltab continued to stare and the crowd continued to cheer and eventually Princess Lois was forced to look away. Zoltab smirked horribly and looked out once more at the crowd.

'But before the ceremony there is entertainment to enjoy. Before you stand four imposters. Four fakes. Four frauds who have tricked their way into Zoltab's domain.'

The crowd broke out again but this time their roars were of fury and blood-curdling hate.

'Ministers and minions. Let what is about to happen to the scum which stand before you be a warning to any who betray the cause of Zoltab.'

He paused. The crowd held their breath, eager with anticipation.

'Death!'

Cheers rolled from the tops of the Terrorsium down over the rows of minions and out into the centre of the ring, rocking the four helpless figures.

'He didn't hear our side of the story,' said Blart indignantly.

Capablanca's frustration at his defeat by Zoltab and his failure to become the greatest wizard of all time boiled over.

'This is all your fault,' he yelled at Beowulf.

'You always feel sorry for yourself,' retorted Beowulf. 'I'm going to die a warrior. I'll never be a knight now.'

'And I should never have listened to you,' Tungsten added. 'You promised to make the iron dwarves the greatest of dwarves. Now my people will stay as the lowest of the low. My father and grandfather and great-grandfather turn in their graves.'

'Oh, shut up, all of you!' yelled Blart. 'I never even wanted to come. I wanted to stay at home with my pigs. But he made me and then he kept trying to cleave me in two and you've been too small ever since I've met you.'

Boiling with rage, Blart aimed a kick at Tungsten. Tungsten threw a punch at Blart. Capablanca yanked Blart's arm. Beo grabbed Capablanca around the neck. Capablanca kicked out and hit Tungsten in the face, sending him tumbling to the ground. Blart, seeing Capablanca gripped by Beo, punched the wizard as hard as he could in the stomach. Tungsten, dazed and unsure what had happened to him, bit Beo in the leg. Beo howled with pain and let go of Capablanca, who swung round and prodded Beo in both eyes. Beo stumbled backwards and fell over the figure of Tungsten. Blart grabbed hold of Capablanca's hair and pulled with all his might. Capablanca's head jerked backwards and he lost his footing and fell over, taking Blart with him.

All four lay on the ground panting for breath.

They heard a new sound, a sound unheard for a long time. Laughter.

Fingers were pointed at them. They could see the faces at the front of the crowd contorted with hysteria. They had come this far and sacrificed this much only to become figures of fun to Zoltab's throng.

'Ministers and minions.'

Blart looked round to see Zoltab looking down at them, and even his face was shaped into a contemptuous smirk.

'When I condemn traitors to death even I, Zoltab, do not expect them to carry out the sentence themselves.'

More laughter erupted from the rows of minions.

'And though it would give me great pleasure to watch them kill each other, we do not have the time – for one of them is little more than a boy, another is an old man, a third is a puny dwarf and the last is a fat oaf. It would take days for them to kill each other as they are so pathetic. I, Zoltab, wish to see the blood of these traitors now and I call upon the Four Horsemen of Zoltab to dispatch them from this world.'

Immediately there was the thunder of hooves. The crowd was silenced, eager to see what would appear.

Four horsemen on great black steeds burst from the tunnel. They galloped towards Zoltab's throne, brought their horses to a shuddering halt and saluted. The crowd went wild, for they were a truly awful sight to behold.

The first sat tall and gaunt in the saddle. His skin was

stretched so tightly over his bones it seemed as though it was about to tear. The fire in his eyes was savage. Armed with a sharp spear, he was starving for blood.

The second was worse to look at. His face was covered with sores and boils. Yellow pus ran from encrusted scabs and black bile flowed from his nose. Armed with a bulbous mace, he was sick for blood.

The third was almost invisible, surrounded as he was by a haze of stinging wasps and deadly mosquitoes. The black cloud of insects swarmed around him wherever he went. Armed with a trident and net, he was burning for blood.

But the fourth was worst of all. For in the saddle sat nothing but a skeleton. A set of remains revivified by some diabolic force, its skull set in a terrible grin that was worse than any expression of hatred could ever be. Armed with a great sword, he was dying for blood.

The crowd continued whooping and yelling and cheering. Here were the champions of Zoltab who would lead them to conquer the world and they would see them in action any second now. The promise of slaughter drove the minions into a frenzy.

If Blart could have stood up he would have done. But he was paralysed with fear. He couldn't believe that these terrible warriors were here to kill him. He, who'd never done any harm to anybody. This wasn't strictly true but it seemed very true to Blart at the time. But as he gulped with terror he knew that there was no getting out of this one. There could be no bargaining and there could be no running away for there was nowhere to run.

'Famine, Disease, Pestilence and Death,' Zoltab's voice boomed around the Terrorsium. 'You, the Four Horsemen of Zoltab. The guilty are before you. Zoltab has judged. Execute the sentence. Kill them.'

The horsemen pulled their horses on to their hind legs and saluted Zoltab once more. Then they wheeled round and charged.

'Let us die like knights!' shouted Beo, pulling himself from the ground and standing four-square, unarmed as he was.

'Let us die like my ancestors!' yelled Tungsten, rising to his feet.

'Let us die like heroes!' cried Capablanca, as he too rose up.

'I can't stand up,' said Blart. 'My legs have stopped working.'

The other three looked down at Blart with contempt. Perhaps the last looks of contempt that he would ever receive.

Chapter 42

Monstrous and terrible, the four horsemen bore down on the stricken victims. Instinctively, Capablanca, Beo and Tungsten threw themselves to the ground and buried their faces in the sand. The horses thundered overhead. They were still alive.

'I knew I shouldn't get up,' said Blart.

The Four Horsemen of Zoltab wheeled round and prepared for another charge. The questors were in urgent need of a good idea.

Capablanca rose to his feet and shouted an order to Beo and Tungsten. Then he turned to Blart.

'Be a decoy, boy.'

Unfortunately, Blart had no idea what he meant by the word 'decoy'.

And there was no time to ask. For the second charge of Zoltab's horsemen had already begun. Blart found that somehow his legs had rediscovered their power to stand. The horsemen advanced. Blart ran, which, though he didn't know it, was exactly what he was supposed to do. The horsemen were moving at a great pace. Disease, Pestilence and Death chased Blart. Famine drove on towards the three others.

Blart was still running away as they thundered past him. From one side of Blart a sword slashed down while from the other a net was thrown to enmesh him. For a moment it seemed that Blart was doomed, but with a feint one way and then a twist another he managed to avoid the horsemen's weapons. Off balance, Blart stumbled to the ground as the horsemen galloped past. Immediately he looked across the ring to witness the fate of the others.

Famine charged towards a stationary Capablanca, his spear pointing directly at the wizard's heart. The crowd roared. Their first victim was to die. Behind Capablanca, Beo swiftly knelt down and clasped his hands to form a step. Tungsten ran towards the warrior and leapt. His foot landed in the step created by Beo's clasped hands. With all his strength the warrior threw Tungsten up and over his back as Capablanca stooped. Tungsten the dwarf flew through the air, sailed over Capablanca, over the horse's head, past the pointed spear and smashed into Famine. The horse carried on. Zoltab's horseman didn't. Tumbling from the horse, he fell, spear slipping from his hand.

For an old man Capablanca was on his feet remarkably quickly. He swooped on the spear. Without stopping he ran towards Zoltab's horseman. The first thing Famine saw when he looked up was Capablanca thrusting the spear into his throat. The four horsemen were now three.

A stunned silence enveloped the crowd. One of their great champions had been defeated. And not only defeated – defeated by a flying dwarf and an old man. Nothing could have surprised them more. But at the end of the Terrorsium the three remaining horsemen were turning once more. They would still defeat these puny unarmed challengers. As the horsemen charged, the crowd found new heart and roared them on again.

Blart ran to join the others. Beo was frantically pulling the spear out of the corpse on the ground. Capablanca and Tungsten were staring at the charging riders. Nobody knew what to do.

'If we could stop one,' shouted Beo, 'I could get a throw at him with this.'

'Can't you magic them or something?' Blart suggested.

'They are horsemen of Zoltab,' panted Capablanca. 'No magic on earth would be powerful enough to work on them.'

The riders sped towards them. How could they survive a third charge unscathed?

'What about their horses?'

Capablanca's expression cleared.

'Boy,' he ordered. 'Stand straight in front of one horse. Tungsten! Distract the others.'

'But I'm good at distracting,' countered Blart.

'Stay there!' ordered Capablanca.

Tungsten ran directly towards the horses. Beo and

Capablanca backed off behind Blart. When the horses were almost upon him Tungsten changed direction. Two of the riders veered off to chase him, but Disease kept coming. Somehow Blart resisted the urge to flee. He faced the terrible beast and its horrific rider with his suppurating sores that oozed yellow pus and he did not flinch.

The horse was almost upon him when there was a flash of blue light. Instantly a great wall of flame appeared in the narrow gap between Blart and the horseman. The terrified horse pulled up short and for one precious moment the rider was still.

There was a zing as Beo threw the spear with all the force in his arm. It sped towards Disease. The rider had no time to duck. It hit him directly in the eye. Such was the power behind the spear that it did not stop until its point protruded from the back of the rider's head. The three horsemen had become two.

But the cheers of the crowd did not falter. The reason was Tungsten. He had acted as a decoy but he had not been as lucky as Blart. The riders had learnt from their mistakes, so that when Tungsten twisted and flung himself to the ground they were prepared. They pulled their horses up right next to him and dismounted. Tungsten was in a terrible position. He made a desperate attempt to rise to his feet, but Pestilence flung down his cruel chain net and Tungsten was trapped beneath it.

Beo snatched up Disease's mace and rushed across the

arena to try to save the dwarf. Blue light flashed from Capablanca's eyes towards Zoltab's remaining riders but his spells had no effect. It was too late. Blart winced as the terrible blows repeatedly fell on the helpless dwarf. One stab from the trident of Pestilence and then a swipe from the sword of Death. The dwarf writhed desperately beneath the net to avoid the vicious blows but there could be no escape from the savage onslaught.

Yet still Beo ran. The crowd suddenly spotted the danger and their cheers turned to shouts of warning. Still Beo ran towards the horsemen. Capablanca ran after him. Blart, feeling rather foolish standing idly in the middle of the arena whilst everybody else was fighting to the death, began to run too. The crowd continued to shout their warnings.

But the lust for blood was too great in Pestilence and Death. They continued hacking at Tungsten. Beo positioned himself behind Pestilence, ignoring the stinging wasps that buzzed around him. He lifted the mace high over his head only to discover it was heavier than any weapon he had ever held before. Just as he was about to let the gigantic blow fall he realised the mace was now controlling him. He teetered, struggling to stay on his feet. But muscles tire and metal balls do not, and slowly the mace dragged Beo backwards. And then suddenly he was gone, tipping over and landing with a thump on his back. Roars of laughter and great whoops greeted his catastrophe.

Pestilence and Death turned round to find another

of their enemies conveniently lying helpless on his back. Surrounded by the buzzing swarm, Pestilence raised his trident.

It was at this point that Blart realised that being young is not always an advantage. He had started running after Capablanca but had overtaken him. This meant that only he was near enough to save Beo from having a trident thrust into his midriff. If Beo had known that all that stood between him and a deadly blow was a potential act of bravery by Blart, he would have closed his eyes, said his prayers and resigned himself to the end.

But, fortunately for Beo, Blart saw the situation not in terms of bravery but in terms of self-pity which as we know Blart was very good at. If Beo died then there would be just him and Capablanca left, and the wizard's magic wasn't working, which made him as much use as any wizened old man in a fight to the death, which is no use at all. If Beo had the self-ishness to get himself killed then he was as good as sentencing Blart and Capablanca to death. So, fuelled with indignation, Blart ran faster than he knew he could and, just before the trident was thrust into the body of the warrior, he threw himself forward.

He torpedoed through the air and smashed into the middle of Pestilence. The horseman of Zoltab crumpled up and fell backwards with Blart on top of him. Straight away Blart felt a sting. And then another. The buzzing angry swarm was defending its master. Within seconds there were so many stings that it was impossible to tell them apart. On his face, on his arms, on his legs, everywhere. Blart tried to shield his face but nothing could stop the onslaught. One wasp sting will not kill anybody, but a thousand will, and Blart was rapidly heading towards that number. He rolled away but the swarm pursued him. Diving at him. Stinging him in his ears and on his eyes. Blart was dying. Nothing could save him.

Except for the wasps themselves. For without warning they buzzed away. Dazed, Blart looked after the departing horde and saw why. For Beo had risen and grasped the great club once more. Pestilence too was on his feet, looking curiously naked without his swarm. As Pestilence thrust his trident, Beo swung the club. Which would land first?

The club smashed into Pestilence's head. The swarm sped towards Beo, each wasp, hornet and mosquito poised to strike their venom into his blood. And then suddenly they stopped. What had been a deadly dagger became a confused mass. Instead of aiming for Beo it buzzed instead over the prone figure of Pestilence. Beo's massive blow was proving fatal and as the horseman died so did the insects, dropping harmlessly around his corpse.

The two horsemen had become one.

'Help!' yelled Capablanca.

And he was in need of it. For though there was only one horseman left, he was the deadliest of them all. Death himself.

'Watch out!' shouted Capablanca. 'If Death's sword or bones so much as touch you, you will die instantly!'

Even as Capablanca spoke, Death's sword scythed towards him. Capablanca jumped backwards just in time. The sword hacked through his cloak but did not touch his body.

Death tried again, this time with a terrifying downward swipe intended to split Capablanca down the middle, but the wizard's reflexes did not fail him and a leap to the side saw the sword smash into the ground.

Capablanca ran towards Beo and Blart.

'Why didn't you tell us that bit about Death before?' demanded Blart. 'I might have touched him by accident.'

'I didn't want to worry you,' snapped Capablanca. 'And stop scratching. It's most off-putting when I'm trying to think.'

Blart was frantically scratching at the stings that were beginning to lump up all over his body.

'He's coming!' shouted Beo. 'What do we do? How do we kill Death?'

'Run!' shouted Blart desperately as Death loomed nearer.

And this turned out to be the best plan. It wasn't very courageous and it didn't look particularly heroic but it kept them alive. Round and round the arena they ran with Death pursuing them on foot. The crowd booed and jeered but the questors kept running. They split up and Death followed Blart. Blart ran until he was exhausted and then Beo distract-ed Death who ran after him. Then when Beo was exhausted he handed him on to Capablanca, who only got a short turn because he was old, before returning him to Blart who had got his breath back. Death, it was turning out, may have been extremely deadly but he wasn't very bright.

But though this delayed the ending, it could not prevent it, for with each run Blart, Beo and Capablanca grew more exhausted. Death continued at the same remorseless pace for Death never tires and Death never sleeps. Sooner or later they would be so weakened that they would be unable to run and then Death would strike them down mercilessly. All three realised that this would be their fate – Capablanca quickly, Beo slowly and Blart very slowly. But what option did they have but to keep running? Life feels very precious when it is about to be taken from you.

'Death, death, death,' chanted the crowd.

Finally, Capablanca was too weary to run any more and it was left to Beo and Blart to carry on distracting the terrible horseman.

And Beo was not built for long-distance running. He was built for short sprints and for face-to-face combat and for drinking beer. His legs would no longer carry his huge bulk. Blart alone had to keep Death running. When he flagged it would all be over.

'Death, death, death.'

And then death came.

Blart stumbled. His legs gave way beneath him and he fell. He could not get up. He was going to die. He buried his head and waited for the final blow.

But it didn't come. This was true torture. Knowing you were going to die and yet being made to wait. Still the final blow didn't come. Unable to wait any longer, Blart rolled over, expecting to see Death standing over him.

But that was not what he saw.

Death had stopped in the centre of the arena. He was swaying from side to side. A spasm shot through him. The bones that had once been his hands grabbed at his chest. He staggered and fell. He did not rise. The final horseman was no more.

The crowd was stunned into silence. Death, their ultimate champion, lay dead on the ground. It couldn't happen. He couldn't die again. But even if it couldn't happen, it had. The minions were transfixed with horror.

Blart, Beo and Capablanca approached the still figure.

'What happened?' asked Beo.

'It is incredible,' said Capablanca. 'The boy has outrun death and triumphed over him. It is impossible and yet it has happened. I do not understand.'

And so unlikely was their survival that the wizard admitted his ignorance of the reason for it without bitterness. They were distracted from contemplating Death's corpse and the mystery of his defeat by an awful groan.

Turning round, they were horrified to see it had come from Tungsten. He lay under the net, bleeding from the terrible wounds that he had received at the hands of Death and

Pestilence. Beo rushed over and pulled the net off him. Up close his wounds were grievous indeed, and there seemed little chance that he could survive. Indeed, it was a miracle that he had lived to see the end of the battle. Capablanca knelt by his side.

'Tungsten,' said Capablanca gently. 'Can you hear me, Tungsten?'

Tungsten's eyes fluttered open and he seemed to recognise his companions.

'You have died nobly,' said Beo.

'Sssh,' hissed Capablanca. 'He isn't dead yet.'

'Sorry,' said Beo. He coughed and tried again. 'You are dying nobly.'

'Oh, for heaven's sake,' snapped Capablanca. 'Hold your tongue if all you can talk about is death.'

Beo looked sulky but he said no more.

'Tungsten,' said Capablanca. 'Is there anything you want to say to us, any message that we can take?'

Tungsten opened his mouth. His three companions inclined their heads to hear his final words.

Tungsten burped.

'What kind of a message is that?' demanded Blart.

'Hush,' insisted Capablanca. 'He is going to speak.'

And Tungsten was. In a tiny voice he said, 'What's my name?'

'Tungsten,' said Blart. 'Your name is Tungsten.'

'Tungsten,' repeated Tungsten. 'Tungsten. Son of Gravel,

Grandson of Slab, Great-Grandson of Tar, Great-Great-Grandson of …'

And there he stopped. His eyes glazed over and his breathing was silenced. Tungsten the dwarf had gone to the Great Mine in the Sky.

'You know,' observed Blart, 'he doesn't look so small now he's dead.'

Chapter 43

'Ministers and minions of Zoltab.'

The three of them jumped as Zoltab's enormous voice shattered the silence.

'So, they have defeated the Four Horsemen of Zoltab. Do not despair. They merely prolong their suffering. For now, I will deal with them myself.'

The crowd's spirits were lifted and they began to cheer once more.

From the tunnels appeared forty guards, each dressed in the black armour of Zoltab, led by Minister Maroczy in his flowing red robes. They marched directly towards the three questors.

Blart looked at Beo. Beo looked at Capablanca. Capablanca looked at Blart. Blart looked back at Capablanca, who avoided his gaze and stared at Beo. Beo flicked his eyes towards Blart. They were looking at each other for an answer to this new problem and it was increasingly obvious that none of them had one.

'Their armour will protect them against my magic,' said Capablanca.

'There are too many even for a warrior of my strength,' said Beo.

'Um,' said Blart.

The crowd's cheering grew wilder as they saw that the traitors were not offering any resistance.

The cohort marched up to Blart, Beo and Capablanca and halted. Maroczy stepped forward.

'Guards, take them to the platform,' he instructed.

The guards marched them across the arena, leaving the body of Tungsten behind. The crowd found a new chant that it accompanied by stamping its feet.

'Go to Zoltab! Go to Zoltab! Go to Zoltab!'

Past the body of Famine. Past the body of Disease, the spear still sticking out of his head. Past the body of Pestilence who had been decapitated by Beo's great blow. Past the body of Death himself.

'Go to Zoltab! Go to Zoltab!'

Up the stone steps which led to Zoltab's platform. They were among the minions now. There were shouts of 'traitor' and they had to cover their faces to ward off stones. If the guards had not been there they would have been torn apart. The noise drummed into their skulls.

'Go to Zoltab! Go to Zoltab!'

And then they stopped.

Blart couldn't see past the guards, but he heard the crowd

quieten and Maroczy announce, 'Lord Zoltab. The traitors are here as you requested.'

'Bring them forth.'

The guards in front of Blart drew to one side. He and Beo and Capablanca were pushed forward. Blart gazed upon the face of Zoltab and knew absolute fear for the first time.

For Zoltab was indeed terrible. Even sitting on his throne he was massive. Much, much bigger than Beo and Beo was the biggest man Blart had ever seen. Zoltab's hands were closed in fists so gigantic that Blart felt that one of them could crush the life from him. Yet one punch would also be deadly for protruding from each armoured knuckle was a sharp steel spike. From Zoltab's shaven head a horrific scar ran down his cheek and his lip was wrinkled into a cold commanding sneer. Blart felt Zoltab's black eyes boring into him. In fear he looked away and for a moment his eyes caught those of Princess Lois. He was amazed to find them still sparkling with defiance. She looked at him with almost frightening intensity. Nobody had ever looked at Blart like that before and for some reason it made Blart feel stronger.

'Kneel,' barked Zoltab.

The three questors knelt and looked up at the dreadful Lord.

'Your names before you die. You, wizard.'

'Capablanca,' replied Capablanca, his voice shaking. 'Wizard of the Order of Caissa.'

'You?'

'Be-Be-Be-Beowulf the Warrior,' stammered Beowulf.

'And you?'

Blart opened his mouth but no words came.

'Do not keep me waiting.'

Please speak, Blart begged his mouth. Please speak.

'Blart.'

'Why are you here?'

'To save the world,' said Blart.

Next to him, Capablanca sighed.

'To save the world,' mocked Zoltab. 'You? A mere boy? Save the world? That is a task for a great and powerful Lord. That is a task for Zoltab.'

The crowd roared its approbation.

'I will give you a new task, Blart,' announced Zoltab, twisting his mouth into a cruel smirk. 'It is not to save the world, Blart. It is to choose how you will die. Behold.'

Two prisoners were dragged into the centre of the arena. Zoltab addressed his minions.

'These traitors are guilty of not digging hard enough.'

The crowd booed.

'Of taking rests.'

The crowd booed louder.

'And leaning on their shovels.'

More boos.

'There can be only one punishment for these offences – death.'

The crowd's boos turned instantly to cheers.

'Let the sentence be carried out.'

There was a black flash from behind Blart. One of the prisoners howled in agony and fell writhing to the ground. Blart had never seen such pain.

The effect on the other minion was not so dramatic. Indeed, at first it was difficult to tell that there was anything happening to him at all. But he had become terribly still. His face was rigid. Something awful was happening to him but Blart had no idea what it was.

'Your choice, Blart. One traitor is being burnt to death. I have set fire to his entrails. He cannot see the flames, he cannot roll on the ground to put them out. But he can feel them consuming him.'

'Stop it!' cried Princess Lois.

Zoltab laughed.

'Does my little punishment offend you?' he asked her mockingly. 'You will grow used to it when you are my wife.'

Princess Lois turned away. Tears burned in her eyes. How she wished she had never left Illyria and all that was good.

Smoke began to pour from the mouth of the minion. His howls filled the arena.

'Could you do that, Wizard?' demanded Zoltab.

'No,' said Capablanca, and his voice shook with rage and terror.

'No. Your weak power is no match for the greatness of Zoltab. You are nothing.'

Blart could not take his eyes from the second minion.

Something horrible was happening to him but what was it?

'The other traitor is slowly freezing. An awful cold is creeping through his body. His liver, his brain and his heart slowly turn to ice. Whilst still alive, he experiences death.'

Blart could not drag his eyes away. Behind him he heard Princess Lois gasp in disbelief at Zoltab's cruelty.

'Blart, I ask you first. How will you die? Either will suffice, but is it to be fire or is it to be ice?'

Capablanca moved nearer to him as though he wished to offer some comfort. Was this it? thought Blart.

It appeared that it was.

'Er …' said Blart.

In some situations it may be a comfort to know how and when you are going to die. But this is not the case when you know that the how is going to be extremely painfully and the when is going to be now.

'Er …' said Blart again.

'Fire or ice? I'm waiting to get married and then conquer the earth.'

'Let Blart live!' interrupted Princess Lois.

'What?' Zoltab rounded on his wife-to-be and gave her a terrible stare.

But this time Princess Lois refused to be quailed. She held her head up high and faced the evil Lord.

'Do it for me,' she demanded. 'I am to be your wife and I ask you for this favour.'

Zoltab looked incredulous.

'You mean that you would marry me voluntarily if I were to pardon this ugly boy?'

Princess Lois swallowed hard.

'I would, My Lord.'

Zoltab lowered his head to consider the offer. Blart looked thankfully at Princess Lois. He could not believe that she was prepared to make this great sacrifice for him.

Zoltab raised his head.

'Thank you for your proposition, Princess. But I would prefer to marry you against your will and kill this boy as well.'

'But if I –' began Princess Lois.

'Silence!' thundered Zoltab. 'I shall brook no more futile delay. How will you die, Blart – fire or ice?'

'Er …' said Blart again.

'We could draw lots, My Lord,' suggested Maroczy.

'Fool!' bellowed Zoltab. 'He must choose. Don't you see that's the beauty?'

'Oh, yes, my lord,' said Maroczy quickly. 'I do …'

And then things happened so fast that Blart didn't catch the end of his sentence.

Chapter 44

There was a sudden movement next to Blart and he was thrust towards Zoltab. The sneer of cold command was wiped from the Dark Lord's face and replaced by surprise. Blart tried to twist his body to see what was happening but it was all too fast. Before he knew it and before Zoltab had time to react, they were face to face. Revolted and terrified, he managed to turn his head. And he saw Capablanca. Raising a knife.

And then he remembered.

For had not Capablanca told him that the only way that Zoltab could be robbed of his powers was to have blood spurt on him directly from the heart of the first-born son of a first-born son of a first-born son all the way back to the start of time? And here was Capablanca bringing down a knife towards his heart. Blart didn't believe it was going to happen. Everything slowed down. Around him the crowd gasped, the guards leapt for Capablanca, Princess Lois screamed and Zoltab flinched. But all Blart saw was the knife travel ever so slowly downwards. He couldn't do it. The knife kept descending. Not after all they'd been through. Still falling. No, no, no.

The knife plunged straight into Blart's heart. Blood splashed everywhere. Over Blart, over Capablanca and over Zoltab. Zoltab gasped and slumped back. The guards and Ministers, so intent a second ago on capturing Capablanca, stopped aghast at the sight of their collapsing leader.

Blart slumped to the floor. He could feel himself growing weaker. He could still see and hear what was going on but, though it was close by, it seemed far away and getting further away all the time.

Grim-faced, Capablanca approached Zoltab. Everybody looked at the blood-spattered Dark Lord. Blart, the last seconds of his life slipping away, lay ignored on the floor.

'Zoltab is defeated,' proclaimed Capablanca. 'It is too late to do anything for him now. He has been destroyed by the blood of a first-born son of a first-born son of a first-born son going all the way back to the beginning of time. I, Capablanca, have ...' Capablanca's voice faltered. He looked towards Blart and his expression became one of doubt and shame as he observed the weakening of the dying boy. 'I, Capablanca, have ...' he began again, but this time a sob caught in his throat and brought an end to his speech. 'I, Capablanca, have destroyed Zoltab, but the price has been truly terrible.'

Unable to look at Blart any more, Capablanca hung his head.

Guards, Ministers, minions – all were too shocked to kill him. They gazed towards their Lord, waiting for a sign that would tell them how to act.

There were waves of black now for Blart. One moment he could see and the next moment he couldn't, even though he was sure he had not closed his eyes. The scene on the podium would return but each time more blurry and more distant. Blart was slipping away from the world.

But he could still hear.

And he heard something. A rumble that became a roar. A roar of laughter.

'I, Capablanca, have saved the world.'

But it was not Capablanca's voice. It belonged to Zoltab.

'You foolish wizard. To think that you could do such a thing. Behold the majesty of Zoltab.'

The darkness parted and Blart could make out Zoltab standing tall and proud whilst Capablanca cowered in the grip of the Dark Lord's guards. It was all for nothing, thought Blart. It hasn't worked. I will die for nothing.

And then Zoltab looked down upon him.

'Wizard, by fire or ice I decreed, and by the hand of Zoltab that is what I shall have.'

Dimly, Blart was aware of a flash of black light from Zoltab's eyes.

And then he seemed to be coming back. The figures on the platform became clearer. The voices were nearer. Blart felt strength returning to his bones. His felt his heartbeat become stronger and the blood move through his veins. And then he was back. Lying on Zoltab's platform with everybody staring at him, and feeling rather foolish. He felt his chest. Where there should have been a hole there was nothing. It was a miracle. He was alive. Blart smiled.

'Do not be so quick to smile. For I have brought you back to life only for a more unpleasant death.'

Blart stopped smiling.

'Could you do that, wizard?' demanded Zoltab, turning his attention to Capablanca. 'Save a boy on the verge of death? Could you do that?'

Humbly, Capablanca shook his head. All his research and his quest had come to nothing. He would not be remembered as the greatest wizard of all. He looked old and beaten.

'But you thought that you could defeat Zoltab. How little you know. But before you die it is time for you to know a little more. Guards. Hold them tight.'

Blart was pulled roughly from the floor by two guards. Others leapt to hold Beo. Capablanca was already being held so the guards shook him about a bit to show they'd been listening.

'Now you will see the depths of your folly. Now you will meet my most senior minister, the Master.'

The tall, thin black-cloaked figure that Blart had last seen in the Great Tunnel of Despair appeared from behind Zoltab's massive throne. He stood by Zoltab's side.

'This is the Master. But to you, Blart, he may have a

different name.'

The Master threw back the hood of his cloak.

'Grandfather!' said Blart in astonishment.

Capablanca groaned.

'But, Grandfather,' said Blart, so shocked to see his relative that he forgot everything else. 'If you're here who's looking after the pigs?'

'Don't call me "Grandfather",' snapped the Master. 'And don't expect to see your pigs again. They were sent to market the day you left.'

'Even Wattle and Daub?'

'Gone to market,' the Master told him brutally. 'Sold, slaughtered, sliced and cooked into pies.'

Tears welled in Blart's eyes.

'Oh, I am a fool,' groaned Capablanca. 'Why did I not see? Why did I not ask what had become of Blart's parents?'

And the moment that Capablanca said this it occurred to Blart that perhaps he should have asked too. Everybody else had parents and he hadn't. And he'd never thought to mention it.

'Blart's parents perished when he was just an ugly baby,' said the Master. 'And I adopted him. For you should know, Capablanca, that greater than the Cavernous Library of Ping is the Even More Cavernous Library of Zing, and it was there that I discovered the secret of the power of the first-born son of the first-born son of the first-born son going back to the beginning of time to rob Zoltab of his power. I traced that boy before you and resolved to keep him from you.'

'You did well, Master,' said Zoltab, 'and you will be handsomely rewarded.'

The Master bowed to his lord and then gestured towards Blart.

'The only thing that could make spending years with this horrible boy worth it is the fact that it has made you safe,' he said reverently.

Blart couldn't believe it. No parents, no pigs, and still people insulted him.

'But,' protested Capablanca, 'I don't understand. I found Blart and you let me take him from you. We got to Zoltab. I splattered Blart's blood all over Zoltab. I know my research was right. I checked it over and over again. Blart's blood should have robbed Zoltab of his power. It doesn't make sense.'

Zoltab laughed so loudly that the arena shook. The whole world could hear him.

'Tell him before he dies,' he commanded.

The Master bowed once more to his lord and then turned to Capablanca.

'Your research was right, wizard. It is indeed true that blood direct from the heart of a first-born son of a first-born son of a first-born son going right back to the beginning of time can rob Zoltab of his powers. And your plan would have worked if it had not been for one thing.'

Here the Master turned to Blart.

'Blart,' he said.

'What?' said Blart.

'I would like you to meet your older brother.'

From behind the throne he came. He looked like Blart but he did not look like Blart. For where Blart's features had made him ugly, slight alterations had made his brother handsome. They were the same height, but, where Blart stood awkwardly, his brother stood tall and proud. Where Blart's face was marked with the lumps of wasps' stings, his brother's complexion was smooth and clear. Where Blart's skin was white and pasty, his brother's was tanned and gleaming.

Blart had never hated anybody more.

'Didn't I always say it?' shouted Beo. 'Didn't I, Capablanca? I said Blart couldn't be a hero. Look at his brother. Now there's a hero for you.'

'I always had my doubts,' confirmed Capablanca reluctantly. 'Blart was so cowardly, so untrustworthy, so useless, so loathsome. But I checked the records. I checked and checked them. There was no mention of Blart having an older brother.'

'Because I destroyed all the evidence,' said the Master smoothly. 'And I killed everybody who had ever known of Blart's brother's existence. I hid him away and so when you came to look you thought the first-born son was Blart. I let you take him because I knew from the start that your quest was a hopeless waste of time. You never had a hero at all.'

309

'Boy,' Capablanca shouted to Blart's brother, 'I beg you to save the world. All you have to do is stab yourself and allow the blood from your heart to pour directly on to Zoltab. His power will be taken from him.'

'Your pleas are useless, Wizard,' replied the Master. 'Blart's brother has been brought up under the protection of Lord Zoltab. He would never hurt him, would you, boy?'

'My loyalty lies with Lord Zoltab,' replied Blart's brother, in such an amiable and polite way that Blart got even more angry.

'Enough,' commanded Zoltab, raising one spiked fist. 'My destiny awaits. I must execute these traitors, get married and conquer the world. Any last requests?'

'You couldn't make me a knight, could you?' asked Beo. Zoltab stared at him.

'Ah, come on,' pleaded Beo. 'What harm would it do?'

'You amuse me, warrior,' replied Zoltab. 'I will grant your request.'

'Beowulf!' exclaimed Capablanca. 'You cannot become a knight of Zoltab. To do so would be to betray our cause.'

Zoltab ignored the wizard's protests.

'To be a knight of Zoltab you must carry the shield of Zoltab and wear the helmet of Zoltab. You, guard. Give him yours.'

A guard removed his helmet and handed over his shield. Beowulf knelt down.

'It's not too late to change your mind,' urged Capablanca.

But Beo did not even look at him. Zoltab raised his huge sword. He touched it on Beo's shoulders and said, 'I dub thee Sir Beowulf, Knight of Zoltab.'

'That's grand,' said Beo.

'Now prepare to die.'

It was at this moment that one of the four guards surrounding Blart turned into a dragon.

Chapter 45

Now this is really stupid, I know you're saying to yourself. I've followed this story all the way through, and I've not always been sure that it was telling me the truth, but I've given it the benefit of the doubt and now, right at the end, for no apparent reason, a guard, a minor character who is of no significance at all, just turns into a dragon. What kind of tale is this?

But you forget that when Blart was in the desert being pulled to his death by a serpent he sent out three spells. The final one freed him, the second turned a man's nose into a carrot, but the first ...

What happened to the first?

As has been proved by Znosko-Borovsky's Third Law of Magic, a spell cannot disappear until it has engaged. In order to engage it must penetrate. And, amazingly improbable as this might seem, Blart's first spell had not yet encountered anything it could penetrate in all the time since he'd inadvertently cast it. Until it hit the guard who, having handed his helmet over to Beo, was no longer protected against magic.

Everybody stared.

The dragon stared back.

Now, as we've already established, dragons aren't dangerous creatures. They are timid and shy, but when timid and shy creatures are placed in a large amphitheatre with a vast crowd staring at them they tend to panic. The dragon flapped its wings.

One wing hit Beo and his guards and knocked them over, the other hit Capablanca and his guards and knocked them over. Everybody else on the platform dived for cover, apart from Zoltab, who had his image to think of, and Blart's brother who, as we know, was predestined to be a hero and therefore knew no fear. The dragon's great wings were beating. Smoke poured from its nose. It flew forward towards Zoltab. The Dark Lord was not prepared to be knocked over in front of his minions. He raised his great sword and thrust it into the dragon's soft belly.

The dragon howled. Its great wings lost their strength and it plummeted back down on to the platform. It could have landed anywhere. But where it did land was plop on the head of Blart's brother, who was squashed so hard that he exploded. Bits of Blart's brother flew everywhere. Everything was splattered with red goo. Blart was. Princess Lois was. Beo was. Capablanca was. The Master was. Maroczy was. The guards were.

But most important of all, Zoltab was.

'No!' he shouted as the blood landed on him, but already his great voice was reduced to a whisper. And this time there was no pretence. He was shrinking into himself. His power was gone. Within seconds, he was smaller than Tungsten the dwarf.

'Quick,' said Capablanca, reacting first. 'We must get Zoltab out of here. We cannot leave him in the hands of his Ministers and minions. They might find a way to reverse the action of the blood.'

'By washing it off,' suggested Blart.

'Don't give them any ideas,' snapped Capablanca. 'Help me get Zoltab out of here.'

'Look!' shouted Princess Lois.

They did as she commanded. Over the far wall of the arena rose a creature that brought a smile to each of the questors' faces. It was black and it was flying.

'Deus ex machina,' shouted Capablanca, which nobody else understood.

'Pig the Horse,' cried Blart, which some people did.

And it was Pig the Horse. Huge, powerful and magnificent. He had escaped from the stables of Zoltab and was coming to the questors' rescue.

None of the minions and Ministers had ever seen a flying horse before. They all watched, dumbstruck, as Pig the Horse flew over them and landed right by Zoltab's throne.

'Quick,' shouted Capablanca. 'We must mount Pig and flee before the Ministers and minions regroup and try to prevent us escaping with Zoltab.'

Capablanca and Beo forced the shrunken figure of Zoltab on to Pig's back. They climbed on behind him.

'Attack,' shouted the Master, who had eventually recovered from the shock of seeing Zoltab shrivel and from the arrival of Pig the Horse. 'We must get Zoltab back. Don't let them get away.'

Beo pulled Princess Lois on to Pig's back. Things were beginning to get crowded up there.

The guards, who had seemed stupefied by the turn of events, responded to the voice of command. They picked themselves up and rushed towards Pig.

Only Blart was left on the ground. He was on the opposite side of the massive throne to Pig the Horse and the others.

'Let's go,' shouted Capablanca.

Capablanca had intended this as encouragement to Blart. Unfortunately such was his urgency that it was transmitted to Pig the Horse, who began to rise into the air.

Without Blart.

Blart ran round the throne towards the rising horse. Behind him charged the minions, outraged and furious at the defeat of Zoltab. Pig the Horse rose higher.

Blart jumped.

Pig rose.

Everybody looked.

Blart caught the tail of the great horse. Howls of anger reverberated from below. Blart looked down to see guards shaking their fists. Pig the Horse rose higher and higher, taking the questors to safety. Blart gritted his teeth and held on to the horse's tail with all his might. Below him the Terrorsium grew smaller and smaller. He couldn't believe it. They had done it. They had defeated Zoltab. They had saved the world.

Chapter 46

'Pull Blart up,' ordered Capablanca.

'Are you sure about that?' asked Beo. 'I mean, it would be different if he was a hero like we all thought he was. But now it turns out that he's just a pain maybe we could leave him hanging.'

'Or push him off,' suggested Princess Lois.

'No,' said Capablanca firmly. 'Blart has been brave and noble.'

'Has he?' asked Beo.

'When?' demanded Princess Lois.

'He didn't moan when I nearly killed him,' pointed out Capablanca.

'Only because he was too busy dying,' countered Beo.

'Could someone help me up now?' asked Blart, who felt that they could save this discussion until he was safely sitting on the back of Pig the Horse.

Nobody answered him.

'But, Princess,' persisted Blart, 'you tried to save me from

Zoltab before.'

'Only because I thought you were the only one who could defeat him,' answered the Princess. 'Don't think it was because I like you.'

'Oh,' said Blart, feeling hurt.

'I don't think we should let him up until we know that he's a hero,' said Princess Lois.

'Right,' agreed Beo.

There was silence on the horse. Capablanca pondered. Blart dangled.

'Eureka!' shouted the wizard suddenly. 'He is a hero, after all.'

'How?' demanded Princess Lois.

'Because,' said Capablanca and then, since he was about to show himself to be very clever, he paused for dramatic effect. Blart wished he'd hurry up. 'Because,' repeated Capablanca, 'I've just worked out that the reason the guard changed into a dragon was because Blart made a mistake in casting a spell when we were trapped in the clutches of serpents. And without that mistake the dragon would never have landed on Blart's brother – sorry about your brother, Blart – and Zoltab would have triumphed.'

'If it wasn't for that pesky kid my plan would have worked,' cursed Zoltab in the tiny shrill voice that was his now he had been deprived of his power.

'Shut up,' all of them chorused at him once more.

'Why?' said Zoltab sulkily. 'What can you do to me? I'm immortal.'

'Don't think I haven't thought of that,' said Capablanca smugly. 'We will build a greater tunnel to encase you and I will cast a great spell and it will be covered by the Cap of Eternal Doom.'

'You wouldn't,' said Zoltab, shocked.

'I will,' said Capablanca firmly.

And Zoltab was silenced.

'My arms are getting very tired now,' Blart reminded them from below.

'He's officially a hero,' announced Capablanca. 'You must save him.'

'Is he really a hero?' asked Princess Lois desperately.

'Yes,' answered Capablanca. 'He's possibly the greatest hero there's ever been.'

'We'll have to pull him up, then,' said Beo reluctantly. 'Now I'm a knight I have a responsibility to treat accredited heroes with a proper respect. They outrank even knights in the chivalric hierarchy.'

'I can't feel my arms at all any more,' pleaded Blart from under Pig the Horse.

'But … but … but …' wailed Princess Lois desperately.

'But what?' snapped Capablanca.

'But if he's a hero and he's saved the world then my parents might try to make me marry him. My mother's always wanted a hero as a son-in-law.'

Blart gulped when he heard this. He was far from sure that marriage to a princess was compatible with pig farming.

'Ten minutes ago you were due to marry the most evil Lord in the world,' pointed out Capablanca. 'Blart's got to be an improvement on that.'

'I don't know,' said Princess Lois grudgingly.

'Help!' cried Blart as he felt his grip on Pig the Horse's tail begin to fail.

'Pull him up,' commanded Capablanca.

And so Sir Beowulf reached down and pulled Blart up on to the back of Pig the Horse, and he even patted him on the back and said, 'Well done,' and admitted that he was quite glad he hadn't cleaved him in two. And Princess Lois said, 'Thank you,' to Blart for saving her, and even conceded that she'd probably rather marry Blart than Zoltab. And Capablanca said he'd go down in history and that all peoples of the earth would be for ever grateful to him.

Blart sat on the back of Pig the Horse with his comrades. The world flew by below them. It looked very small and vulnerable as they passed over it. And it had been. But now it wasn't. Because of Blart. Blart was a hero. Blart had saved the world.

And he never let anyone forget it.

THE END